Bolan drove his right fist into the man's jaw

The Okinawan toppled backward and collapsed to the floor. The fourth man had dropped into a low fighting stance, and his hands were stiffened into blunt axes. He looked grimly determined, but the Executioner could see in the man's eyes that he had lost the will to fight. Bolan straightened and stared at his adversary.

"Tell you what, Jack. Do me a favor."

The man blinked, but he didn't drop his fighting stance. "What kind of favor?"

"I want you to deliver a message for me."

The Okinawan's eyes narrowed warily. Two of his men lay moaning on the floor. A third was unconscious. "What kind of message?"

Bolan's smile stayed fixed, but his tone grew as cold as the grave. "Tell Ryuchi Taido I'm here in Okinawa, and I'm coming to kill him."

MACK BOLAN ®
The Executioner

DON PENDLETON'S
THE EXECUTIONER®
VENGEANCE RISING

THE
POWER
TRILOGY
BOOK III

A GOLD EAGLE BOOK FROM
WORLDWIDE®

TORONTO • NEW YORK • LONDON
AMSTERDAM • PARIS • SYDNEY • HAMBURG
STOCKHOLM • ATHENS • TOKYO • MILAN
MADRID • WARSAW • BUDAPEST • AUCKLAND

First edition August 1998
ISBN 0-373-64236-9

Special thanks and acknowledgment to
Chuck Rogers for his contribution to this work.

VENGEANCE RISING

For mere vengeance I would do nothing. This nation is too great for mere revenge. But for the security of the future I would do everything.

—John Abram Garfield
1831-1881

Those who sit back and wait for events to unfold face a bleak and uncertain future. To have any hope of controlling one's destiny, one must take action.

—Mack Bolan

THE
MACK BOLAN®
LEGEND

Nothing less than a war could have fashioned the destiny of the man called Mack Bolan. Bolan earned the Executioner title in the jungle hell of Vietnam.

But this soldier also wore another name—Sergeant Mercy. He was so tagged because of the compassion he showed to wounded comrades-in-arms and Vietnamese civilians.

Mack Bolan's second tour of duty ended prematurely when he was given emergency leave to return home and bury his family, victims of the Mob. Then he declared a one-man war against the Mafia.

He confronted the Families head-on from coast to coast, and soon a hope of victory began to appear. But Bolan had broken society's every rule. That same society started gunning for this elusive warrior—to no avail.

So Bolan was offered amnesty to work within the system against terrorism. This time, as an employee of Uncle Sam, Bolan became Colonel John Phoenix. With a command center at Stony Man Farm in Virginia, he and his new allies—Able Team and Phoenix Force—waged relentless war on a new adversary: the KGB.

But when his one true love, April Rose, died at the hands of the Soviet terror machine, Bolan severed all ties with Establishment authority.

Now, after a lengthy lone-wolf struggle and much soul-searching, the Executioner has agreed to enter an "arm's-length" alliance with his government once more, reserving the right to pursue personal missions in his Everlasting War.

PROLOGUE

Okinawa

The Executioner's eyes slitted as four men entered the bar. Wind blasted in through the open door, the pall of cigarette smoke swirled and the rain that had been hammering the corrugated-steel roof for the past hour splashed in behind them. The four men shook off yellow slickers and laughed boisterously as they strode to the narrow bar. The saloon was a run-down establishment near the docks, and it was popular with local workers, sailors and occasional off-duty United States servicemen. Unshaved and dressed in a faded Hawaiian shirt, khaki pants and filthy construction boots, Mack Bolan looked extremely off duty.

It was midafternoon, and only a few locals sat at the bar. Bolan had a table to himself facing the door with his back to the wall. He had spent the past hour nursing a sweating bottle of Japanese beer as he waited. The humidity inside had to be nearly one hundred percent, and the lone ceiling fan had no effect on either the humidity or the eighty-nine-degree heat.

It was high summer in Okinawa.

Bolan scrutinized the men as they ordered beer. They didn't sit. The new arrivals were native Okinawans, and they were dressed as dockworkers. Their stocky physiques were heavily muscled, and their work coveralls and boots were grimy and sweat-soaked. Bolan almost raised an eyebrow. He noticed the men weren't wearing gloves, and their hands didn't appear to be particularly dirty. The tallest of the four men raised his beer to his lips, and the Executioner's gaze narrowed as he took in the heavy calluses on the man's knuckles. Calluses in themselves proved nothing, other than the fact that most dockworkers had them on their palms rather than the knuckles of their fists. The four men also had extremely good posture, and walked with a grace and ease that belied their heavy muscles and scruffy appearance.

The big American was prepared to lay a bet that all four of them were trained in martial arts. That told him something about the way things were about to go. This was likely to be an interrogation, rather than an execution. Bolan grimaced. It was most likely to be an interrogation that would start with a savage beating.

The tall man with the callused knuckles set down his beer and made a show of leisurely looking around the bar. His gaze finally came to a rest on Bolan. The man had a bullet-shaped head with close-cropped hair, and he turned a startlingly white smile on Bolan. There was no friendliness in the smile whatsoever. He spoke with heavily accented English.

"Hey, GI, what are you doing around here? You lost?"

Bolan smiled back amiably. "I'm not a GI."

The Okinawan scowled. Bolan continued to smile in a friendly fashion.

The Okinawan scratched his chin. "You know, I asked you what you were doing around here, Jack."

Bolan shrugged. "I'm having a beer."

The man folded his arms across his chest and sighed. "You know something, Jack? I don't think I like you too much." He leaned back against the bar as he looked at two of his companions. "Ito, Goro." He jerked his head toward Bolan, and the meaning was very clear.

Ito and Goro stepped away from the bar. The two men seemed to be identical twins, with flat faces and heavy brows. They also wore matching, unpleasant smiles as they leisurely approached the table where Bolan sat.

The big American sat with his left leg crossed over his

right underneath the table. As Goro came within six feet, the Executioner snapped out his left leg and sent the bar table shooting across the floor. He kept his beer bottle in his hand. Goro bent and caught the table before it hit him in the groin, but Bolan had already risen from his chair. He took one step forward and rammed the heavy cleated sole of his right boot into his adversary's face.

Goro's head snapped back, and he collapsed to the floor. Ito leaped forward with a snarl and threw a heavy round-kick at Bolan's head. It was the move of a talented amateur. There was a saying that a true master laughed at a high kick and a closed fist. Bolan had learned his deadly fighting techniques the hard way.

He took the thundering kick across his forearms, and the force of it rattled his bones. He stepped in with his own kick, and it barely skimmed four inches off the floor. The steel toe of his boot smashed into the Okinawan's shin with the crack of shattering bone. The Executioner whipped the beer bottle in his hand into Ito's temple and drove him to his knees.

Bolan scooped up the chair from behind him and kept moving forward. The eyes of the man at the bar widened with surprise. His remaining companion let out a piercing scream and lunged. The Executioner threw the chair between them, and the third man's fist smashed the flimsy chair to kindling. These men were fighters, trained to kill with a single blow, and Bolan didn't want to trade punches with them. He raised his knee as if he were going to kick. His opponent lowered his hand slightly, and Bolan spit in the man's face.

The Okinawan flinched in anger, and in that split second Bolan drove his right fist into the man's jaw with every ounce of strength in his body. The Okinawan toppled backward and collapsed to the floor, his eyes rolling in his head.

Bolan faced the remaining man at the bar. The few locals had scattered and pressed themselves against the wall and stared aghast. The bartender stood frozen behind his bar. The last man had dropped into a low fighting stance, and his hands were stiffened into blunt axes. He looked grimly determined, but Bolan could see in the man's eyes that he had lost the will to fight. Bolan straightened and smiled at the Okinawan.

"Tell you what, Jack. Do me a favor."

The Okinawan blinked, but he didn't drop his fighting stance. "What kind of favor?"

"I want you to deliver a message for me."

The Okinawan's eyes narrowed warily. Two of his men lay moaning on the floor. The third lay unconscious. "What kind of message?"

Bolan's smile stayed fixed, but his tone grew as cold as the grave. "Tell Ryuchi Taido I'm here in Okinawa and I'm coming to kill him."

1

Tokyo

Yonekawa Shirata sat and stared at the walls of his Tokyo office. The tiny room on the thirty-second floor didn't have a window. He glanced about for what had to be the hundredth time at the severe gray walls and remembered an old American sports program whose opening credits talked of the thrill of victory and the agony of defeat. Shirata had been given field command of an operation that, if successful, would have shifted world power to the East. As the commander, victory would have made him one of the wealthiest and most powerful men on the planet. The operation had failed in Europe and been utterly smashed in the United States. He had barely escaped southern California with his life, and returned to face his superiors in Japan an abject failure. Shirata stared forlornly at the clock on his desk. Even in his worst nightmare he would never have guessed that the agony of defeat would be excruciating boredom.

Shirata shook his head. They should have just ordered him to commit suicide and been done with it. He had been a field operative of outstanding talent in the cutthroat world of the giant business cartels, and then a paramilitary and espionage commander. He had bribed, stolen, extorted, spied and killed on five continents. Being shoved behind a desk to push mountains of meaningless paper in one of the Tokyo branches was more than his soul could bear.

He glanced with irritation at his phone as his intercom

buzzed. He loathed the intercom. It was used only by his secretary. She was an old and ugly woman with a sharp tongue. She knew nothing of his past or what he had done, but she had worked in the building for many years, and she knew anyone who was assigned to work in the gray window-less office was being punished for failure. Her tone of voice and the thinly veiled contempt in her eyes never let him forget that she knew his shame. Shirata waited several long seconds to deliberately irritate her, then spoke into the voice-activated speaker.

"What do you want?"

For once her tone was respectful, and Shirata raised an eyebrow as she spoke. "Yonekawa-san, you have a visitor."

Shirata blinked. He never had visitors. "Send him in."

He was further startled as his secretary opened the door, then bowed low. Shirata had to make a physical effort to keep his face neutral as his visitor entered. It was the old man. Shirata shot to his feet and bowed deeply at the waist. The old man grunted and nodded his head almost imperceptibly in return. "I see you have grown more respectful since your transfer, Shirata."

The secretary bowed low again and closed the door behind her as she left. The old man peered around the small office with distaste. Rinjiro Iasu was one of the directors of the Nishiki-Tetsuo Corporation. He was also the man who was in charge of most of the business cartel's illegal operations. Shirata had been directly under his command and had been the head of paramilitary operations. The fact that the old man was visiting him here in this office was extremely significant.

Shirata tightened the reins on his composure as the old man took the chair in front of the desk. Shirata followed the old man's lead and sat. "How may I be of service to you, Rinjiro-sama?"

The old man's frown deepened. "The American is here."

Shirata's eyes flew wide. He didn't have to have be told which American. The American commando had spelled disaster for the whole operation, and had figured prominently in Shirata's nightmares for the past three months of his punishment. Shirata cleared his throat. "He is here? In Tokyo?"

"No. He is currently in Okinawa."

Shirata frowned. "What is he doing there?"

The old man's mouth twisted slightly in grim amusement. "He is causing trouble."

"What kind of trouble?"

The old man sighed. "As you know, Okinawa is a transfer point for a number of our operations. Particularly our illegal ones. I believe it was you who set up our gun-smuggling operation there."

Shirata nodded. It had been one of his first actions as an employee of Nishiki-Tetsuo more than two decades earlier.

The old man sat back in his chair. "He arrived in Okinawa. None of our operatives there had any idea who he was. He was just some strange American who was asking lots of questions and flashing large sums of money for information about Nishiki-Tetsuo operations in the islands. Our Okinawan head of security sent a few men to interrogate the American. They were local muscle, and highly trained karate men." The old man's scowl deepened. "The American made mincemeat of them, in hand-to-hand combat no less."

Shirata grimaced. "We are sure it was the commando?"

The old man grunted. "We have two reasons to believe so." He pulled a folded piece of paper from the inside pocket of his suit and pushed it across the table. "This is the composite sketch our artist came up with after interviewing the defeated operatives."

Shirata unfolded the paper. He had only glimpsed the commando once or twice in the heat of combat. But during the operations in Europe and America, survivors of the American's counterattacks had given similar descriptions. Shirata looked at the sketch before him, and his blood went cold.

There was no doubt in his mind that this was his greatest foe. Shirata cleared his throat. "You said we have other evidence?"

"Yes." The old man's grim smile returned. "He told one of our Okinawan operatives to deliver a message."

"What was the message?"

"It was a message for your old friend. The American said, 'Tell Ryuchi Taido I'm here in Okinawa and I'm coming to kill him.'"

Shirata was silent for a moment. "The American is challenging us to fight, and he is doing it in our own backyard."

"Indeed." The old man nodded. "As we suspected, the Americans have made no overt move toward retaliation. However, we attempted to use a flulike Ebola virus against the United States as a weapon, and threatened millions of American lives. They cannot let that go unanswered. But they suspect that our government had no idea of what we were attempting. For that matter, they probably also know that we form only one aspect of the Nishiki-Tetsuo Corporation. They cannot declare war on Japan, and they are not about to officially sanction or economically attack one of Japan's biggest business cartels. I also believe they do not want their people or the rest of the world to know of our attack."

Shirata shrugged. "Yes, but what can one man do against us here?" He almost instantly regretted the remark. The old man scowled deeply.

"The American almost single-handedly defeated our operations in Europe and the United States. Now he is here, in Asia, and has already humiliated our local operatives in Okinawa. He says he intends to kill Taido. I believe him. If he can manage to find out who was directly involved in the operation in the United States, he will undoubtedly intend to kill you and me, as well." The old man raised an eyebrow. "You do not find this cause for concern, Shirata?"

Shirata kept his eyes on the tabletop. "Indeed, Rinjiro-sama. It is cause for concern."

"I am glad you think so."

"What do we intend to do about the situation?"

The old man shrugged. "It is obvious. We must kill him. His government has sent him because he is deniable in case of exposure. He is expendable, and they know we have a vested interest in killing him. However, he cannot pass for Japanese. He cannot penetrate our operations as a spy. His only choice, as you say, is to challenge us in our own backyard, and hopefully expose us at the same time.''

Shirata calculated. ''He will be acting alone, or perhaps with a few agents, but he will have the entire intelligence arsenal of the United States at his disposal. We must be very careful. The CIA, the NSA and anything else the United States can bring to bear is undoubtedly scrutinizing every action of Nishiki-Tetsuo.'' Shirata could almost feel the gray walls around him falling away. Finally there would be action again. He kept his elation to himself and nodded. ''How may I be of assistance?''

The old man stared at Shirata long and hard. ''Shirata, your failures in both Europe and the United States were monumental.''

Shirata couldn't suppress a flinch. The old man's tone softened slightly as he continued. ''As field commander, the responsibility was yours. However, you and I both know that you were the scapegoat. None of the board, including myself, intended to take the fall for the failure. You and I also know that in Japan there is no one who is better at what you do than yourself. No one questions this. It was one of the reasons I vetoed the board's decision to have you killed, and one of the reasons they accepted my veto. However disgraceful your recent failures have been, you are too useful a weapon to throw away.''

Shirata didn't blink. He had wondered why no one had put a bullet in his brain, or given him a dagger to rip his belly after he had provided his report of the disaster in Los Angeles. He had suspected it might have been the old man, and now he knew. It was also a case of the old man letting Shirata know that he owed him his life.

''You are the one most capable of dealing with the American. The board has discussed it. Kill the American, and we shall consider returning you to your former station. Fail...''

The old man's grim amusement returned. "Fail, and both of us shall probably be dead."

Shirata nodded as plans already began to form in his mind. The old man studied him acutely. "What do you intend to do?"

"First I think I shall go find Taido."

2

Mack Bolan moved through the night like a shadow in the dark alleys of the Okinawan wharves of Naha. The night-vision goggles he wore lit up the night, and the silenced 9 mm Colt submachine gun he cradled could fire as silently as he moved. The M-203 grenade launcher clipped under its barrel would announce his presence like thunder if necessary. Naha was the largest city on the island of Okinawa. It was a nexus of Asian trade, and the site of a major American military presence in the Far East.

Smuggling was big business in Naha.

The United States Army, Navy, Air Force and the Marines all had bases on Okinawa. All of them maintained their own security, and like all military bases around the world, peacetime security wasn't always what it should be.

The fact of the matter was some U.S. weapons were disappearing. The loss of matériel from military bases was almost to be expected, and in some places, such as the former Soviet Union, it was endemic. However, United States military security was better than most, and it was cause for concern when Stinger antiaircraft missiles of the Third Marine Division were missing.

The Stinger was the most sophisticated shoulder-fired antiaircraft missile in the world. It was light, easily portable, simple enough to use and so effective that illiterate Afghani tribesmen had kept the Soviet air war above ten thousand feet after their introduction. The Stinger was an almost perfect weapon for terrorists and guerrilla fighters, and stolen Stingers commanded top dollar around the world.

You couldn't just bribe the sergeant of the guard to report them missing or destroyed in shipment. To get them, you would need people inside at high levels, large amounts of money and a sophisticated smuggling system to get them out of containment and off the base. The average gunrunner just couldn't manage it.

Bolan had a suspicion that the hard-core elements of Nishiki-Tetsuo Corporation could. The attempt on the lives of the British Royal Family had revealed that they had connections with various terrorist organizations, and the renegade element of an international business cartel that wanted to change the world order just couldn't have too many Stinger missiles lying around.

Bolan moved on through the night.

An operation like this would normally be hard to penetrate. Bolan was alone and he couldn't pass for Japanese. However, he had the entire resources of the United States intelligence services backing him as a silent partner. Weapons smuggling would probably be one of the smaller operations in the Nishiki-Tetsuo range of illegal activities, and it was amazing what kind of information you could get out of the locals when you started opening briefcases that held one million dollars in bundles of hundred-dollar bills.

The Executioner crouched and peered at the warehouse across the alley.

It didn't look like much. The structure could have been there since World War II. Its sides of corrugated steel had long ago been painted a red that had dulled to nearly match the rust creeping up the walls. It was a low, rambling affair with a tiny square office sticking up out of the top. For such a ramshackle affair, security seemed extremely tight. Bolan had observed men with suspicious bulges under their shirts lounging around the loading dock. In the view of his night-vision goggles, beams of dim light crossed the sliding doors of the dock at neck, waist and shin height. A similar set of triple beams stood across the lone side door Bolan examined now.

Normally the security lasers would be invisible to the human eye, but in the light-enhanced view of the night-vision goggles, the beams stood out like ghostly bars of light guarding the doors. Anything that passed through the doors would break the beams and sound the alarm.

Bolan decided to bypass the doors altogether.

He moved through the darkness to the back of the warehouse, where there were no doors or beams. There were no lights, either, just darkness and a blank steel wall. Bolan slung his submachine gun and uncoiled a rope from his pack. He snapped out the tines of a lightweight, padded aluminum grapnel and examined his target. Near the eaves the steel box of an old-fashioned ventilator housing rose out the roof, and on its top the slitted-onion shape of its windmill turned listlessly in the offshore breeze. Bolan let out a little bit of rope as he swung the grapnel and let fly. The grapnel was padded with foam rubber to silence it, but to Bolan it still sounded overly loud as it hit the top of the ventilator and skidded across the housing. He slowly pulled back on the rope, which suddenly went taut as the grapnel's tines hooked on something. Bolan slowly leaned back and put his weight on the rope. The grapnel stuck fast. He swiftly scrambled up the knotted rope and then froze as he reached the top.

The four edges of the roof were boxed by the dimly glowing lines of security lasers an inch from his face.

Only the two-foot elevation of the ventilator housing had kept the rope from breaking the beam. Bolan gingerly hooked a leg up on the eaves and placed his foot against the top of the warehouse wall. He pulled his body up by the rope into a standing position, then carefully stepped over the security beam. He unhooked his grapnel and coiled the rope behind him as he glanced about. There were no guards on the roof, and no light spilled from the windows of the narrow office that had been constructed there. Bolan moved slowly. The soft rubber soles of his boots were designed for silence and traction, but he could feel the metal of the roof flexing under his weight. His stride turned into a slow-motion shuffle as he slid his feet across the roof.

The office had four windows that looked out, one in each direction. Bolan would have bet anything that there were trip wires in the frames. However, the dirty glass itself didn't seem to have any filaments in it.

The soldier took out his glass cutter and a suction cup with a pistol grip. He placed the cup against the glass and pumped the bellows button with his thumb. The pump emptied out the air in the cup and set up a powerful vacuum. He ran the cutter around the glass close to the wooden frame, then stepped back quickly. The pane of glass came away with a brittle-sounding snick, and Bolan grunted as he took the awkward weight in one hand. He set down the pane carefully and released the vacuum seal, then put his tools back in his pack and unslung his weapon.

The Executioner stepped through the vacant window frame and entered the warehouse. The top office was cramped. A single desk held a computer, and a filing cabinet stood in one corner. Bolan noted with interest that there was a sawed-off pump shotgun with a pistol grip stock sitting on the desk, as well. Gun control in Japan and Okinawa was extremely tight, though Japan had a thriving small-arms industry. It made smuggling weapons both in and out of the country big business. The fact that such a weapon was lying out and ready for use in a warehouse told Bolan that security had recently been stepped up, and they had been told to expect trouble.

There was a single door to the office. Bolan took out a small syringe and squirted oil onto the hinges. A moment later he opened the door. A tiny landing opened onto a rickety set of wooden stairs that led down into the dimly lit cavern of the warehouse. Only a few lights were on, so Bolan turned down the gain on his night-vision goggles and glanced around. The walls of the warehouse were lined with pallets and crates.

He headed down the stairs and moved to a row of pallets.

Large, chest-high cylinders that looked like barrels of woven string sat in a row. Each bore Japanese characters on its sides, with stickers in English proclaiming them to be tuns of sake. Bolan pulled out his fighting knife and cut away the top of the woven outer barrel. He pushed the blade between two of the top staves, then popped off a thin piece of planking. No fumes of rice wine rose to meet him. He distinctly smelled gun oil. Bolan pulled a penlight from his web gear and shone it inside the barrel.

Over a dozen M-16 rifles stood up neatly in wire racking.

Bolan nodded to himself. The rifles had probably been stolen from one of the military bases and were destined for Japan's black market to help slake the Japanese Yakuza gangsters' almost insatiable thirst for firearms. But it was the goods destined for foreign export that Bolan was most interested in.

A Stinger missile launcher was five and a half feet long. Bolan glanced around the warehouse for likely containers. It didn't take him long. A pallet along the back wall contained eight crates that were each six feet long, secured to the pallet with heavy web straps that had locking buckles. The straps parted beneath the serrated blade of Bolan's fighting knife. He pried up one of the crate lids and peered inside, seeing two loaded Stinger missile launchers with their grips and targeting units attached. The Marines were missing six launchers with grips and sighting units, and nearly three times that number of spare, loaded launch tubes.

Bolan removed one of the loaded missile launchers and reached into his pack. United States military hardware had clearly been stolen, but he couldn't go to the authorities with this. He was operating illegally in Japanese territory, and he had little faith that the Okinawan authorities were beyond Nishiki-Tetsuo influence. There was no way Bolan could carry out all of the missiles on his back, but he wasn't going let them stay in Nishiki-Tetsuo hands, either.

The Executioner began to pull explosives out of his pack. He quickly pushed a detonator into a stick of C-4 plastic explosive and placed it in the center of the crates of Stingers. A single stick of C-4 was unlikely to destroy much hardware by itself, but on the other hand, each Stinger missile had a 6.6-pound high-explosive fragmentation warhead, and those warheads were backed by fully fueled solid-propellant rocket motors.

The secondary explosions ought to be significant.

Things were about to get hot, and Bolan didn't want to try to get out the front or side door when the fireworks started. He didn't want to be trapped on the roof, either. He needed a bolt-hole, and he had brought one with him. The Executioner took the Stinger and moved to the side of the back of the warehouse and uncoiled several lengths of flexible linear-shaped charge explosive and took out his tape. Bolan measured out a five-foot hoop and taped it securely to the back wall. The wall itself was rusted corrugated iron and should prove no significant opposition to the charge. He pushed a detonator pin into the bottom of the hoop and then took cover behind a stack of metal drums. Bolan took his remote detonator box out of his web gear and slid the clear plastic safety shield off the detonator button, then pushed down the red button with a click.

There was a loud thump, and muffled orange light pulsed through the dim warehouse. A second later there was another, louder thump, and then a third. Fire flared, and crackling and hissing sounds joined the din as the Stinger rocket motors began to ignite. As the Stinger warheads blew, they tore open other missiles, and the rocket fuel ignited to detonate more warheads like a string of massive rocket-propelled firecrackers. Lethal metal fragments from the warheads tore through the air and shrieked sparks off the walls as chunks of burning solid-rocket fuel from the ruptured rocket motors flew in fiery streaks.

Bolan pulled a pair of white-phosphorus grenades from his belt and pulled the pins. He lobbed the bombs over the barrels, and seconds later the warehouse erupted into white-hot smoke and burning streamers of molten phosphorus. The interior of the warehouse was quickly becoming an inferno. The metal walls began to burn, and the old wooden infrastructure was going up like kindling. The smoke and fire suddenly sucked in on itself, then pulsed violently and blew higher as the pressure changed in the building.

Someone had opened the doors to the loading dock.

Bolan stared through the flames and tried to make out the competition.

Six men entered the warehouse on the run. They wore body armor over their coveralls and riot helmets with the visors pulled down. They sprinted fearlessly through the flames with automatic rifles held at shoulder height and the muzzles scanning the fiery interior. Bolan grimaced. These weren't ordinary security guards. They were hitting the warehouse like a professional entry team that had been expecting him.

He pushed the detonator button again, and behind him the flexible charge hissed in a hoop of yellow fire. A five-foot lozenge of wall fell away, and Bolan hefted his liberated Stinger and jumped into the alley outside. He pulled his last white-phosphorus grenade and dropped it back through the hole behind him to cover his exit. The Executioner moved at a dead run toward the front of the warehouse. Orange, yellow and white light leaked into the night through the shrapnel holes in the warehouse walls and lit up the alley in slanting, lurid rays.

The big American kept to the shadows and headed for the docks. Behind him the warehouse was burning out of control, and small-arms ammunition had begun cooking off and firing like popcorn. There would probably be very little left to salvage. Bolan suddenly flattened himself against a wall as he detected a thumping sound in the air over the fire and explosions.

A helicopter seemed to drop out of nowhere and hovered over the warehouse. It lingered for one moment, then rotated on its axis and dipped its nose in Bolan's direction. The Executioner broke from cover and raced for the docks. They had found his bolt-hole, and they knew the direction he had taken.

The ground troops would be following swiftly on his heels, as well.

Bolan ran on as a searchlight blazed into life under the helicopter's chin and its beam probed the narrow alleys looking for him. The back alleys behind Naha's wharves were narrow, but they offered little in the way of cover. The searchlight swept back and forth as it searched for the perpetrator. Bolan could smell the sea over the stink of the alleys, and he knew he was close to the docks.

An accusing circle of light swung over him as he ran, then whipped back. Bolan quickly turned a corner as a burst from a machine gun tore into the alleyway. The helicopter slowed and tracked its light as Bolan played a desperate game of tag. The aircraft rose higher and began to edge out toward the water. The soldier's eyes narrowed as he ran. The helicopter was taking a defensive position. Once he went out onto the docks, he would be out in the open and an easy target. If the helicopter was standing off to guard the docks, then ground teams couldn't be very far behind him.

Bolan sprinted into an alley that led out to the water and stopped. The helicopter hovered and tracked its lights across the docks. He raised the purloined Stinger to his shoulder and centered the optical sight on the aircraft. Bolan activated the infrared sensor as blinding light suddenly silhouetted him. He squinted and held his position as the Stinger targeting unit gave him a high-pitched, steady tone.

The Stinger's infrared sensor had acquired the helicopter's engine exhaust.

The long, slender missile hissed out of its launch tube and quickly accelerated to Mach 2. The helicopter's pilot started to jink his aircraft as he saw the fiery streak, but he was too late. The Stinger smashed into the upper engine cowling and detonated. Orange fire erupted over the water, and the aircraft dipped and shuddered, then began to plunge downward as its twisted rotors lost lift.

Bolan tucked the spent launch tube under his arm and ran for the water. He could hear people shouting behind him, but so far he was still out of the line of sight. Bolan ran down the wharf and scanned for his pier. Five hundred yards away he saw the white fishing schooner he had mentally marked earlier, and redoubled his speed. Behind him he heard the first crack of small-arms fire.

The Executioner reached his pier, his boots thundering on the old planks as he ran. More weapons began to fire as he sprinted all out. He clutched the Stinger launch tube in both hands and leaped as he ran out of pier.

Dark water closed over him as his weapons, gear and the missile launcher pulled him toward the bottom.

3

The lights and music of the Tokyo bar pulsed loud and bright enough to wake the dead. Ryuchi Taido drank sake and wallowed pleasantly in his misery. He was a short man, even by Japanese standards, but his powerful, ropy physique was nothing short of orangutanlike. A short, full beard and mustache and a flat face betrayed an ancestry mixed with that of the original Japanese Ainu aboriginal people, or, as it was rumored behind his back, there had been some mixed breeding during one of the Mongolian invasions.

Taido poured another cup of sake and peered disgustedly around the bar. He thought about the money he had left and deliberated on whether he wanted more drink or the Filipina hostess who was making eyes at him. In this downtown, expense-account hellhole they both cost almost the same. Taido sighed and decided on more drink. He snapped his fingers as a shadow fell across his table. "More sake."

A deep voice replied, "You've had enough."

Taido grinned and his knuckles cracked as his hands clenched into fists. Destroying one of the Thai kickboxers the club used for bouncers was just the kind of exercise he needed at the moment. He smiled happily as he balled up his fists. "Hey, tell you what. I think I will shove your—" Taido's hands unclenched, and his jaw dropped as he looked up at his adversary. Rinjiro Shirata was smiling at him, the smile not quite reaching his eyes.

"You look well, for a slobbering drunk, Taido."

The smaller man regained some composure and lolled back

in his chair. At six feet, Shirata was tall for a Japanese. The man's face had been extensively altered through surgery. The epicanthic fold of his eyes had been removed, and his skin color subtly changed. In repose his face was an eerily blank slate that could be changed at a moment's notice. Taido had personally seen Shirata change from a blond, blue-eyed European to an olive-complected Latin, then back to an Asian again in an hour's time. In a matter of minutes, he could pass as a member of nearly any Asian subgroup down to mannerisms and dialect. Shirata was a chameleon, and he was a stone-cold killer, as well. It was odd to find himself confronting his former superior in a Tokyo hostess bar. Taido grinned up at Shirata. "You know, after California, I would have thought you would have ripped open your belly, or be at the bottom of Tokyo Bay with a bullet in your brain."

Shirata's smile came close to being genuine. In the highly stratified and ritualized world of Japanese crime and espionage, Taido's impudence was legendary. If that impudence was still intact, then the man was probably still a useful asset, despite his current state. Shirata folded his arms. "Worse. They put me in the gray office."

Taido looked genuinely shocked. "The rat bastards." Taido enjoyed using English expletives, and his Mongoloid face suddenly split into a massive, horse-toothed grin. "Let us go kill them."

Shirata snorted. He had little doubt that all he had to do was nod, and Taido would attempt to kill the entire governing board of Nishiki-Tetsuo. "There is someone else who needs killing first."

"Oh?"

"Yes. The American."

"Which American?"

Shirata's tone lowered an octave. "*The* American."

"Oh. That American." Taido considered that for several grave moments. "Yes, I agree. He needs killing. Where is he?"

"In Okinawa."

"Okinawa? What is he doing there?"

"Yesterday he took out some of our local security boys."

Taido frowned. "I trained our local security in Okinawa."

Shirata nodded sagely. "Yes. I know."

Taido shook his head. "Stupid bastards, I bet they tried to use their karate on him and got themselves shot to pieces."

"Indeed, they tried to use karate on him, but he defeated them with his bare hands."

Taido blinked. "Oh."

"We also have reason to believe that an hour ago the American took out one of our warehouses on the docks of Naha. The warehouse contained over a million dollars' worth of illegal weapons that were ready for shipment, including a half-dozen Stinger missiles we had managed to acquire from the United States Marines. The warehouse was burned to the ground, and except for a few rifles and handguns, nearly all of the weapons were irreparably damaged or destroyed. In the past half hour it has already cost Nishiki-Tetsuo over a million yen to smooth this out with the Okinawan authorities in Naha."

Taido snorted. "I can imagine."

"He also shot down one of our helicopters during his escape."

Taido nodded with great seriousness. "He has a habit of doing that."

"He also left a message with one of your boys."

"Oh?"

"Yes, he said to tell Ryuchi Taido that he was coming to kill him."

Taido seemed to sober up considerably. "He knows my identity?"

"It seems so."

Taido chewed on his lower lip reflectively. "They must have gotten photographs of us during our North American operation, probably in Mexico."

"I agree. I suspect they have photographs of myself, as well, but I do not believe they can readily identify me."

Taido grunted. "Mmm. I gather that the old One Heaven bastards consider this situation intolerable."

Shirata grimaced. They were in a noisy bar, and he had made sure that he hadn't been followed. But he didn't like Taido shooting off his mouth. During World War II there had been a slogan among the Japanese people: "Bring the eight corners of the earth under one heaven." The "old One Heaven bastards" Taido referred to comprised the inner sanctum of Nishiki-Tetsuo Corporation, controlling its illegal and paramilitary operations. Their goal was nothing short of Asia's ascendance as the dominant power on the planet. Japan, naturally enough, would be at its head, and the inner circle would rule at the pinnacle.

Shirata's open hand lashed out like a whip across Taido's face.

"Watch your mouth, runt."

Taido's head snapped around from the blow. The little man's eyes flared wide with rage, and his face purpled as blood trickled into his beard and mustache. Shirata locked his eyes implacably with Taido's. Long seconds passed, then the little man bowed his head stiffly. "My apologies, Shirata-san. My conduct was inexcusable."

Shirata ignored the apology. "You are correct, the board considers the situation intolerable. The American is here in Asia, undoubtedly with the unofficial support of his government. He has already attacked Nishiki-Tetsuo twice in the past twenty-four hours and he will continue to attack us. I believe he intends to kill you, me and the inner circle if he can find out who they are. He needs to be killed immediately. I have been given this responsibility, and I believe your services would prove valuable. I require a yes or no from you, immediately."

Taido nodded and rubbed his chin. Despite the blow that was already swelling the left side of his face, he was immensely pleased at the prospect of being back in business. "What do you want me to do?"

Shirata smiled again. "Use your contacts. I want a hit team

assembled immediately. One that cannot be linked with Nishiki-Tetsuo. You have friends among the Yakuza, as well as organizations outside of Japan. Get some of them who you think are reliable. Get as many as you think you need, and remember it may take more than one team to bring down the American.''

Taido grinned. He had several men in mind already. ''Tell me, do we know where the American is now?''

Shirata sighed. ''No. He disappeared without a trace after he shot down the helicopter. However, I have little doubt that we will hear from him again very soon.''

MACK BOLAN HAD SHOWERED and was dressing as the chief petty officer of the United States Navy submarine *Sam Houston* knocked on his door and stuck his head into the cabin. ''Sir, we are at periscope depth, and your secure satellite link has been established in the communications compartment. There's a fresh pot of coffee, too.''

Bolan nodded. ''Thank you, Chief, I'll be right there.''

The pickup had gone off without a hitch. A pair of United States Navy SEALs had been lurking in the Naha harbor parked in a four-man swimmer delivery vehicle with a spare set of scuba tanks. Finding Bolan after he had plunged off of the dock hadn't been difficult. The burning helicopter crashing into the water had been an excellent beacon. The converted Navy SEAL delivery submarine *Sam Houston* had been waiting for them.

Bolan scooped up the spent Stinger launch tube from his bunk and headed for the communications room. The *Sam Houston* had once been a fleet ballistic-missile submarine of the Ethan Allen class. The Navy had converted her for SEAL special operations, and two floodable hangar decks had been added for their special-purpose vehicles. The boat was small for a missile submarine by modern standards, but the converted boomer had been designed from the get-go with stealth in mind, and it fit the SEALs' insertion needs extremely well.

It fit the Executioner's needs perfectly.

He moved forward through the cramped corridors toward the communications compartment. Sailors stood aside for the big man as he walked down the passageway with a missile launcher over his shoulder.

An ensign opened up the communications compartment door as Bolan approached. The interior was a cramped closet of a room, and the captain and the communications officer stood over an impressive bank of communications consoles with steaming mugs of coffee in their hands. The captain looked up from a console and smiled as Bolan propped the Stinger launch tube in a corner. The captain was a short, broadly built man with an iron gray crew cut. He looked Bolan up and down once and grunted. He had been ordered to pick up and deliver the mysterious big man at interesting ports of call on several occasions. "Evening. Is it still Belasko?"

Bolan shrugged and grinned. "Sure, Captain, why not?" Belasko was an alias he often used, and on the *Sam Houston* it was as good as any. "Thanks for picking me up. It was starting to get a little hairy back there."

"Nothing to it. There isn't anyone in this stretch of ocean who could give us any static." The captain grinned. "Other than flaming helicopters raining out of the sky on top of my divers, it went like clockwork." He nodded toward the communications console. "Your call is waiting."

The captain and the communications officer left the compartment, and the wheel of the bulkhead turned to seal the room. Bolan pushed a button on the console and spoke into the intercom as he poured himself a cup of coffee. "This is Striker."

Barbara Price's voice came through crystal clear as the satellite bounced her voice from the rolling hills of Virginia to the western edge of the Pacific Ocean. "We read you loud and clear, Striker. How are you?"

"Fine. We have a confirmation on the missing Stingers."

Price sounded pleased. It was she who had suggested that the missing missiles might be in Nishiki-Tetsuo hands. It had been a gamble, and it had payed off. "Aaron is linked right now with United States Ordnance and Logistics computers. Did you manage to get a serial or lot number?"

"I happen to have a launcher right here."

He could almost hear Price grinning. "Care to read the serial number to me?"

Bolan read off a series of numbers and letters, and he could hear the clicking computer keys in Virginia. He took a sip of coffee and waited. Price's voice rose triumphantly. "Got it. We have a confirmation. That launcher matches one of those missing from U.S. Marine Corps inventory. They were supposed to have been diverted from U.S. inventory in South Korea, but were reported lost in shipment."

"Someone seems to have found them."

"How many did you see?"

"At least half a dozen launchers, with reloads."

"That fits my numbers. What's their status now?"

"Destroyed, along with a large assortment of small arms and explosives. Most of which seemed to have come out of United States military inventory."

"It seems we have something of an accounting-control problem in South Korea."

Bolan nodded to himself. "It kind of does, but then again, it's a lead I can use."

"What do you want from my end?"

The big man had already given that some thought. "I need names of officers and enlisted men who had anything to do with the storage and transport of those missiles, no matter how minor the capacity, as well as anyone from the South Korean military who might have been involved. I'm going to need a couple of uniforms waiting for me, and a full load of armament with a full complement of spare equipment." Bolan smiled and scratched his chin. "A pilot I can trust wouldn't hurt, either."

"I think I can do something about that."

Bolan finished his coffee and rose from his seat. "I'll contact you again in twenty-four hours. Striker out.'' The Executioner spun the heavy bulkhead's wheel.

The captain stood on the other side of the door. ''So, what can I do for you, Belasko?''

The Executioner glanced at his watch and checked the internal compass. He jerked his thumb west. ''How fast can you get me to Seoul?''

PUBLIC SECURITY Investigation Agency Agent Honda Mitsuko's rage smoldered like the remains of the burned-out building before her. There had been weapons in the warehouse—of that she was absolutely certain. The acrid odors of burned rocket propellant and high explosives rose above the smell of smoke and rotting fish, permeating the entire wharf.

The Okinawan chief police inspector grinned at her in an oily fashion. ''Is there anything else I can assist you with, Agent Mitsuko?''

Mitsuko yearned to pull her collapsible baton from her purse and beat the grinning Okinawan about the face and neck. She bowed deeply at the waist and smiled demurely instead. ''Thank you for your assistance, Chief Inspector. Please, accept my card and contact me if there is anything else you wish to add to your statement.''

The chief inspector gave her a shallow bow as they exchanged business cards, and his greasy smile remained plastered on his face. Mitsuko stood up and loomed over the little man. She was five foot nine, tall for a woman, and huge for a Japanese. That and her looks had allowed her to pay her way through law school with runway modeling in the Tokyo fashion scene. As a PSIA agent, she often used her height and her looks to her advantage. Many Japanese men found her intimidating. Unfortunately neither her more obvious talents nor the badge of a PSIA field agent seemed to be having much effect on the chief inspector. Mitsuko suspected someone had propped up his backbone with a large sum of yen.

She turned on her heel and strode away in disgust. An entire warehouse had burned down on the Naha wharf, and the fireworks of exploding munitions had been seen and heard for miles. Yet the local authorities were sticking by their story that the warehouse had contained only industrial chemicals that had caught fire and exploded. Someone had engineered a massive cleanup before her arrival. The cleanup was still going on even as she had spoken with the inspector. Her request for an injunction against the cleanup until she could get a full investigative team flown in from Tokyo had officially been denied by the Naha authorities. By the time the legal red tape was cleared, there would be hardly any evidence left.

The Japanese security agent's fury burned in the pit of her stomach. Money had been paid. The warehouse was legally owned by a small Okinawan shipping firm, but Mitsuko had little doubt about who the real owner was or who could finance and organize such a massive cover-up so quickly. The PSIA had been watching the organization, impotently, for some time now.

Its name was Nishiki-Tetsuo.

She grimaced as the sweltering afternoon broke into a downpour of rain that felt as warm and salty as sweat. She stepped under some eaves and watched the bulldozer destroy what remained of her evidence. Despite the massive cover-up, Mitsuko had managed to find several interesting things. Most of the fallen walls had been removed before her arrival. However, Mitsuko had seen a section of one wall as it was being bulldozed and compacted, and the corrugated iron was obviously bullet ridden. That would do her little good. The metal had been squeezed out of all recognition before she could get out her camera. There was one thing she had managed to get a photo of, and it had given her great pause. As she had walked around the fire's perimeter, she had found a round, five-foot section of wall that seemed to have been neatly burned away from the warehouse wall and left fallen in the adjoining alley.

Mitsuko didn't believe that the fire had been an accident, nor did she believe that the owners had for some reason deliberately destroyed their own building. Someone had broken in and done this, then broken out. Mitsuko's frown deepened. She had been investigating Nishiki-Tetsuo for more than a year and a half, and what her instincts told her was almost inconceivable. The illegal arm of one of Japan's most powerful business cartels had been openly attacked. No Yakuza gangsters would be insane enough to try something that brazen, and a rival cartel would have used Byzantine business maneuvering or perhaps corporate assassination. Mitsuko's stomach tightened as she pulled her cellular phone out of her purse and dialed the PSIA Tokyo office.

Someone had just declared war.

4

South Korea

The Special Forces officer marched across the Marine base like a brick wall. He was a full-bird colonel with the almost permanent, deep-water mahogany tan of an officer who spent very little time behind a desk. Iron gray hair framed his skull like a helmet, and his eyes were hidden behind mirrored sunglasses. The creases in his dress whites would have cut glass. Despite the physique that filled out his uniform, the colonel moved with the deceptive ease of a special-operations soldier. United States Marines scrambled to get out of his way and avoid any kind of attention. Beneath his mustache, the colonel also wore the leering half grimace of an officer who was always looking for someone to paint rocks.

The grimace Bolan wore was real. The summer heat and dust of Korea was just about as stifling as the humidity of Okinawa, and the dye he had used on his hair was making his scalp itch. The skin dye that gave him the bronze tan was guaranteed not to run with sweat, but Bolan decided it was time to get in out of the heat. He whirled on a hapless, bespectacled young Marine. "You! Private!"

The private snapped to parade-ground attention. "Sir! Yes, sir!"

"Where's your goddamn armory, son?"

The Marine quickly pointed to a squat, massive concrete structure fifty yards away. "Sir! Over there! Past the truck park! You can't miss it! Sir!"

Bolan nodded. "Thank you, Private. Carry on."

The private hurried away. Bolan strode past the truck park and entered the armory. A blast of air-conditioned air hit him like a wall as he entered the building. A corporal sat behind a desk and stood and saluted Bolan a bit uncertainly. "Good afternoon, Colonel."

Bolan reached into his metal briefcase and pulled out his orders. They were more than likely to pass a cursory glance. However, if questioned and bucked up the chain of command, they would be denied. The corporal scrutinized the orders, then looked at Bolan. The Executioner had a few aces. He looked every inch a Special Forces colonel. Every military man who sat behind a desk knew that Special Forces officers could appear at almost any time and anywhere with weird and wonderful orders. It was also common military knowledge that it wasn't wise to mess with Special Forces officers. Due to the very nature of their operations, they often had strange and powerful connections out of all proportion to their rank. They were also equally famous for their long memories and highly personalized sense of vengeance.

The corporal adopted a courteous smile. "Welcome to Korea, Colonel. How may I be of assistance?"

"Where can I find Gunnery Sergeant Burdick?"

"I believe he's in the east storage room, sir. Would you like me to announce you?"

Bolan shook his head. "No, thank you. I'd like to surprise him."

"Through the door, take the hallway to your left, straight down. Room 101. You can't miss it, sir."

"Thank you." Bolan left the corporal and headed down the hallway. The man in command of the armory was undoubtedly a captain, but like a great deal of the military's operations, its day-to-day running depended on sergeants. Bolan's nostrils flared as he approached the door. There was the distinct smell of cigar smoke in the air, and he recognized the aroma of Cubans. It was the Executioner's first piece of corroborating evidence that Burdick was engaged in black-market trading. Bolan flung open the door to room 101 without knocking.

A large, florid man with his red hair clipped close his skull nearly jumped up out of his seat. "What's the—?"

Bolan could read Burdick like a book. The Marine had a big face with small features, and his small eyes narrowed even more as they took in Bolan and the uniform and decorations he was wearing. The sergeant was a large man, over six feet tall with the arms and chest of a man who spent a lot of time doing heavy upper-body work with the weights. However, the paunch that strained the front of his uniform and his narrow legs betrayed his laziness and false, top-heavy strength. He seemed like the kind of man who bullied subordinates and scraped before superiors with equal facility. An ingratiating smile plastered itself across Burdick's face as he saluted. "Sorry, Colonel, you startled me. Have a seat." He shoved his cigar to the other side of his mouth as Bolan returned his salute and sat. "What can I do for you?"

Bolan smiled. "Cubans?"

Burdick shrugged. "They were a gift. Would you care for one?"

"No, no, thank you. What I could use is a man who has the ability to move ordnance."

The sergeant's eyes grew guarded. "Well, that's my job, Colonel. What kind of orders are we looking at?"

Bolan sat back in his chair. "I don't have orders. What I have are Javelins."

"You have Javelins?"

"I have a half dozen of them, with twice that number of prepackaged missile reloads."

The sergeant leaned back in his chair, and Bolan watched the wheels in his mind turn. The Javelin was the United States military's latest shoulder-launched anti-armored-vehicle weapon. It was a fire-and-forget weapon, with no need for trailing guidance wires or for the user to keep the sights on the target once it was fired. On approaching the target, the Javelin's missile would pop up over the target, then strike down through the roof of the vehicle where its armor was thin and at a vulnerable flat angle. The Javelin had just begun to be issued in 1995, and it was meeting with great success. On the black market, Javelins could easily fetch anywhere between fifty to one hundred thousand dollars apiece. Being newly issued, they were also very rare.

Burdick looked across the desk at Bolan with mild interest. "Where did you happen to acquire half a dozen Javelins, Colonel?"

Bolan shrugged. "Special Forces extensively tests just about every weapon in U.S. inventory, often before they're ever issued to regular troops. A lot of that testing goes through me and my team. During testing, some of this equipment is lost in jumps, at sea, in mountains and swamps. I happen to have six Javelins that no longer officially exist."

Burdick gazed at Bolan long and hard, trying to detect a setup. "Well, Colonel, what you've just suggested is highly illegal. Is there any reason why I shouldn't call the MPs and report the story you just told me to the captain?"

Bolan smiled and put his briefcase on the desk. He flipped its latches and spun the case to face Burdick. The sergeant's eyes flew wide as Bolan opened the case. "I've got forty thousand reasons why not." Burdick cleared his throat as he stared at the bundles of one-hundred-dollar bills that lined the case. "That's just for keeping your mouth shut and listening to what I have to say."

Burdick shut the case and steepled his thick fingers over it. "I'm listening."

Bolan's tone became conspiratorial. "I heard a little something through channels about some missing Marine Corps Stingers. I'm sure there's nothing that can be proved, but to be honest, my nose is leading me in your general direction. And I need a man who can move ordnance like that."

Burdick scowled. He obviously wasn't pleased at being so easily picked out.

Bolan shrugged. "But for the sake of argument, let's forget

about the Stingers. My question is, Sergeant, are you interested in what I have?''

Burdick tapped his fingers together in thought. "Just for the sake of argument, I'd estimate that six Javelins, with reloads, could bring in at least six hundred thousand. Maybe more.''

Bolan nodded, although it sounded like a very conservative estimate to him. He had little doubt that Burdick would inflate the asking price with the customer, then skim off the top. "How do you feel about thirty percent of the action, plus expenses? Not counting the forty grand I just gave you.''

Burdick smiled. "Forty percent of the take sounds better. I'm the one taking all the risks.''

Bolan smiled back coldly. "Thirty-five, and you have no idea what risk is.''

Burdick blinked, but his smile stayed in place. "Sounds reasonable.''

"Deal?''

"Deal.''

Bolan nodded at the case. "Why don't you go ahead and count it.''

Burdick popped open the case and began riffling the bundles of hundreds. Bolan's voice lowered. "One other thing.'' The Marine sergeant looked up to find himself facing the gaping muzzle of a .44 Magnum Desert Eagle pistol.

"If you try to screw me, I'll kill you. Even if you kill me, my men will come and kill you. Do you understand?''

Burdick swallowed as he stared down the barrel of the massive nonregulation pistol. "Yeah, sure, no problem.''

The pistol never wavered from the point between Burdick's eyes. "I want you to get in contact with the people you sold the Stingers to. I want you to give them first dibs.''

Burdick didn't bother denying his role. "Hey, sure, like I said, no problem. I made a killing on those Stingers, and I'd bet they'd be interested in your merchandise. They'd be my first pick anyway.''

Bolan lowered the pistol. "I just don't want there to be

any misunderstandings between us, Sergeant.'' Bolan pointed the Desert Eagle's muzzle back at the briefcase. ''Why don't you go ahead and count it? You and I are about to go into business together.''

SHIRATA STARED HARD at the men Taido had gathered. There were ten of them, the majority Japanese Yakuza gangsters. Four of the larger ones were Koreans. The Korean minority in Japan was heavily discriminated against, and often allowed access only to the most menial of jobs that Japanese citizens didn't want. Crime was one of the few occupations in Japan that they could excel at. Shirata nodded. They would be useful in the current situation. He motioned Taido over to him and spoke low. ''These men are untraceable to Nishiki-Tetsuo?''

''Of course. That is what you specified. None of these men are members of the gangs loyal to the cartel.'' The little man's grin widened. ''I chose these men because they personally owe me favors.''

Taido had a large and convoluted web of contacts among some of the worst elements in Japan. It was one of the things that made him useful. Shirata nodded. ''Good. I want you to take them to Korea.''

''Korea? I thought we were going to Okinawa.''

''The American disappeared after the attack. I have no reason to believe he will have stayed there. He will be looking to attack us someplace else.''

''Then perhaps we should stay here in Tokyo. It seems more likely he would come to attack us here.''

''I do not believe he knows who exactly to attack here in Tokyo. He needs to acquire more information.''

Taido frowned. ''I understand, but why Korea?''

Shirata folded his arms. ''Our agents in Seoul have informed us that the same contact who sold us the Stingers has approached them with a consignment of Javelin antitank missiles.''

Taido pondered this. ''I do not see the connection. It is

hard to believe that the Marines had any knowledge of how and where we were transporting the Stingers in Okinawa.''

"True, but they were tracked and destroyed. If that was done once, it could be done again.''

Taido nodded. "Very well, what do you want me to do?''

"Go to Korea. Take your team and reinforce it once you are there. Surround the transaction site. If the transaction seems legitimate, take the consignment of missiles for a reasonable price and be ready, watch for tails. If anything seems strange, or you see the American, kill him and kill anyone with him.''

5

Burdick drove the Hummer up through the foothills outside of southern Seoul. The big city had given way to the suburbs, then hills began to rise toward the mountains. A hodgepodge of small towns and villages nestled in the tiny valleys that lay in the shadows of the mountains. The area was typical; almost the entire country of South Korea was a series of mountains and valleys. The mountains ahead shimmered in the midday heat, and the Hummer's tires raised clouds of red dust behind them. Burdick glanced over at his passenger as the big man checked the loads in his M-4 Ranger carbine. "You expecting trouble, Colonel?"

"You can't be too careful, Sergeant."

"I hear you." Burdick slapped the Colt .45 automatic by his side. "This is the one I let them see." Then he tapped his shirt under his left arm. "Over here's the one they don't."

Bolan suppressed a smile. Over the past forty-eight hours, Gunnery Sergeant Burdick had proved himself so unrepentantly corrupt it almost made him lovable. The sergeant was also keeping a Marine Corps Mossberg 12-gauge shotgun as extra insurance behind the driver's seat. The Marine reached up and tapped a knuckle against the top of the Hummer's cab. He had noticed that the Hummer the big man had requisitioned had the full complement of interior Kevlar armor. The gunner's hatch in the roof was open, and he was starting to believe it wasn't just for ventilation. "Is there something you aren't telling me, Colonel?"

"Who are the folks we're dealing with?"

The Marine rolled with the change of subject. "The man we should be dealing with is named Si, a former Korean Blue Dragon Marines sergeant. Big bastard, bigger than you, Colonel, and by reputation he's plenty mean. Business-wise he's no pushover, but he's always dealt square with me. It was him I sold the Stingers to, and like I said, I made a killing on that one. Si likes to buy quality equipment, and he always pays in American dollars."

Bolan nodded. The Korean armed forces had a reputation for toughness, and Blue Dragon Marines were among their elite troops. Even U.S. Navy SEALs respected them. "Does Si ever have any Japanese with him?"

Burdick frowned. "No, not so's I've ever noticed. But I'd bet my left nut that Si's got Japanese backing. The Koreans get their hands on all kinds of military stuff, ours, as well as Communist-bloc stuff from China and North Korea. But it's the Japanese boys who can really move ordnance around Asia and the Pacific. Their connections are global. Like I said, Si pays top dollar, and we aren't talking surplus Chinese rifles. We're talking Stingers and Javelins, high-tech stuff, U.S. military issue. You just know he isn't turning this stuff around and giving it away free to some goddamn revolutionary bean farmers. If he's paying top dollar, then so are his clients."

"You think Si is the front man for a larger operation?"

"I'd bet my ass on it, Colonel, and I'd bet my ass that black-market weapons aren't his only source of income. He's got a pretty heavy reputation."

Bolan nodded. Burdick didn't know it, but he *was* betting his ass on this one. The Hummer rounded a hill and began to descend into a shallow dale.

Burdick shifted his cigar to the other side of his mouth. "This is it."

The unpaved road led to a strip of houses and shops that clung to either side of a narrow, rutted street. The buildings were old, built low and walled with timber and stone. The little hamlet could have passed for medieval except for the presence of bicycles and a few very old cars. Bolan scanned the area. Except for a few dogs lying in the shade and a couple of chickens, nothing seemed to be moving. "What's the deal with this place?"

Burdick shrugged. "It's where I dropped off the Stingers. I think Si pretty much owns the village and everyone in it."

"And where is everybody?"

The sergeant glanced up and down the narrow street. "Don't know. It's hot, it's midday."

"Maybe your friend Si told them to stay inside."

"Could be. What we're doing isn't exactly legal."

"Do you like it?"

Burdick grunted and stopped the Hummer. "No, I don't. Things were a lot friendlier last time. But like it or not, here he comes."

At the other end of the hamlet, dust boiled up in the street, and a big black Mercedes sedan with tinted windows pulled into view. A second, burgundy Mercedes followed it, and a flatbed truck with a canvas awning pulled up at the rear of the approaching convoy. Bolan scanned the surrounding hills. "Does Si always bring two cars?"

Burdick shook his head. "Not when I've done business with him."

The two cars pulled to a halt fifty yards away. They parked next to each other and completely blocked off the street. The truck pulled up behind them. All of them appeared to have kept their engines running.

Burdick chewed his cigar. "What do you say we get out of here?"

The Executioner took a glance through the side mirror. "I don't see anything yet, but I'm willing to bet there is something behind us."

The big Marine's face tightened. "So it's an ambush."

"Maybe." Bolan watched the two automobiles facing them. It looked like everything might be going according to plan. "Maybe it's just extra security. Maybe they've had some problems you haven't heard about."

"Goddamn it." Burdick shook his head. "No disrespect,

Colonel, but I had a bad feeling about you the moment you walked into my armory. If this is an ambush, and Si is leading it, you and I are screwed.''

Bolan locked gazes with the Marine and held it. "Sergeant, you've got to have faith.''

Burdick's eyes widened, and he swallowed hard. "Well, what the hell, but goddamn it, Colonel, you're scaring the hell out me.''

"Stay close to the vehicle. Keep your shotgun nearby.'' Bolan pulled his mirrored aviator sunglasses over his eyes. "They know you. You do the talking.''

"Goddamn it.'' Burdick opened his door. "Here we go.''

Bolan and Burdick stepped out of the Hummer and faced the vehicles down the street. Both men stayed within a footstep of the Hummer's armored doors. A moment later the doors of the two cars began to open and men started to pile out of them. Most of them appeared to be Koreans, though Bolan thought several in the back could be large Japanese. None of the eight men carried weapons in their hands, but all of them wore jackets in the midday heat. After several seconds a man unfolded himself from the burgundy Mercedes's passenger seat. He was well over six and a half feet tall, with a head that was almost square, and his hair was shaved close to his skull. The big Korean stared down the street at the two Americans from behind dark glasses. He looked from Burdick to Bolan, then back to the Marine again.

He shouted above the idling of his vehicle's engines. "Hey! Fatso! How come you look so nervous?''

Burdick smiled cagily and shouted back. "What's with all the extra security, Si? I scare you that much?''

The tall Korean smiled and shrugged. "I've had some problems on my end, Burdick. I can't be too careful.'' The dark glasses turned to Bolan. "Who's your friend?''

"This is the colonel I told you about.''

Si nodded. "You got some Javelins for me, Colonel?''

Bolan smiled. "Show me the money.''

Si grinned back. "You got it, big guy." The big Korean turned to one of his men, who held up a small suitcase.

Aaron Kurtzman's voice spoke in the earpiece Bolan was wearing. "Striker, the satellite has two more vehicles, sedans, right around the hill blocking your exit."

Bolan spoke very low, almost without moving his lips. The microphone taped to the base of his throat transmitted back across the link in the Hummer. "Tell me what I'm not seeing down the street."

"Hold on." There was a second's pause. Back at Stony Man Farm in Virginia, Kurtzman was patched into a high-resolution observation satellite that had been tracking Bolan's vehicle since he had turned on his homing beacon ten minutes earlier. "Striker, men with rifles are deploying out of the back of the truck. I suggest you take action."

"Roger. Send in backup."

"ETA three minutes, Striker."

Bolan roared at Burdick. "Get back in the Hummer."

Burdick didn't have to be told twice. Bolan drew his .44 Magnum Desert Eagle pistol from his waistband at the small of his back and shot the man with the suitcase. He fell forward, and a 9 mm Uzi submachine gun with its stock folded tumbled to the dust. Si dropped to the ground after it, and his men began to draw handguns from under their jackets.

The sergeant had yanked his shotgun from behind his seat, and the big 12-gauge roared. Another Korean fell, then they began to return fire in earnest. Bolan leaped into the cab, and Burdick hurled his shotgun back in the Hummer, jumped in quickly behind it and slammed the door. Bullets began to rattle the vehicle's armor like a hailstorm. The Hummer began to rock slightly as automatic rifles began to tear into its frontal armor, and the bulletproof windshield began to go opaque with lead spalling from all the rounds hitting it.

"Jesus Christ!" Burdick had pulled his .45 automatic from its holster, and he gunned the Hummer's engine. "What the hell do we do now?"

Bolan pulled his Ranger carbine from the floor and folded the telescoping stock. "We sit tight. Here, fire back."

Burdick took the carbine incredulously. He knew the Hummer's armor was designed to stop small-arms fire, but the powerful vehicle was sitting in place and taking a terrible beating. Soon enough its Kevlar armor would begin to fail. His eyes widened as Bolan slid between the front seats and moved to the back of the vehicle. "Where the hell are you going?"

"Fire back, Sergeant. I need a second or two."

Burdick's eyes flared wide as he realized what Bolan was doing. "You got it." The big Marine stuck the carbine out the driver's window and began to spray short bursts down the street. The Hummer continued to rock on its chassis as every Korean with a weapon fired into it as fast as he could empty his gun and reload.

The Executioner flipped open the top crate containing the Javelins and pulled out one of the launch tubes. The quarters were extremely cramped in the back of the Hummer, but Bolan manhandled the forty-pound antiarmor weapon around and onto his shoulder. "Where's Si?"

"What?"

"Where's your friend?"

Burdick yelled back over his shoulder as he fired the carbine out the window. "I think he's in the red car!"

Bolan powered up the Javelin's optical sight. "Fire the grenade launcher. I need their heads down for a minute." Burdick grunted and triggered off the Ranger carbine's M-203. The weapon nearly jerked out of his hands from the recoil, and the Koreans hit the dirt at the launcher's sound. A split second later the 40 mm fragmentation grenade detonated in front of the two Mercedeses with a pale yellow flash, sending lethal metal fragments flying in all directions. Yellow sparks flashed off of the cars' bodies.

"Those cars are armored!" Burdick yelled.

Bolan didn't doubt it for a second as he rose through the Hummer's roof hatch. He reshouldered the Javelin and quickly sighted down the street. The range was fifty yards, and the black Mercedes filled the Javelin's optical sight. The range was point-blank, and the target was a lightly armored stationary civilian vehicle. It was a blazing-hot day, and the Javelin's heat seeker had a clear lock as heat shimmers rose from the Mercedes's idling engine. Bolan pressed the trigger.

The missile's ejection motor popped it out of the launch tube, and the main rocket motor fired. With a sizzling shriek the missile accelerated to Mach 1, and Bolan dropped the spent launcher and slid back down into the Hummer.

The Javelin followed its protocol to a T. At the last fraction of a second before impact, the missile's guidance fins pulled it up, then yanked it back down in a high G maneuver that would have left a human pilot unconscious. The missile hit the roof of the Mercedes, and its six-pound shaped-charge warhead detonated. A stream of molten metal and superheated gas filled the interior of the Mercedes and blew out its doors and windows. The entire car was engulfed in flame from the inside and rose several feet into the air, then fell back in a blazing hulk. The gunmen who weren't caught in the explosion scrambled for cover as flaming debris rained all over the street.

Bolan pulled a second Javelin from its crate as Kurtzman's voice spoke in his earpiece. "Striker! Enemy vehicles behind you are closing in!"

"I'm on it." Bolan shouldered the second Javelin and rose through the hatch. "Burdick! We've got trouble behind us! Keep our friends in front occupied!"

"You got it!" Burdick drew both of his .45 automatics and leaned out the driver's window. Bolan turned and sighted down the road approaching the village. Dust rose in rooster tails as a pair of former Korean army jeeps came boiling around the hill. Both vehicles had pedestal-mounted machine guns and men manning them. Orange flame flickered from the lead vehicle's weapon, and Bolan locked on the Javelin's optical sight and returned fire. The Javelin streaked up the road, then rose and fell upon its target. The jeep was an open vehicle, and as the Javelin's warhead detonated, the vehicle disappeared in the fireball and flew apart. The jeep behind it drove directly into the flaming debris and flipped over the side of the narrow road.

Bolan dropped the launcher and ducked back down in the Hummer for another. Burdick had fired his pistols dry and had retrieved his shotgun. "Looks like Si's making a run for it!"

The Executioner nodded as he pulled open a crate and heaved another Javelin onto his shoulder. He rose through the roof hatch and surveyed the street. The burgundy Mercedes was grinding up dust under its wheels as the driver desperately threw it in reverse. The truck behind it was quickly reversing down the street, as well. Bolan put his sights on the truck and fired. The missile shrieked down the street and rose over the truck. It whipped back down, and the truck heaved and shuddered as the missile flew through the canvas awning and detonated against the truck bed. The truck twisted up into a V-shape as the antiarmor warhead broke its back and crippled its chassis. The canvas awning and the truck cabin began to burn in earnest.

The burgundy Mercedes cranked itself about in a bootlegger's turn, and metal screamed as it scraped past the burning hulk of the truck. A cloud of red dust rose as the car broke free and peeled out down the road beyond.

Burdick snarled. "He's getting away!"

Bolan had been slightly concerned that Si's car might have been trapped in the narrow street by burning debris. "Good."

Burdick blinked. "You don't want to get him?"

The Executioner shook his head. "Not immediately."

The sergeant mulled that over, and a concerned look crossed his face as he fed fresh shells into his shotgun. "What about your leftovers?"

The surviving gunmen had risen up from behind cover. They had been abandoned, and their only hope of escape lay straight through Bolan. They raised their weapons and began to move grimly. There were more than a dozen of them. Burdick racked the reloaded shotgun's action. "They're going to swarm us!"

Bolan pressed a finger against the mike taped to his throat. "Jack, where are you?"

Jack Grimaldi's voice spoke loud and clear in Bolan's ear. "I'm right behind you."

As the Koreans began to fire, a shadow suddenly passed over as a Hughes 500 Defender scout helicopter materialized from behind the hills. The little dragonflylike helicopter sported a 7.62 mm Gatling gun pod on each of its stub wings, and both weapons roared into life with a sound like ripping canvas. The street erupted into geysers of dust as full-metal-jacketed bullets hailed down at a combined rate of sixteen thousand rounds per minute. Grimaldi, the ace Stony Man pilot, held down the triggers for five seconds. To the men on the ground it seemed like an eternity as the street in front of them was chewed by the lethal hailstorm. The guns suddenly stopped, and there was no sound but the thumping of the hovering helicopter's rotors. The Defender also mounted the bell of a public-address system under one of its stub wings. A voice spoke in Korean, then repeated itself in Japanese. "Drop your weapons immediately. Kneel and put your hands behind your heads."

The gunmen dropped and assumed the position. Burdick gaped at Bolan. "This was all a setup!"

Bolan regarded the Marine dryly. "So, figured that out, huh?"

Burdick glanced up at the Hughes as it covered the kneeling men with its machine guns. "Who's in the helicopter?"

"A friend of mine, and a Korean American CIA officer from the embassy in Seoul."

Burdick nodded thoughtfully. His thick chest rose, then fell with a sigh. "All right, Colonel. What's going to happen to me?"

Bolan considered Burdick for a long hard moment. The Marine had stolen United States military matériel and sold them on the black market to the highest bidder. He was a criminal—of that there was no doubt—and he had gone along on the operation unawares, and motivated by greed. However, when things had hit the fan, he hadn't turned and run, and he had fought bravely. The Executioner's face hardened. "You're facing a court-martial, Sergeant. You've been selling advanced weapons that don't belong to you or to enemies of the United States."

Burdick swallowed hard. He had no illusions. United States military courts took a dim view of those kinds of crimes. He would be an old man before he got out of Leavenworth Federal Penitentiary. Bolan's voice stayed hard, but his eyes narrowed slightly. "But you have a choice."

The sergeant squared his jaw. "What kind of choice?"

"You take an early retirement from the Marines, effective immediately, and I'll let you keep the money I gave you up front for a fresh start in something legitimate in your new civilian life."

Burdick saw what was coming. "And in the meantime I work for you."

"You've got it. It's a simple deal. You tell me everything I want to know, and you do exactly what I say. You screw up, you don't see daylight for twenty years. You turn on me, I kill you. You kill me, and Military Intelligence will be hunting you down for the rest of your life, and when they find you, they tell friends of mine where you are. Do we understand each other?"

Burdick looked Bolan in the eye and didn't flinch. "I understand."

"Do we have a deal?"

"Deal."

Bolan checked his watch. "Our observation satellite will only be able to track Si's car for about another ten minutes before it passes over the horizon. We need to hand Si off to a tail lower down."

"And when he goes to ground?"

The Executioner picked up his carbine and slid in a fresh magazine. "We're going to be there."

6

The old farmer kept his head down and cringed before the South Korean military police sergeant. The Korean officer yelled several questions at him, and the little old man bowed and scraped and said that he didn't know anything. He presented his papers and whimpered that he was just on his way to Seoul when gangsters had tried to blow up the village. The Korean officer grunted, then moved on to the next villager without returning the aged man's bow.

The old man was just another fool come down from the hills. His homespun pants were held up by a length of rope, and a knotted towel was twisted around his head. His back seemed permanently bowed from carrying heavy loads, streaks of gray shot through his hair and beard and his skin was burned to a leatherlike mahogany from decades of manual labor in the sun. He didn't look at all like one of the most dangerous men in the Pacific Rim.

Ryuchi Taido smiled at himself. He was very good at playing a peasant. Even the locals believed he was just an old farmer passing through on his way to Seoul. Taido kept his head down and watched from under his eyebrows as Si's gunmen were rounded up and loaded into military-police vans.

The American had been here. Taido had seen the commando with his own eyes. He had watched the confrontation from inside the village's one inn, and he had almost taken a shot at the American himself until the missiles began to fly and the street had turned into an inferno. Taido shook his head ruefully. They had known ahead of time the deal was for Javelin antiarmor weapons, and yet even Taido himself hadn't expected the weapons to be used against them. It had been a grievous oversight. He looked again at the battered, lead-smeared hide of the Hummer where it still sat in the middle of the street. It had been a perfectly laid-out trap, until the American had shown up in an armored vehicle loaded with guided missiles, and a helicopter gunship. Taido had watched helplessly as the commando and the Marine had wiped out nearly half a platoon of well-armed men and then taken off in the helicopter once the South Korean military authorities had arrived.

Taido found himself developing a profound respect for the American. He was extremely devious.

Taido sighed. Shirata wouldn't be pleased, but at least Si had escaped. Perhaps part of the situation would be salvageable.

Taido's eyes suddenly narrowed at the thought. Si shouldn't have escaped. Si should be scattered, charred bits of cooling meat at the moment. He had been a sitting duck for many long seconds while his driver struggled to get his car out of the narrow street. Taido's gaze swept past the smoldering ruin of the truck and the road beyond. The American would have had a clear field for a hundred-yard shot even after Si had broken free. Taido doubted the commando had run out of ammunition, either. The deal had been for a half a dozen Javelins, and the Americans had used only three. No, Si was still alive because the American wanted him alive, and running. Si was being tracked.

Taido's fists clenched at his sides as another South Korean military policeman bumped past him. Si would run to the safehouse, and Taido had to get a message there warning them, as well as a message out to Shirata. He grimaced as two policemen with rifles stopped almost right next to him and began to smoke cigarettes. He had to get to his transmitter back at the inn. There was still a chance to set up another ambush.

Time was now everything.

THE EXECUTIONER MOVED at a smooth run over the brown broken ground of the Korean highlands that loomed over Seoul. Grimaldi ran easily beside him. Burdick wheezed and gulped air, but he grimly kept up with them. Beside Burdick was their Korean CIA attaché. Kim Park was almost exactly the same height and build as Grimaldi, and he was a former Korean Blue Dragon Marine sergeant. As such, he had a bone to pick with the renegade, Si.

Si hadn't gone far. He didn't have to. The roads in the highlands formed twisting, often unpaved mazes that writhed around and through the hills and peaks, then dipped sharply into little valleys and canyons. His defensive driving was excellent, and he knew the territory well. He would have lost even the most skillful of tails. He hadn't lost the nearly all-seeing eye of the satellite, and Kurtzman was on the ball. Si had gone to ground in another little hamlet almost identical to the first one except at a higher elevation.

Bolan pulled to a halt. According to his mental map, the hamlet should be just around the next ridge. He turned to Park. "What do you think?"

"He'll be on a high state of alert, and I think there will be sentries posted."

Burdick was stooped over with his hands on his knees as he took in shuddering breaths. They had set the helicopter down two miles away, and it had been some time since the Marine sergeant had done any marching, much less a two-mile run over broken ground. He straightened painfully. "If this is his safehouse, you've got to figure he owns the village. When you came in with a Hummer and started firing missiles, the villagers kept their heads down. But now we're just four men on foot. Si may have some of the villagers armed and actively working for him. We'd better count on him having some backup."

Bolan nodded. Stealth would be the best way. "They'll be watching the road, and we don't have the satellite anymore.

We'll climb this ridge and take a lay of the land.'' The rest of the team nodded, and the four men began to climb. Bolan led the way up the steep grade of the ridge face, staying along the line of solid rock and avoiding the loose scree that could tumble and give them away. He reached the crest and lay prone as he drew his binoculars. The Executioner took a long hard look at the hamlet.

Two hundred yards away the little hamlet clung to one side of a hill. A dirt road snaked along the hillside, and at both ends of the little valley a pair of armed men watched the approaches to the village. Si's burgundy Mercedes was parked under the shelter of a covered corral, and several displaced cows were tethered to a post outside. One structure in the middle of the hamlet was a two-story affair with a peaked loft. The loft had a single window, and someone inside was careless enough to leave the muzzle of his M-60 machine gun sticking out over the sill. Everything in the village was still.

Grimaldi sprawled out next to Bolan and swept his own binoculars up and down the village. "You saw the M-60 in the window?"

Bolan kept his eyes on the building. "Kind of hard to miss. I'm betting Si's inside."

"How do you want to play it?"

"I want to sneak in as close as we can, but that M-60 is going to be trouble. It commands the whole street."

Bolan jerked his head at the big Marine. "Burdick."

"What's up?"

Bolan held out his Ranger carbine, with the M-203 mounted under the barrel.

"Jack, Kim and I are going to go down and rustle up your friend Si. We're going in quiet, but I want that machine-gun nest out of commission when we hit them. You think you can lob a frag in there on my signal?"

Burdick peered steadily at the distant window, then nodded. "Not a problem."

"Good. Give me your shotgun." Bolan traded weapons with Burdick and hefted the big 12-gauge. The Mossberg had been modified to U.S. Marine Corps specifications, with an 8-round extended magazine and rifle sights and a black, parkerized finish. Bolan handed Burdick his bandolier of 40 mm grenades and spare magazines. "Your radio is on-line?"

Burdick tapped the earpiece Bolan had given him. "Loud and clear."

"All right. You're our fire support, Sergeant. Take out the machine gun, then hit the sentries. On my signal."

"You got it."

Grimaldi cradled his silenced MAC-10, and Park held an M-16 rifle with practiced familiarity. Bolan nodded at the two men. "You two take the north side of the road, and I'll take the south. On my signal. Let's do it."

The three men began to slowly move back down the ridge, then split as they moved to cover both sides of the road in and out of the village. Bolan moved silently across the rock escarpment until he came back down to level ground. He could see the road where it led around the bend and into the village. The Executioner could hear voices as he moved closer to the rocky bend. The two sentries were talking in Korean. Bolan could smell their cigarette smoke, and a wisp of it came around the rock, borne on the afternoon breeze. Bolan doubted the two men could be more than five yards around the rock. He whispered into his throat mike. "Jack, are you in position?"

"Waiting on you, Striker."

Bolan glanced up the ridge where Burdick lay out of sight. "What's our status, Sergeant?"

"Nothing is moving in the village. Your guys are standing almost right around the corner. Weapons slung. On the north side they have their weapons in their hands, but they don't act like they are expecting trouble."

Bolan flicked off his shotgun's safety. "All right. We'll try it quiet. Be ready, Burdick. Team two, go."

The Executioner stepped around the corner. The two Koreans goggled in alarm as the big man appeared in front of them. One of them opened his mouth to yell, and Bolan rammed the shotgun's muzzle into his midsection. The man's shout came out as a strangled wheeze as he collapsed to his hands and knees. The other gunman took a step back and tried to whip his M-16 around on its sling. Bolan took a step forward, whipped the butt of the Mossberg up and brought the Korean hardman to the ground, unconscious with a shattered jaw. The Executioner turned on the first gunman and brought the shotgun's buttstock back down behind the man's ear. The sentry fell on his face and lay unmoving.

Bolan spoke into his mike. "Jack, status."

The pilot sounded pleased with himself. "Both sentries down. We—"

Burdick's voice cut through urgently. "Striker! Get down!"

A machine gun snarled, and a long burst of automatic fire stitched the dirt road as Bolan threw himself back against the rocks. Orange flame strobed from a second-story window in the hamlet. On top of the ridge, Burdick's M-203 grenade launcher thumped. The machine gunner's second burst was cut short as the 40 mm fragmentation grenade looped through the window and detonated with a muffled crack. Pale yellow light lit up the window and the machine gun fell silent.

Bolan cursed silently. They had lost the element of surprise. Speed was their only asset now. He sprinted down the narrow street and hugged the fronts of the houses.

At the other end of the village, Grimaldi and Park were charging in. They moved to the opposite side of the street from Bolan to stay out of each other's line of fire. Bolan watched as lines of tracer smoke streaked down from the ridge as Burdick put a round into a street-level window of a building. The building's door flew open, and a man with an M-16 aimed up at the ridge. The enemy didn't know yet that they were being attacked at street level, as well. Bolan brought up the big 12-gauge shotgun and put the front sight on the man's chest. The weapon bucked and roared, and the gunman twisted and fell as he took nearly the full pattern of buckshot.

Down the street Park's M-16 ripped into life as he engaged an unseen opponent along one of the narrow side streets. A rifle barrel appeared in one of the first-floor windows of the big building and began to traverse the street as Bolan put a round of buckshot through the dark opening. Sparks flew off the weapon's muzzle, and it clattered onto the street as it seemed to jump out of its owner's hand. The enemy definitely knew they were there now.

Another door flew open down the street, and a half-dressed man lunged out firing a pistol in each hand. Bolan didn't hear the shots from Grimaldi's silenced MAC-10, but he saw the man stagger and fall as he took the burst. Bolan shot the man behind him before he could bring the M-16 rifle he clutched to bear. The Executioner spoke into his mike. "We take the big house now! Before they have time to mount any kind of counterattack."

"Affirmative, Striker!"

Grimaldi and Park pounded down the street as Bolan pulled a flash-stun grenade from his bandolier and yanked the pin. "Cover me!"

The Executioner charged down the middle of the street toward the big house. Every window was a potential sniper hole, but Bolan kept his attention on his target and relied on his team to cover him. He ran up to the big house and tossed the grenade through a shattered window. The darkened interior lit up in a brilliant white flash, and the surviving windows on the ground floor blew out from the blast wave.

The front door was made of an ancient and very heavy single piece of wood. Bolan raised the shotgun and put a round of buckshot into the top and bottom hinges. The soft black iron hinges twisted and tore in their moorings, and the door tilted in its frame. Bolan dropped the shotgun and unleathered both his .44 Desert Eagle and 9 mm Beretta 93-R pistols as he kicked the door.

Three men and a pair of screaming women were inside. One of the men lay dead on the floor by the window where Bolan's shotgun blast had disarmed and downed him. Another man was on his hands and knees and seemed to have been in the center of the flash-stun grenade's detonation. The third man weaved slightly on his feet, but he held an Uzi subma- chine gun in his hand. He was half-blinded by the flash, but he could still see light and dark. Bolan stepped aside as the man nearly emptied his weapon at the doorway and put a burst of his own from the Beretta into the man's chest. The two women sat in the corner clutching each other and scream- ing continuously. Bolan walked up to the man on his knees and kicked away the M-16 rifle the blinded gunman was grop- ing for. He rapped the butt of the Desert Eagle against the side of the man's head, rendering him unconscious.

Grimaldi's voice spoke in Bolan's earpiece. "We're com- ing in behind you."

Bolan nodded and kept his weapon trained on the stairs. "You're clear!"

Grimaldi entered the room, followed by Park, then knelt by the doorjamb with his weapon trained on the street outside. Bolan cocked an ear. The street outside seemed suddenly very quiet. "What have we got, Burdick?"

"Nothing's moving, Striker. We've got—" Burdick's voice dropped to a snarl and his weapon let off a burst up on the ridge. "Belay that! We've got movement! Five or six men! Armed! They've moved into the stable!"

The street outside erupted as the gunmen returned Bur- dick's fire. Bolan nodded. The Mercedes was in the stable. Si was making a break for it. He pulled a grenade from his bandolier.

"Kim! Get those women out here! Now!"

Park roared in Korean and brandished his M-16. The women's shrieking rose an octave and they fled out through the back door. Bolan suspected Si and his men had gone the same way, but he couldn't afford to leave anyone upstairs coming down behind them. He popped the pin on the CS tear- gas grenade and dropped it to the floor. "Kim! Jack! Take the back! Burdick—I'm coming out the front!"

"Affirmative, Striker!"

Bolan moved to the front door as the gas grenade began to spin and hiss on the floor. Down the street a man was leaning out of the corral and firing at Burdick's position with a U.S. Army semiautomatic sniper rifle.

Burdick's voice came grimly through the earpiece. "I'm taking heavy fire!"

Bolan knelt and flicked the Beretta's selector switch to semiauto. The target was thirty-five yards away, and he braced his hand on a water barrel as he fired. The sniper jerked as the 9 mm hollowpoint slug hit him, and the big American followed up with a quick second shot that put the man on the ground. Bolan began to move quickly down the street with his pistols held ready in front of him. Up on the ridge Burdick began to lay down covering fire again.

The Executioner heard weapons firing behind the row of buildings, and he knew that Park and Grimaldi were engaging the enemy from the rear.

Grimaldi's voice spoke in Bolan's ear. "They're in the car, Striker. It's armored. What Kim and I have won't stop it, it's coming your way!"

Bolan dropped the Beretta as he heard the tear of tires on dirt and the roar of the Mercedes's engine. Gears screamed, and the armored sedan smashed the corral's fence and fishtailed into the street. Bolan raised the Desert Eagle and spoke into his mike. "Burdick, load a willie pete."

A shooter leaned out of the passenger's window, holding an AKS-47 rifle with its stock folded. Bolan fired. The conical, steel-jacketed, metal-piercing .44 Magnum round was designed to penetrate thin-skinned armored vehicles. The shooter's chest didn't put up much resistance, and he sagged limply in the window frame as the car accelerated and his weapon fell to the dust. Bolan adjusted his aim and put the front sight of his massive pistol on the driver's side of the tinted windshield. He fired, and the darkened bulletproof windshield spiderwebbed with cracks as the metal-piercing bullet hit it.

The car wasn't stopping. Bolan lowered his aim and began

to fire into the Mercedes's grille as the car tore toward him. "Burdick, take the car."

"You got it." The M-203 thumped up on the ridge.

Bolan squeezed the trigger of the Beretta slowly and methodically, and round after round smashed through the Mercedes's grille. The engine screamed as something inside came loose, but the car showed no signs of slowing. The street suddenly erupted into fireworks as Burdick's white-phosphorus grenade smashed into the Mercedes's hood. White-hot smoke and streamers of burning phosphorus fountained into the air, and the Mercedes disappeared for a moment in the ball of burning gas and smoke. The vehicle erupted out of the phosphorus cloud and careered forward clearly out of control. The entire front of the car was engulfed in yellow fire as it skewed off of the dirt road and sideswiped a stone storefront. The car spun and spewed up dust as it plowed to a halt.

For a moment nothing moved except the flickering flames and gray smoke billowing off the car's hood and windshield. Bolan kept his weapon trained on the vehicle. The doors flew open, and a pair of Uzis were tossed out. Two men fell out choking and coughing behind them. A third fell out a moment later from the rear door. There was no sign of the driver. Park's voice roared in Korean from down the street. Bolan couldn't be sure of what he said, but two of the men scooted away from their weapons on their hands and knees. Si's hand stayed near his weapon. Kim shouted again, then Si's eyes met Bolan's over the muzzle of the Desert Eagle.

Si scooted over by his men.

Bolan kept his weapon trained on the three men. "Kim! Tell them to move away from the car! When the fire reaches the gas tank, it's going to go!"

Park barked out instructions, and the three gangsters quickly began to crawl across the street away from the car. A few seconds later the car shuddered with a muffled boom, and the orange fire of burning gasoline bloomed from under the chassis and expanded out into the street. The Koreans instinctively threw themselves down, then almost immediately rose again and redoubled their crawling speed. Si led them, and the big Korean halted as he almost ran into the Executioner. He looked up past the muzzle of the big pistol and into Bolan's face. Whatever he saw there didn't inspire him with confidence. Si cleared his throat and swallowed hard. "I surrender."

Park strode forward and nonchalantly kicked Si square in the temple. The big Korean toppled backward, blood drooling down his face. The Korean armed forces weren't known for gentle interrogations. Bolan held up a restraining hand as Si shook his head dazedly. Park relented and took a step back. He continued to glare at the man he considered a traitor to the Blue Dragon Marines.

Bolan had no doubt that Park would cheerfully beat Si to death with his hands and feet. Grimaldi took a position with his back to a wall and kept his submachine gun trained on the street as the Executioner looked down coldly at the Korean gangster. "Tell any of your men still in hiding to throw down their weapons and come out."

Si sighed heavily. "Most of the men in the village work for me, one way or the other. But you took out my shooters."

Bolan took a mental head count and the total seemed about right. Si couldn't have taken more than four men with him out of the first ambush, and he doubted he would have more than four or five men under arms in a remote village, but it didn't pay to take chances. He spoke into his mike. "Burdick, if anything goes bad down here, drop a frag on Si and his two friends."

Burdick's voice came back in Bolan's ear. "You got it."

Si's eyes widened. "Burdick is the shooter up there?"

Bolan stepped forward and shoved the Desert Eagle between Si's eyes. "Burdick is playing on the home team now, but he isn't your problem at the moment. I am." The Executioner jerked his head toward Park. "My friend would like to hang you upside down by your ankles and kick you to death, but I don't have time for that. You're either going to tell me everything I want to know, or I'm going to blow your head off. Do you want to cooperate?''

Si seemed to shrink several inches, and his shoulders sagged. ''I want to cooperate.''

Bolan nodded. ''Good.''

He looked up at Grimaldi. ''Go get the chopper.''

7

The U.S. Navy Viking jet tore across the Sea of Japan at well over five hundred miles per hour. Its twin turbofan engines howled as they redlined at full emergency power. Grimaldi had taken the Hughes 500 helicopter screaming down from the Korean highlands and headed straight for the coast. The U.S. Navy aircraft carrier *Carl Vinson* was on maneuvers in the Far East and had received the overheating helicopter, and had the Viking antisubmarine jet warmed up and waiting in the catapult. A pair of Navy pilots sat in the back of the bird and looked confused as civilians took over their aircraft. Their orders were terse and confusing: take over the plane once it was landed, and claim that they had flown it and had experienced technical difficulties. Bolan checked his watch and made a mental calculation. It had taken an hour to reach the *Carl Vinson* by helicopter, and Grimaldi had the Viking jet screaming over the water at optimum altitude with the throttles all the way forward. With luck they would be in Osaka in half an hour. Bolan frowned.

The enemy held all the cards. They had the manpower, the firepower and the home-court advantage. Bolan had only two cards to play—sheer gall and speed. His only chance was to mount a rolling, lightning war, one that would keep the enemy off its feet as he attacked from out of the blue and then leapfrogged to attack again while the enemy was still reeling. Blitzkrieg was the name of the game, and at present, Bolan had an army of three. Luckily his tiny army had worldwide assets to call upon. They also had Si. Faced with the choice of cooperation or death, the Korean hardman had readily spilled everything he knew. He was by no means a major player in the illegal arm of Nishiki-Tetsuo, but he knew enough of where his end of the operation ended up in Osaka to generate some leads. Si was now in a Korean army military stockade under the not-so-gentle care of Kim Park. Si had saved his skin, but Bolan didn't envy him.

The Executioner checked his watch again, and his frown deepened. Time was the crucial factor. Every second that passed might mean that the information they had gotten from Si was no longer current, and that the enemy could cover its tracks or set up a massive ambush. Bolan relaxed. They would reach Japan as quickly as Grimaldi could get them there. What he needed now was more information. Bolan smiled as the red light on his satellite link started blinking almost as if on cue. He opened the line. "What have you got for me?"

Barbara Price sounded pleased with herself. "Well, we can't legally connect Kojima Enterprises with Nishiki-Tetsuo, nor does the CIA or Interpol have any kind of information on Kojima Enterprises that leads them to believe they are engaged in illegal activities."

Bolan nodded to himself. Nishiki-Tetsuo was extremely effective at covering its tracks. "So exactly what do you have for me?"

"We've got confirmation. The address your informant gave you is correct. There is a Kojima Enterprises facility in Osaka where he said it was, and the CIA has had it under observation for the past forty-five minutes and is continuing to monitor."

"Any unusual activity?"

"No. No one seems to be having a fire sale, and we haven't detected any signs of major movement. The place is acting like it's business as usual."

Bolan considered. "According to Si, the Kojima Enterprises facility in Osaka is where a lot of the weapons he procures in mainland Asia go for transfer and sale to Japanese domestic criminals. He said he also believes that facility is a storage and transfer point for significant quantities of illegal drugs, mostly heroin.''

Price didn't sound totally convinced. "You believe him?"

"He had a gun to his head when he told me. He seemed very sincere.''

"What do you intend to do?''

"We really have only two options. We can pull back and try to find another chink in Nishiki-Tetsuo's armor, or I take this lead and hit Kojima Enterprises right now.''

"You already know this, Striker, but this isn't going to be like rooting Korean gunrunners out of little mountain villages. You'll be attacking a Japanese civilian business concern on Japanese soil in a major city. We have absolutely no proof of any kind of wrongdoing against the United States other than the word of one minor Korean gunrunner, much less any kind of permission to take action from the Japanese government. Our CIA agents in Japan are only authorized to observe and pass on information to you through us. The White House is unwilling to let CIA agents become directly involved and risk being compromised. If you drive up to the U.S. Embassy with half the Japanese police on your tail, they're not going to open the gates. You're almost totally alone on this one.''

"What do you mean, 'almost totally'?''

"Well, we've sent you some deniable backup.''

"Oh, really? Who?''

"Akira Tokaido landed in Tokyo yesterday.''

Bolan raised an eyebrow. "I thought direct use of the cybernetic team in field operations was officially frowned upon.''

"Oh, it is, but this is a pretty unusual operation, and besides, sooner or later you're going to need someone who looks Japanese. A bunch of big Americans with guns can't run around indefinitely without some kind of local connection.'' Price's tone became serious. "He may be part of the cybernetic team, but he's just like the rest of us on the Farm. Deniable and expendable. He volunteered.''

Expendability was a grim fact they had all accepted when

they took the job. Bolan looked at his watch again. "All right, link up with Akira. See if he's clever enough to figure out some kind of safe haven after we extract."

"I'm on it."

Bolan nodded. "Good. I'm hitting Kojima Enterprises in thirty minutes."

Osaka, Japan

YUKIO TADASHI SAT at his desk, and the phone trembled in his hand. He was the head of security for Kojima Enterprises, and he looked the part. He had been a sumo wrestler in his youth, and while he had never risen high in the rankings, his massive bulk was very useful in his present job. He had slimmed down considerably from his competition days, and was now a comparatively svelte five foot eleven and three hundred pounds. Tadashi had started off as a bone-breaker, and through sheer hard work and talent had risen to his current position. His primary responsibility was securing the illegal goods stored in the Kojima facility and safeguarding their transfer. He also kept unauthorized people out of unauthorized areas, bribed the local authorities, bullied the local workers and sank an occasional troublemaker to the bottom of Osaka harbor. Tadashi was very good at his job, and he was feared and respected in both the legal and illegal business communities in Osaka. Fear and respect burst out of his pores as he listened to the voice on the phone. The voice frightened him.

Tadashi had never seen the face that belonged to the voice. He didn't know the voice's name. The only thing he knew was the sound of the voice itself. He didn't hear it often, but when he did, the voice automatically made him very nervous. The voice spoke perfect Japanese, except that it spoke with an almost machinelike lack of inflection. It never made any attempt to identify itself. It was simply the only voice that ever spoke over this particular secure line. Very early in Tadashi's tenure as head of security, it had been made very clear to him that for all intents and purposes, the voice on the secure line was the voice of God. Tadashi's obedience was to be unquestioning and immediate. The voice was speaking to him now, and the security man was absolutely appalled at what it was telling him.

He wiped his brow with the back of his hand. "Excuse me, sir. Could you please repeat that?"

There was no pause. "Which of my instructions have you failed to understand?"

Tadashi swallowed with difficulty. "You wish me to destroy all five hundred kilograms of heroin we have in storage, as well as the remaining consignments of cocaine and methamphetamines. Without trace."

"That is correct."

Tadashi pulled out his silk handkerchief and wiped his profusely sweating brow again. "You want me to take all weapons being stored at the facility and load them in container barges, then scuttle the barges in Osaka harbor and sink the weapons."

"That is correct."

The security man's jaw opened and closed several times. The voice on the phone spoke to him again. "Listen to me very carefully. The Kojima Enterprises facility in Osaka will be attacked within the next twenty-four hours. We have already sent you backup. However, we believe the attack will be brazen. With shooting, the police will come. We may not be able to contain the resulting investigation with bribery. I suspect our enemy knows this. I suspect he is counting on it. All traces of contraband in the facility must be removed or destroyed. Arm your men and secure the facility grounds immediately. Do you understand?"

Tadashi frowned and glanced up. He cocked his head and squinted out the window. His eyes flew wide.

The voice spoke again. "I said, do you understand?"

The security chief had a feeling like a cold wind moving through his guts. "Sir, an unidentified helicopter is flying straight at the building at high speed."

THE ROOF of the Kojima Enterprises main building almost seem to fall upward toward Bolan as Grimaldi dropped the hijacked Kawasaki executive helicopter like a stone. The Executioner shouted over the roar of the rotors and the rush of air through the open doors. "Last chance, Barb! Do we have any change in status?"

"CIA says still no unusual activity at the Kojima facility. The only thing unusual is that they can see you."

Bolan nodded to himself. "We're going in! Drop the bird, Jack!"

Just before it seemed the helicopter was going to slam through the top of the roof, the rotors roared and Grimaldi pulled up the nose. A second later the airframe shuddered as the skids slammed onto the roof.

Bolan leaped out the door. "Let's move!"

Burdick jumped out behind Bolan with an M-4 carbine and M-203 grenade launcher of his own, and a second later Grimaldi leaped out of the cockpit. All three men wore armor over their raid suits, and gas masks rested on their straps over the tops of their heads. The helicopter's rotors were still turning and the engine whined in a high idle as the three-man team deployed. On reaching Osaka, Grimaldi had landed the Viking, and the Navy pilots had dutifully gotten out and told the airport police that they had been diverted off course by catastrophic instrument failures. As soon as they had gone off in the security jeep to discuss this mysterious phenomenon with Japanese airport authorities, Bolan and his team had slipped out of the Viking jet's weapons bay and stolen the first helicopter they had come upon.

Even Bolan had to admit the operation was starting to get extremely fast and loose.

The big man moved across the helicopter pad toward the roof access door at a run. He reached into a pouch of his web gear and pulled out a small shaped charge. The security door was white-painted steel with a computerized combination lock. Bolan slapped the shaped charge against the top hinge and pushed a detonator pin into the lump of plastic explosive.

He stepped away, then pushed the button on the detonation box strapped to his web gear. The charge went off with a sharp crack, and the steel door sagged with its top corner blackened and folded inward. Bolan put his boot into the door, and the bottom hinge screamed as it twisted and gave way.

He turned to Grimaldi and Burdick. "What I want are any kind of sensitive files. According to Si, the illegal stuff is being stored at the bottom. We leave that for the authorities to find." Bolan glanced behind him. There was a civilian helicopter with the Kojima Enterprises logo parked on a second pad twenty yards from the helicopter they had stolen.

Bolan jerked his head at it. "Speaking of attracting the authorities, Burdick, burn that chopper."

The big Marine turned and fired his M-203, then the three men moved into the stairwell. The 40 mm white-phosphorus grenade smashed against the helicopter's side and detonated with a boom. Streamers of superheated white smoke and burning phosphorus shot into the air over the Kojima building. The helicopter began to burn in earnest. Bolan and his team took the stairs three at a time as they descended to the building's top floor. They came to another steel door, and Bolan pulled out another charge. "All right, masks on."

The three men pulled their gas masks down over their heads as Bolan detonated the charge on the door. He smashed down the sagging door, then quickly stepped back around the jamb. Burdick and Grimaldi pressed themselves on either side of the door as gunfire erupted from inside and bullets whined and sparked against the wall of the stairwell behind them. Grimaldi hurled a flash-stun grenade around the doorway, and Bolan tossed in a CS tear-gas grenade behind it. Blinding white light pulsed, and the stairwell roared with the thunderclap. Bolan came around the corner with his teammates behind him.

Two men in coveralls reeled on their feet with revolvers in their hands. They were temporarily blinded and deafened, and they were already gagging and choking as the gray CS gas rose up and expanded through the hallway like a noxious fog. Bolan stepped up and planted his boot in one of the security men's chests and sent him flying off of his feet. Bolan grabbed the other man by the front of his coverall and swung him around into the wall with bone-jarring force. He leaned into the man's swollen and tearing face and shouted through his gas mask in rough Japanese. "Where is main security?"

The man coughed and stuttered a stream of words. Bolan frowned. He had operated in Japan before, and prior to this mission he had done a three-week cram course at the CIA language school in Virginia, but even he had to admit that Japanese was a hard language and his grasp of it was woefully lacking for his mission, particularly for interrogating choking and half-deafened natives in a combat situation. He would have to keep it simple. "Room number!"

"Eleven! Room number eleven!"

"Floor!"

"This floor! This floor!"

Bolan whipped his elbow into the man's jaw and sent him sliding down the wall into an unconscious sitting position. There was a very real possibility that other than a hardened cadre, most of the guards at this facility wouldn't be aware of Kojima Enterprises's illegal operation, much less its connection with the activities of Nishiki-Tetsuo. Even while they tried to burn down the operation, civilian casualties had to be avoided at all costs. Bolan glanced down the hall. The hallway itself was long and narrow, with doors along both sides and a pair of double doors at both ends. The big man looked back over his shoulder. The double door down the hallway read 11. That way led to the front of the building. A security suite would have a top-floor vantage looking out across the facility. There would be a security station on the ground floor and below, as well, but here at the top would be the real security nexus, and very close by would be the sensitive materials that Bolan and his team could get their hands on quickly. If there was anyone inside, they would be destroying sensitive files and calling up reinforcements. "Jack! Do the door!"

Grimaldi moved down the hall with a shaped charge in his hand.

Bolan jerked his head back down the hall toward the stairs. "Burdick! Cover our rear!" The Marine swung the M-4's twin muzzles to cover the hallway as Bolan moved in behind Grimaldi. The pilot slapped the charge against the seam between the two doors and pushed in a detonator pin. He and Bolan stepped to either side of the doorway, and Grimaldi pushed the button on the small black detonator box clipped to his chest strap.

The door blew inward on its hinges, and immediately a long, sustained burst of high-powered riflefire tore into the hallway from within the security suite. As Bolan lobbed in a tear-gas grenade, Grimaldi unclipped a second one and tossed it inside. There was another long roar of automatic riflefire, then Bolan distinctly heard the clack of an automatic rifle's action slamming open on an empty chamber. The big man swung into the room with his M-4 carbine raised to his shoulder.

A Japanese man of even more impressive girth than Burdick stood behind a desk coughing, with tears streaming out of his eyes as he tried to fumble a fresh magazine into an M-16 assault rifle. Bolan strode through the expanding gas cloud and rammed the muzzle of his carbine into the man's chest and drove him back down into his padded chair. He slapped aside the muzzle of the man's empty rifle and kept the muzzle of his own carbine firmly jammed into the man's chest. He roared a word in Japanese. "Files!"

The massive Japanese coughed and shook his head as he said something Bolan couldn't make out. The Executioner pushed the muzzle of his carbine harder into the man's chest. Seconds were quickly ticking away. "Files!"

The man shook his head again and pointed into the hallway. Bolan yanked him to his feet and dragged him back out of the room. The man stumbled toward the next door and pointed at it. The door was painted to look like wood, but it was steel and had no knob. Beside the door was a computer keypad that activated the coded lock. Bolan raised his carbine again. His meaning was clear. With streaming eyes the big man punched a code into the door lock. The door opened, and air hissed out of the hermetically sealed room, carrying the sour stench of burned incendiary.

Grimaldi yelled through his mask. "What have we got, Striker?"

Bolan cursed as he looked in the room. In the modern world, it was almost impossible to be sure that a file had been totally erased. Somewhere on a computer disk, the ghosts of erased data could be retrieved with special software and high-powered scanners. The surest way to erase sensitive information was literally to destroy it. The small, secure storage room consisted of several banks of steel safes set into the walls. The burned-metal stench told Bolan everything. The safes had been set with incendiary charges. Before the fat man had begun to fire at them through the doorway, he had managed to send the destruct signal. Everything in the safes was now molten slag.

Bolan whirled. Time was running out. They couldn't afford to run around the complex looking for clues. They had to do their damage and get out. Bolan marched the big man back to the security suite, then he scanned the bank of the console inset in the desk. Bolan shoved the man and yelled a word in Japanese. "Fire!"

The big man coughed and wheezed in the tear gas. Bolan yanked his head up by the hair and pointed his carbine at the ceiling. The man nodded and pointed to a button on the console. Bolan shoved him over to Grimaldi, then punched the button. A high, whining alarm began to shrill throughout the building, and a moment later a small nozzle descended almost seamlessly out of the ceiling and began to spray out high-pressure streams of water. All down the hallway more nozzles descended, and the floor suddenly began to resemble a teak-lined, pile-carpeted car wash. Bolan suspected that even now the alarm had also been sent to the Osaka fire department. The Executioner moved to the window and looked down. Seconds later Kojima Enterprises employees began to stream out of the building in impressively orderly lines. The employees looked back over their shoulders as smoke rose into the sky from the burning helicopter on the roof. Bolan's eyes narrowed. This was good, but it wasn't enough.

A fire and a burned-up helicopter could be explained fairly easily, and its investigation contained. What was required here was something impossible to cover up, something that would be in every newspaper and fill the evening newscasts in Tokyo. Bolan slung his carbine and hoisted the big security man's oversize chair over his head. He took two lunging strides and heaved the chair through the window. The glass shattered outward, and the chair tumbled into space. Down below, several people on the ground screamed. Bolan went and stood in the shattered window for several long seconds and let the hundreds of onlookers on the ground see the masked and armored man standing over them. He suddenly whipped his carbine around on its sling and brought it to his shoulder. He leveled the double muzzles of carbine and grenade launcher on the crowd.

Screaming broke out in earnest, and the orderly evacuation lines broke apart as Kojima Enterprises employees began to run in all directions. The M-4 snarled in Bolan's hands as he fired long bursts over the heads of the crowd. The carbine clacked open on empty, and he flipped up the ladder sight of the M-203 and aimed at a white sedan in the parking lot. The M-203 roared, and the 40 mm grenade arced out over the grounds. A second later the sedan disappeared in white-hot smoke and burning streamers of fire. The screaming below intensified. Bolan loaded another grenade and burned a minivan near the Kojima truck docks. He fired a third and a fourth round, and smoke and fire rose in plumes into the sky from a loose ring around the Kojima grounds. Secondary explosions filled the air as the vehicles' gas tanks caught fire and exploded. Other vehicles began to burn as they were dowsed with streamers of exploding gasoline and burning phosphorus.

Grimaldi leaned out and peered down at the carnage while he kept his gun on the Japanese security man. The flames rose, and Kojima employees began to run back toward the building away from the expanding ring of fire. Black smoke began to fill the sky. "Looks like a Godzilla movie."

Bolan nodded.

Grimaldi's eyes narrowed behind his mask. "What about the files?"

The big man shook his head. "They're toast."

"What now?"

The Executioner turned and looked at the big Japanese. "Let's take our friend and get out of here."

8

Yonekawa Shirata sat in the "war room" of a Nishiki-Tetsuo-owned skyscraper in Tokyo. He was becoming profoundly disturbed. The old man was on the line, and he wasn't pleased. "Do you have any idea of how bad this is?"

Shirata was all too aware of how bad the situation was. He had spent the past eight hours attempting to do damage control. Despite his best efforts, the situation was completely out of control. The Kojima Enterprises facility had been utterly compromised. Hundreds of witnesses had watched as an armed gunman fired down upon them and then blew up half of the company's parking lot. There had been no way to keep out the police. The perpetrators had flown off in a stolen helicopter, but the Japanese police had stormed the building anyway in full riot gear and gone from room to room on every floor of the facility. Five hundred kilograms of heroin, seventy-five of cocaine and several truckloads of illegal firearms had been found on the premises. PSIA agents were crawling all over the facility. More than half of the Kojima Enterprises executive staff was being held by the police without bail, and they were being held incommunicado, as well. Shirata still couldn't account for many of the executives and security men who were involved in the illegal business at the Kojima facility. Even the highest-level police that Nishiki-Tetsuo had bought and paid for could do little or nothing. This kind of situation had simply never happened in modern Japan. It was on every television channel and the front-page headline of every newspaper.

Shirata steeled himself to accept the old man's anger. "The situation is not as bad as it could be."

There was an incredulous silence from the old man's end. "Oh?"

"Yes, the loss of Kojima Enterprises is a genuine blow to us. It was a major import and distribution site. I am sure, all told, that we stand to lose untold millions of yen. However, I was in contact with the head of security during the actual attack. He managed to send the destruct codes to the sensitive files before I lost contact with him. Our cybernetics team has verified that the destruct codes were sent and the incendiary charges fired. All evidence that could have connected Kojima Enterprises with Nishiki-Tetsuo has been destroyed. Those executives who knew of the connection were chosen for their loyalty. They will not turn over on us. They know there is no place they can hide, and they know the benefits they will receive for keeping their mouths shut."

The old man was silent for long moments. "Where is the Kojima head of security now?"

Shirata sighed. "Dead or in jail with the rest, I suppose."

"Verify that."

"I will. Also I have found out some things that may interest you. This afternoon, little more than half an hour before the attack on the Kojima facility, a United States Navy Viking antisubmarine jet made an emergency landing in Osaka, claiming instrument failure."

The old man grunted. "That is interesting, but can you connect the two?"

"Not positively, but the jet was stationed aboard the United States Navy carrier *Carl Vinson.* The boat is presently on maneuvers off the coast of Korea. It is interesting that this supposedly stricken U.S. Navy jet found it necessary to fly all the way across the island of Honshu and land in Osaka. There are half a dozen other airports, much closer, that they could have landed at. Also, within ten minutes of the U.S. jet's landing, a Kawasaki business helicopter was stolen from the airport. Almost all the eyewitnesses on the ground at Kojima saw the gunmen flee from the roof in a helicopter. Many of the witnesses were able to make out the markings on the helicopter, and it has been positively identified as the same aircraft that was stolen at the airport.''

"Mmm. The Americans used a helicopter in Korea. They flew it to the *Carl Vinson*, then flew the Viking jet here to Japan. When the plane landed in Osaka, they were hiding in the weapons bay."

"I believe that is what happened."

"Yes, it would explain how they were able to catch us with our pants down at Kojima. Where is the Navy jet now?"

"The pilots were debriefed by the airport authorities, then the jet was refueled and the pilots were released. They flew the aircraft back to the *Carl Vinson*."

The old man's voice grew colder. "Where is this Korean who has betrayed us, Si?"

"I believe he is in the custody of the South Korean military police."

"See to it that he is killed."

"I will see to it immediately."

"Good." The old man's voice lowered. "This situation is intolerable, Shirata. Everything the American has done in the past is nothing, little more than irritations. Now he has attacked us here, in Japan, in a major city, in broad daylight. He has compromised a major operation of ours and cost us millions of yen. Once again he has struck and escaped without a trace. You and I both know he will not stop. I believe you did everything possible in this situation, Shirata. That will be enough to save your life from the board. Many members are becoming nervous. They are more concerned now with ending this situation than assigning blame, but you must find this American, and you must kill him quickly." The old man's voice hardened again. "He is an American, operating almost alone in a foreign land. He cannot pass for Japanese. He cannot hide for long. Nor can he afford to. He must show himself to attack us. We have his description. If the American Marine, Burdick, is still with him, we have his description, as well.

Use every connection you have. I want every cop and every criminal we own in every major city on Honshu looking for him. Find him, Shirata! Kill him!''

Shirata modulated his voice to radiate ruthless efficiency. "Taido will be here within the hour. We will find the American. We will kill him."

"Do not fail."

The line clicked dead, and Shirata set the receiver down. It rang again almost immediately. "Yes?"

His personal secretary and chief communications officer was on the line. She was a vast improvement over the disrespectful old hag he had endured during his tenure of punishment in the gray office. "Shirata-san!"

"Yes."

"I have a communication from Osaka."

Shirata frowned. He had given strict orders that there were to be no communications from Osaka routed here. "Who is it?"

"It is Yukio Tadashi, the head of security from the Kojima facility. I thought you would wish to speak to him personally."

Shirata sat up in his chair. "Patch him through on the secure line immediately."

There was a moment's pause, and the line clicked. It was unmistakably Tadashi. "Sir, I—"

Shirata cut him off. "Why are you not dead or in jail?"

The security chief sounded miserable. "I destroyed the files as you ordered, and then went down to try to destroy the contraband. When everything began to explode, I decided it would be better for me to escape and report directly to you rather than be captured by the police or killed by the American."

Shirata's breath hissed inward. "You saw the American?"

"He was hard to miss. He was big, and he was shooting and setting everything on fire. There was a smaller man with him. When they escaped, I believe the smaller man was piloting the helicopter." Tadashi paused a moment and took a deep breath. "There was another man as well, a big man. They were all wearing gas masks, but I could see the back of his head. He had red hair."

Shirata's fist clenched. That would have been Burdick. He had gone cowboy on them in Korea, and now Shirata was almost certain the old man's suspicion that the Marine was operating with the American was correct. Shirata's jaw clenched. The penny-ante black marketer had decided to turn hero. It was a decision he was going to regret. Shirata's eyes suddenly narrowed. "Where have you been?"

Tadashi sounded even more miserable. "First there were fire trucks, and right behind them swarms of police. I made it outside of the grounds, but there were police cars everywhere. They were setting up blockades on all the streets near the facility. I am known in Osaka. I did not believe I could allow myself to be seen, and I was not sure I could get past them. I spent the last eight hours in a trash container behind a noodle shop. I got out when it was dark and went to find a secure place to report from."

"Where are you now?"

"At a whorehouse I know not far from the facility. The girls here know me very well. I have had them close up shop for the night. I believe I am safe for the moment."

Shirata thought for several moments. "You have acted correctly, Yukio. You will leave the number where you can be reached with the woman who patched you through to me. I will contact you shortly, and see to your extraction from Osaka."

"Yes, sir. I will await your orders."

Shirata cut the line. There were three of them. The commando, Burdick and an unidentified pilot. According to police reports, the helicopter had flown from the roof of the Kojima facility and headed west. Shirata didn't believe they had gone far. With the files at Kojima destroyed, the Americans no longer had any clues to work with. They would have to try to generate new leads, and here, on Japan's big island, that would be much different than the cowboy games they had played in Korea.

Shirata leaned back in his chair. Tokyo was his turf, and the Americans were now wanted fugitives in a foreign land. To get a new lead on Nishiki-Tetsuo, they would have to stick their necks way out. Without leads, their task was without doubt impossible. Shirata doubted that would stop them. The Americans wanted vengeance. They wouldn't leave until they got it. It would be their undoing. The commando had made an impressive series of attacks, but his trail was dead, and now he was left with only the most desperate of options.

It was time to see how this American enjoyed being the hunted.

AKIRA TOKAIDO SAT cross-legged on the floor with a notebook computer in his lap. He was surrounded by three large suitcases, which were all open. A tangle of wires snaked out between them, connecting them with one another, the notebook computer in his lap and a telephone on the bed with an abnormal number of input jacks. Each suitcase was filled with a mind-numbing array of electronics gear. Tokaido was grinning from ear to ear. Yukio Tadashi sat on the bed next to the telephone. He was nearly cross-eyed from continually staring at the front sight of Bolan's Beretta 93-R pistol. The gun's muzzle hovered an inch from the center of his eyebrows. Tadashi had done very well. He had stayed with the script, and even managed to ad-lib when it had been called for. A pistol was often an amazing motivator. Burdick stood behind the big Japanese with his shotgun. Grimaldi was perched in the windowsill peering out into the night through the drawn blinds.

The Executioner kept the gun where it was while he turned to Tokaido. "Did we get it?"

The young computer expert nodded happily. "Oh, we got it, all right. A clean trace."

"Who was our friend here talking to?"

"Someone in Tokyo."

Bolan had already suspected that. "Can you be more specific?"

"The Nishiki-Tetsuo Tokyo building. The corporate offices. Whoever our friend was talking to was using a LAN, or local area network. It's a series of linked computers, and let me tell you, the Nishiki-Tetsuo setup is state-of-the-art. This particular LAN is one of their corporate office's main secure communications nets, and it's a generation ahead of everything except the most experimental stuff we have back in the States." Tokaido watched information scroll across his computer screen and shook his head in wonder. "I came over here hoping I would be able to help you hack into their system, and I can tell you right now, without our buddy Yukio here helping on the phone, it probably would've taken me a long time to get in, and chances are I would've been discovered in the first sixty seconds."

Bolan nodded. He had gambled that whoever was in charge of dealing with his attacks would be desperate to speak with the head of security from the Kojima Enterprises facility. The gamble had paid off. The enemy had been too eager, and had opened a chink in its own armor. Bolan had no doubt that Nishiki-Tetsuo had a fortress of electronic security around its covert communications systems, but that was simply no match against the mind of Akira Tokaido armed with an open line into the system. "What else can you get me?"

Tokaido chewed his lip as fingers blurred across his keypad. "Right now I'm trying to fool their LAN into believing that me and my computer are just another part of their network, and I'd like to do that without setting off any alarms or leaving any trace."

"Can you get me more specific information?"

The young man's eyes flew back and forth as data scrolled down his screen. "That depends. Some of this stuff is coded, and a lot of the information is coded on a need-to-know basis even between the computers within the LAN itself. Stuff like illegal-weapon shipping dates, who they've had killed recently, their directory of who was responsible for using Ebola as weapon against the United States—all that is going to take time, if it's possible at all with what I have to work with here.''

"What if we fly you back to the States and get you hooked up back at the Farm?''

Tokaido shook his head. "To do that, I'm going to have to disconnect, and once I do, I can't promise you I can get back in. With all of the fun and games you've been running on Nishiki-Tetsuo, they have to be on a war footing. They may be changing their security codes daily. If I disconnect and then try to get in again, it may be our system that gets broken into and our location pinned down. I don't like to admit it, but with the gear they have, they might well be able to do it without my ever knowing it. In my opinion, we've got gold, right here and now. I don't think we can afford to risk it by moving. But that's just my opinion. You're the boss."

Bolan shook his head. Tokaido was the expert in this situation, and the Executioner had profound respect for his abilities. "No, we'll do it your way. Tell me, what can you get me, here and now? We've got to keep moving, and we have to keep hitting them. If we get tied down for too long, we're dead meat.''

"Well, how about schematics of the corporate office building, the probable physical location of the security LAN I've hacked into and maybe even the actual office suite where the other party on the phone was located?''

Bolan grinned. "Is that all?''

"Give me a minute.'' Tokaido suddenly looked up from his computer. "There is one thing we have to consider.''

"What's that?''

He let out a breath from between his teeth. "That what we might have here is crap, and that it's us that have been caught with our pants down. It's well within the realm of possibility that we were detected by Nishiki-Tetsuo security the second we got on-line, and that we've been located, and they're sending some boys over right now.''

It wasn't a happy thought. Bolan holstered his pistol and folded his arms across his chest as he examined the odds. "I'm betting they haven't. You have fifteen minutes to get whatever you can, and then we're out of here."

All three men looked up at Bolan. Burdick shrugged his big shoulders. Grimaldi gave Bolan a what-the-hell grin. "So, we're going to Tokyo."

The Executioner nodded. "We're going to Tokyo."

Burdick jerked a thumb at Tadashi. "What about fat boy?"

Bolan smiled and looked over at Tokaido and his equipment. "You can open up another secure line on that rig, can't you?"

"It'll take me ten seconds, tops."

Bolan nodded. "I think our friend here needs to make another phone call."

9

PSIA Agent Honda Mitsuko was nearly beside herself with both anger and excitement as her fingers flew across her keyboard. The attack on Kojima Enterprises was the biggest thing that had come into the agency's domain since the nerve-gas attacks by the fanatic religious cult in the subways of Tokyo. She had long suspected a tie-in between Kojima Enterprises and Nishiki-Tetsuo, but she had never been able to prove anything, and up to the present time, Kojima Enterprises had never been suspected of any illegal dealings anyway. Everyone in the PSIA, and nearly the entire Japanese government and business community, knew that Nishiki-Tetsuo had vast secret holdings beyond those that were known or even suspected.

But this opened the floodgates of inquiry. The men involved had stolen a helicopter and attacked a major Japanese business in broad daylight with automatic weapons and explosives. They had gone straight to the top floor and used tear gas and hand-to-hand tactics to overwhelm the security force. The attackers had gone out of their way to avoid casualties. It hadn't been the work of some berserk Buddhist death cult. Mitsuko frowned. And that was what a number of people both in the police and the government were already trying to allege. She didn't believe that for a second.

The attackers had set the helicopter on the roof on fire. They had burned and blown up cars in the parking lot, but only ones that were far away from the fleeing employees. She was willing to bet that it was the attackers themselves who had set off the fire alarm. They had fired their guns over the heads of the civilians. Mitsuko grinned in amusement. What they had done was create a gigantic ruckus, one that couldn't be covered up, and it had allowed the illegal weapons and drugs being stored on the premises to be found before there was even a chance of them being concealed.

It was a ruckus just like the one on the wharves of Naha a few short days ago.

Except this time they had gone for Nishiki-Tetsuo's secure files. The door to the secure room had been open, and the destruct sequence had burned all computer disks and files in the safes. Mitsuko doubted the attackers had gotten away with anything sensitive, but they had certainly tried.

Mitsuko leaned back in her chair. She couldn't prove that the warehouse in Okinawa had been owned by Nishiki-Tetsuo, nor could she prove that Kojima Enterprises was owned by Nishiki-Tetsuo, either. The arrested Kojima executives all told the same monotonously similar story. Their combination of loyalty and fear was impressive. Mitsuko knew one thing deep in her bones, and that was someone had declared war on Nishiki-Tetsuo. She had caught the Kojima employees in one discrepancy. All the arrested executives stated the same thing. They knew nothing about the drugs and weapons being stored. They hardly had even heard of Nishiki-Tetsuo, much less of any connection between the giant corporation and Kojima Enterprises, and they believed they had been attacked by Japanese, perhaps Yakuza gangsters. Several claimed to have seen them.

But the PSIA had also talked to the security guards who had been incapacitated by the attackers. They had been taken from the facility by the police while they were still unconscious, and had been unable to get the official story that Kojima was trying to spread. The guards had been gassed, and perhaps their eyewitness account was suspect, but both of them said the same thing. Their attackers had been large. One of the guards claimed that one of the attackers had red hair. Both said they believed the attackers had been Caucasians.

That was highly irregular. Mitsuko could accept that one Japanese corporation would use guerrilla warfare to destroy or discredit a competitor, but the use of foreign mercenaries was unheard of. One of the reasons that the Japanese crime syndicates had been so hard to break or penetrate was that they kept everything in the family, and all operations were in-house. They might use foreigners on foreign soil, with suitable intermediaries and cutouts between them, but foreign mercenaries on Japanese soil was unthinkable. So, the question was, just who was at war with Nishiki-Tetsuo, and what had been done to cause foreigners to make outrageous, nearly suicidal attacks in the Japanese home islands?

Mitsuko's intercom buzzed, and the PSIA telecommunications operator spoke quickly. "Agent Mitsuko!"

"Yes, Kobu, what is it?"

"I have an urgent communication for you."

"Urgent? From whom?"

"I do not know. They say they have sensitive information for the PSIA agent in charge of investigations of the Kojima Enterprises situation."

Mitsuko frowned. She would love to take the call, but she had been clearly delineated as a distant third-in-command in the situation. Her investigative skills were unquestioned, but she was a woman. She wouldn't lead interrogations or do any debriefings to the media. "You should direct the call to Senior Agent Takahashi, or his assistant, Kobu. You know that."

Kobu was undeterred. "Yes, exactly so. However, the informants mentioned Nishiki-Tetsuo. I thought you should know."

Mitsuko snapped upright in her chair. "Thank you, Kobu. Connect me immediately."

"I am connecting you now."

Mitsuko grinned. Kobu liked her, and she flirted with him outrageously. It was beginning to pay off. The line clicked and the voice spoke in a slow, distinct Japanese baritone. "To whom am I speaking?"

"This is Agent Honda Mitsuko of the Public Security Investigation Agency. How may I assist you?"

"Do you speak English?"

Mitsuko's eyebrows rose. Her trained ear told her that the voice was being fed through a voice scrambler, but she didn't skip a beat as she changed languages. "Yes, I do. What can I do for you?"

"I have Yukio Tadashi, the head of security for the Osaka branch of Kojima Enterprises, in my care. He wishes to confess his sins, and has many interesting things to tell you."

Mitsuko kept her voice calm. She knew that Yukio Tadashi hadn't been found at the scene, but not very many people outside of the PSIA and the upper levels of the Osaka police would. "I would be very interested in speaking with Yukio Tadashi. How may I get hold of him?"

"I am going to give you an address. Do you have a pen?"

"Yes, please go ahead." Mitsuko wrote as she was given a terse set of directions to a place in the city of Hongu. She racked her brain as she wrote down directions to an inn she had never heard of. She believed Hongu was in Wakayama Prefecture. Her eyes flicked up to the map of Japan that dominated the wall next to her desk. Hongu was a small city, and was located up in the foothills near Yoshino-Kumano National Park. Mitsuko did some mental calculations. Hongu was within helicopter range of Osaka. Wakayama Prefecture was also sparsely populated by main-island standards. Once clear of Osaka Bay, it would be possible for the attackers to have hugged the coastline and then dive inland up through the mountains and fields of Wakayama and landed outside of Hongu without being spotted.

The voice interrupted her musings. "Do you have it?"

Mitsuko tried to think of a way to keep them on the line. "I need—"

The phone line cut abruptly. Mitsuko stabbed the button of her intercom. "Kobu! Tell me you put a trace on that call!"

Kobu almost sounded hurt. "Of course I put a trace on the call."

"And?"

Kobu sighed. "He was not on long enough for a complete trace. His voice was being run through a scrambler. I believe he suspected his call would be traced when he placed it."

"What do you have?"

"The call came from the Wayakama Prefecture."

Mitsuko bolted out of her chair. "I need a helicopter fueled and ready to go in fifteen minutes, with an investigative team on board. I want the Hongu police to surround the following address, and have a forensics team standing by." Mitsuko gave Kobu the address and then punched off her intercom. Things were getting more interesting by the minute.

THE STOLEN HELICOPTER made a straight course over the midnight skyline of Tokyo. Bolan and Burdick sat in the back armed and armored, with a full battle load. Grimaldi flew the chopper in. As Bolan and his three-man strike team flew into the attack, Akira Tokaido was arranging a bolt-hole for them through the CIA. They hadn't had time to set anything up. They would just have to hope Tokaido had something for them once they were airborne again.

Bolan turned to Burdick. "All right. Same situation as before. I want to raise a stink and get whatever information we can. We still don't know who the real players are, and I want to avoid casualties until we do."

Burdick nodded. He didn't like having his hands tied in a combat situation, but the big man was calling all the shots. "You got it, boss. Gas them, get the goods and get out."

"Right." A ghost of a smile played across the Executioner's face. Burdick might be a semireformed criminal, but he was still a United States Marine. It made him extremely mission oriented. "This is downtown Tokyo, Sergeant. We don't have any margin for error. The police are right down the street. We're in and out. Ten minutes, tops." He stabbed his finger on the building blueprint Tokaido had hacked out of the Nishiki-Tetsuo computer LAN. "We go straight for the office suite Akira traced our phone conversation to. I want computer disks, files, day planners, anything. But remember, ten minutes, tops. I want this sharp and surgical, and I don't care if you've found the Holy Grail. Ten minutes, and the bus is leaving.''

Burdick grinned from ear to ear. "You got it. We're in and out.''

Grimaldi craned his head back around the pilot's seat. "ETA two minutes.''

Bolan watched as skyscrapers flew past in blurred towers of light. Flying into Tokyo hadn't been difficult. Tokyo was one of the largest cities in the world, and at any time of day or night helicopters were in the air, ranging from private business, to police, to the local news choppers. Grimaldi stayed low and between buildings to avoid the local air-traffic-control radars. The pilot was grinning. "Nishiki-Tetsuo corporate office, dead ahead!''

Bolan glanced forward as Grimaldi brought the chopper up to land on the roof. The Nishiki-Tetsuo building wasn't the largest skyscraper in Tokyo, but it was massive. Lights outside the building lit its exterior, but the endless rows of black glass revealed nothing of the interior. It was distinctly fortresslike for a business building.

The chopper surged up and over the roof, and Grimaldi circled low. The roof had a small forest of communications antennae and several large satellite dishes. It also had an embarrassment of helicopter pads. There were four of them, and three were occupied. Bolan's eyes slitted. "Jack, this chopper's serial numbers are known. Pick one of those three over there that you like and hot-wire it. We'll burn the rest on the pads to confuse things.''

Grimaldi nodded. "I like the way you think, and I like that Dauphin over there.''

Bolan glanced at the aircraft. The Aérospatiale Dauphin was one of the sleekest-looking commercial helicopters available and one of the fastest. "You've got ten minutes to bust into it.''

The Stony Man pilot landed the squat Kawasaki on the empty pad. "Get out of my bird, and I'm all over it."

Bolan flung open the door. "Let's move, Sergeant!"

Burdick took his shotgun in both hands and leaped out behind Bolan. The two men sprinted to the secondary roof-access door they had marked on the blueprint, pulling their gas masks over their faces as they ran. Tokaido hadn't been able to hack out specific secure computer files when he had broken into the Nishiki-Tetsuo LAN, but he had learned just about everything there was to know about the building itself, including its security access codes. Bolan skidded to a halt in front of the white outer security door and punched a set of numbers into a keypad set into the wall next to the door. There was a metallic clicking, and the door hissed open a crack as it unlocked. Bolan moved down the stairs with his M-4 carbine leveled. When they reached another door, the Executioner punched in a different set of numbers. The floor they wanted was six down from the roof, and on that floor was the office suite that Yukio Tadashi had been connected to when he had phoned in. The Executioner was very curious to see just who and what might be in that office.

Bolan and Burdick moved unopposed from floor to floor down the gray concrete stairwell. There were surveillance cameras on the roof, but so far Bolan had heard no alarms. He spoke into his throat mike. "Jack, how are we doing?"

The pilot's voice came back in Bolan's earpiece. "I'm in the Dauphin. It's been fueled and I'm warming it up. I left the doors to the Kawasaki open, including the gas cap, and the engine is running. One willie pete, and she'll burn like kindling."

"Watch your tail. Someone has got to figure out there's an unauthorized helicopter on the roof."

"I'm watching."

Bolan checked the symbol written on the next door with the one on his blueprint. It was the suite they wanted. He took out a tear-gas grenade, and Burdick followed suit. The

Executioner reached up and punched in the door's security code. The lock clicked, and he shoved the door open.

A striking-looking Japanese woman wearing an exquisitely tailored tweed jacket was trying to open the nearest office door with her hands full of files. She turned to look at the stairwell, and her jaw dropped as she saw Bolan masked and in full battle gear pointing the twin muzzles of a carbine-grenade-launcher combo at her. The loudest sound in the hallway was the sound of the woman swallowing as she turned pale. Bolan raised his hand holding the tear-gas grenade and put a silencing finger to his mask's main filter. The woman gaped but nodded.

Seconds were ticking by, but the woman represented an opportunity. In Osaka, the head of security had managed to hit the destruct codes before Bolan could get any real information. The Executioner wasn't about to let that happen again. He jerked his head at the door. The woman nodded fearfully and opened it. As Bolan suspected, the room was full of files, but they weren't the ones he really wanted. Burdick came in and closed the door behind them. Bolan flexed his limited Japanese.

"Who do you work for?"

The woman shook slightly, and her eyes widened even farther. Her voice came out in a whisper. "Shirata-sama."

"Secretary?"

"Yes, personal secretary."

Grimaldi's voice spoke in Bolan's ear. "Five minutes, Striker."

"Roger that, I'm working an angle."

The woman's eyes widened farther and Bolan loomed over her. "You speak English?"

The woman swallowed again. "Some."

Bolan brought out his blueprint and handed it to Burdick. The Marine held up the map. The office that had taken the phone call from Tadashi was circled in red pencil. Bolan pointed at the file room they were presently in on the blueprint. "We are here. Shirata's office—" Bolan stabbed his finger on the red circle "—here?"

The woman began to vibrate in absolute terror. Bolan grimaced. He couldn't afford to be gentle. He pushed the barrel of the carbine into the woman's stomach and flicked off the safety. "Shirata! Here?"

Tears began to roll down the woman's face, and she began to whimper in a mix of Japanese and English. "*Hai*, yes, is Shirata-sama's office, please, yes. Do not shoot."

Bolan pointed to what looked like the reception office in front of it. "You, here?"

"Yes, yes. I there."

Bolan glanced at the white phone on the wall. It was time to get Shirata-sama away from the destruct button. "Call him. Tell him to come here."

The woman shook her head and shuddered as she cried. "No! Please no!"

Bolan pressed the muzzle of the M-4 firmly into her stomach. "Do it, or I cut you in half."

The woman reached a trembling hand for the phone. Bolan shook his head. She was a sobbing, hysterical mess. He would have to make that work for him. "Tell Shirata you're hurt. You need help."

The woman picked up the phone and punched one number. Bolan moved to her side and put his ear to the other side of the receiver while he kept his carbine pressed firmly into her side. A voice spoke in Japanese. "What?"

The woman spit out a torrent of Japanese. Bolan caught the words "fall," "broken," "can't walk" and "help me." He couldn't tell what the rest was, and he gambled her terror was keeping her from sending any kind of warning. Bolan screwed the muzzle of the carbine hard into her side, and she yelped piteously as she repeated the word "please" into the phone. Bolan heard the word "wait" through the receiver, and the line clicked dead.

"What did you say?"

The woman collapsed to the floor weeping and pointed at her foot. "Say fall, twist ankle, broken."

Bolan pulled her to her feet. The office was down at the end of the hall. Bolan counted five seconds and opened the file-room door. He pushed the woman partially through the doorway. "Call out."

He saw her eyes widen in recognition as she looked down the hall.

"Shirata-sama—"

Bolan put his foot against the back of her knee and pushed. The woman toppled forward in the middle of calling out and fell to the floor with a strangled yelp. A second later Bolan stepped into the hallway with Burdick beside him. Two men came to a halt twenty feet away. The taller one wore an impeccable blue suit and had to be Shirata. The shorter one wore a black leather jacket and jeans and could be no one other than Ryuchi Taido. The Executioner fired.

Flame ripped from the muzzle of the M-4 carbine, and Taido tumbled backward as a short burst walked up his chest. A .45 automatic had appeared like magic in the other man's hand. It barked three times in rapid succession, and Burdick staggered backward. Bolan turned his weapon on the other man, who threw himself behind Taido and lunged at the nearest office door. The M-4 snarled in Bolan's hands as he put another burst into Taido. Shirata held up Taido with one hand, yanked the office door open, then pulled his companion through behind him. Wood chipped and splintered as the door slammed and Bolan put another burst into it.

Grimaldi's voice was tense in the Executioner's ear. "Three minutes, Striker! And I hear you shooting!"

"Roger that, I'm working!"

Bolan weighed the odds. He wanted Shirata. The man could well be the key to everything. But Shirata was armed and barricaded, and Bolan doubted he could take the man alive in the present situation. Bolan wanted Nishiki-Tetsuo, and right now information was a bigger trophy than Shirata's head. He turned to Burdick, who was steadying himself against the wall. His armor had taken the three hits to his torso, but Bolan knew from bitter experience that even through armor, .45s hit hard.

"Burdick, keep firing through that door. I'm going for the files." Burdick's shotgun roared as Bolan charged down the hall.

The Executioner rehooked his gas mask into his web gear as he came to the last office. According to the blueprint, it would be a corner office and face east toward Tokyo Bay. Bolan put his boot into the door and it flew open. There was little inside except a half-moon-shaped reception desk, two chairs and a water cooler. He strode past the desk to a massive double door of polished teak and slammed the heel of his boot into it.

The door shuddered, and with a second kick there was a cracking squeal. With a third kick the doors flew open. The office inside was Spartan in the extreme. A large oaken desk held two computer terminals, and two chairs faced the desk. A huge tinted window faced the Tokyo skyline and the bay beyond. Along the far wall was a single door. According to the blueprint, there were three adjoining rooms. Bolan consulted the blueprint. One door would open into a private bath. Bolan glanced at the blank wall where the other two doors should be. Behind one of them would be an access to the Nishiki-Tetsuo LAN.

Grimaldi almost sounded nervous in Bolan's ear. "Two minutes!"

"Right." Bolan uncoiled his roll of flexible shaped charge and made two hoops. He peeled open the adhesive strip and pressed two open three-foot hoops against the walls where the doors ought to have been. He shoved a detonator pin into each hoop, then stepped back as he pushed the detonator on his web gear. There were two echoing cracks, and yellow fire hissed in circles on the wall. Bolan stepped forward and put his foot into the first blackened circle. A section of steel door fell inward. Inside was a small room dominated by a queen-size bed, the walls and the ceiling mirrored.

Bolan moved to the other door and smashed in the sagging metal. This time he had hit pay dirt. Three linked computer terminals stood like obelisks in an otherwise empty room. He writhed through the hole in the door and rolled to his feet. Three terminals, and he had no time and even less experience as a computer hacker. He needed something he could carry away. His eyes tracked around the walls and came to a single chromed safe door the size of a telephone book. Bolan took out a lump of C-4 plastique.

Akira Tokaido hadn't been able to get the combinations to any of the safes in the building, and Bolan suspected the destruct charges would fire if the safe was tampered with. He was just going to have to blow it open and hope for the best. Bolan pushed the C-4 against the lock and pressed a detonator pin into it. He took the last of his flexible charge and tracked it around the seams of the safe door. There was a very good chance that the destruct charges would fire when Bolan's own charges blew. He didn't want to waste time on a jammed and mangled door. He wanted the door gone. Bolan pushed another detonator pin into the flexible charge and flattened against the wall.

"One minute, Striker!"

Bolan pushed the detonator button.

The charges fired simultaneously with booms and hissing cracks. The flexible charge burned around the safe door's edges, and the C-4 exploded against the door itself. The door sheared free from its hinges, rebounded against its moorings and flew across the room. Bolan whipped around. There was a shrieking hiss of the incendiary charges firing, and he plunged his hands into the safe as the interior lit up like a kiln. The gloves of his raid suit were fireproof Nomex, but they couldn't stop the searing transfer of heat as Bolan's fingers closed on several objects. He cursed at the white-hot pain and yanked his hands out of the inferno inside the safe. The objects fell burning to the floor. Two of them were small leather folios and were already burned out. The other two were small plastic boxes. One had been thoroughly consumed.

Bolan scooped up the other as it burned and ripped it open. The plastic broke apart in his grip, and five computer disks fell out. Two were twisted and warped by heat, and another looked badly damaged. The other two seemed to be intact, but Bolan knew the intense heat might well have destroyed their delicate contents. He grabbed the three disks and shoved them into a pouch of his web gear.

"Burdick! We're out of here!"

"Affirmative!"

Bolan ignored the pain in his hands as he crawled back through the hole in the door. He yanked a willie pete grenade from his web gear and pulled the pin. He dropped the grenade behind him as he ran through the reception office, and white phosphorus bloomed behind him as he ran into the hall. Seconds later a fire alarm began to resound through the halls. Burdick knelt in the hallway, his shotgun covering the door Shirata had ducked into. The woman still knelt on the floor, sobbing hysterically. Fire sprinklers descended from the ceiling and began to spray. Bolan jerked his head. "Put her in the file room!"

Burdick grabbed the woman and shoved her in the file room. Bolan took out his tear-gas grenade and pulled the pin. He tossed the bomb down the hallway, then began to fire his weapon on full-auto into the walls and ceiling. Burdick emptied his shotgun into the overhead light fixtures.

Bolan smiled under his mask. He wanted Tokyo's chief fire inspector to find lots of bullet holes. The carbine clacked open in Bolan's hands, and he reached for a fresh magazine as he moved to the stairwell. Burdick followed the big man, reloading his shotgun while on the move.

Bolan took the stairs two at a time, and floor by floor they ascended to the roof. He dropped a tear-gas grenade down the stairwell behind them, and it fell clattering and hissing to the landing below. "What have you got, Jack?"

"So far so good. We—" Grimaldi's voice rose. "I've got company! Three men, dressed like security guards. They're looking at me real hard, and waving at me to get out."

"We're almost there. Sit tight." Bolan moved up the last staircase. He was willing to bet that those men didn't know what had happened in the office suite six floors below. They had probably been sent up to check out the unauthorized helicopter on the roof. Bolan flicked off the safety of his M-203 grenade launcher as he came within sight of the roof door.

"What's happening, Jack?"

"I'm waving and smiling in a friendly fashion."

"What are they doing?"

"They're pulling revolvers, and they ain't smiling."

Bolan booted the door open and strode onto the roof. Three men in pale blue uniforms stood with their backs to him, all holding pistols. They were pointing their revolvers at the cockpit of the Dauphin helicopter. Grimaldi sat inside and grinned at them while shaking his head in a vaguely confused and noncomprehending manner. The security guards waved their free hands at the pilot with increasing agitation. The rotors of the Dauphin were turning, and so were the rotors of the stolen Kawasaki. The security guards hadn't heard Bolan and Burdick emerge onto the roof.

Burdick raised his shotgun. Bolan made a cutting motion with his hand and slung his own carbine. The sergeant slung his shotgun. The two men walked toward the guards as Bolan took a flash-stun grenade from his bandolier.

Grimaldi looked past the guards and noted the grenade in Bolan's hand. He nodded at the guards and cut power. The rotors began to slow, and the engine whine began dying down rapidly. The guards lowered their pistols slightly. Bolan lobbed his grenade underhand, and it arced over the guards' heads and fell a few yards in front of them. The Executioner held his forearm before his eyes, and Burdick did the same. White light strobed across the roof, and the blinded guards stumbled back from the thunder of the report.

Bolan walked up to one of the guards and grabbed his gun hand. He rammed his hip into the guard and threw him bodily over his shoulder and slammed him into the roof. Burdick swatted the revolver out of the hands of another man and put him down with a boot to the groin. The third guard still had his hands before his eyes and was shaking his head to clear it. Bolan drove his fist into the man's solar plexus. The guard dropped his pistol and fell backward, clutching his chest in blind agony.

The Dauphin's engine whined back into life as Grimaldi shoved the throttles forward. Bolan and Burdick piled into the helicopter. Grimaldi's teeth flashed from ear to ear. "You're fifteen seconds late! You got the goods?"

Grimaldi's grin was infectious, and Bolan smiled as he pulled off his gas mask. "Possibly."

Burdick roared over the rotors. "We've got company! And it's not uniformed security goons!"

Bolan trained his carbine out the door. Four men had appeared out of the primary door to the roof. Burdick was right; they weren't wearing uniforms. They were wearing well-tailored business suits. They were also wearing sunglasses, and rather than revolvers each man had a high-powered rifle in his hand. Bolan fired his grenade launcher, the interior of the helicopter shuddering with the muzzle-blast. The gunmen saw the flash and recognized it as a grenade. They threw themselves to the rooftop in four different directions, and the flash-stun grenade detonated in a clap of thunder and white light.

The Dauphin rose into the air, and the men on the ground rolled to their feet and shouldered their rifles. They were well disciplined, well armed and were wearing eye protection. The enemy was adapting to Bolan's tactics.

The Executioner yawned at the ringing in his ears and shouted at Grimaldi. "Did you rig the Kawasaki?"

Grimaldi nodded as he rammed the throttles full forward and strove to take the helicopter up. "I rigged all three of them! Willie petes and C-4!"

"Blow them!"

There was a sound like hail hitting the fuselage, and a bullet sparked on the interior of the cabin as it punched through the Dauphin's skin. Muzzle-flashes strobed below them, and the helicopter began taking multiple hits. Burdick fell to the cabin floor with a gasp. Grimaldi hit the button on his detonator box three times in rapid succession.

Below them the Kawasaki helicopter seemed to crumple inward and then explode out again into flame. The other two helicopters quickly followed suit. The men on the roof threw themselves down again as the Kawasaki helicopter's fuel tank blew. Streamers of fire flew into the air, and bits of burning helicopter arced up and then down again. With the second and the third helicopters exploding, the rooftop was an Armageddon of burning aviation fuel and twisted, flying metal. Bolan's stomach lurched as Grimaldi took the Dauphin into a hard turn and dived away from the Nishiki-Tetsuo building. Plumes of fire and smoke rose over the Tokyo skyline as the roof of the building became a massive burning beacon for all of the city to see.

Bolan knelt over Burdick. The big Marine was gasping and clutching his side. The Executioner pulled his combat knife and cut away Burdick's web gear, then ripped open the Velcro tabs of his armor. The sergeant winced as Bolan pulled away his armor. The bullet had hit him low and in the side. The armor had held, but the impact had injured him. The skin of his side was a swelling, spreading purple that was almost black.

Grimaldi's voice was grim as he shouted from the cockpit, and Bolan could dimly hear alarms through the ringing in his ears. "Striker! I'm losing engine number two, and number one is overheating! They hit us good!"

Bolan nodded and switched his frequencies. "Akira, we made the strike and we're out, but we're in a crippled bird and Burdick's got busted ribs. We need an escape route immediately."

Tokaido's voice sounded strained. "I think I've got something for you. Can Burdick ride a motorcycle?"

"If not, he's going to learn real fast."

"Is Jack on the line?"

Grimaldi's voice was strained, as well, as he fought with

the wounded helicopter over downtown Tokyo. "I'm listening."

"Which way are you headed?"

"East. Directly away from the Nishiki-Tetsuo building."

Tokaido sighed. "Good. Do exactly what I say."

10

Shirata crouched behind his desk with his Colt .45 automatic in his hand. The fire sprinklers rained down on him and the prone and wheezing body of Ryuchi Taido. Taido had fortuitously been wearing a ceramic-body-armor insert under his now perforated jacket. His armor had held, but he had taken a pair of 3-round bursts from a high-powered automatic rifle. The following day his flesh would look as if he had been beaten with a baseball bat. That was, if they lived to see it. Shirata waited. He had called his own private security force and dispatched a team to the roof and one to this floor. The hallway had been silent for many long moments.

A muffled voice shouted from outside. "Shirata-san!"

"Yes, I am inside." Shirata rose and unlocked the bullet-riddled door. He stepped back as the stink of tear gas assailed him and gray wisps of it began to curl into the room. Outside the door four men in gas masks with automatic rifles stood at attention. One of them quickly thrust forth a black canvas bag. Shirata pulled out the gas mask and quickly settled it over his face. He pointed at Taido. "Get him out of the gas. Get him medical attention."

Two of the men slung their rifles and scooped Taido up off of the floor. Shirata entered the hallway. The walls were pockmarked with bullet holes. Down the hallway the door to his office suite had been kicked in, and despite the fire sprinklers the reception area and his own office beyond were burning in earnest. Shirata could smell the white phosphorus. "Where is my secretary?"

"She is in the filing room."

Shirata's face was composed but his voice was cold steel. "Get her out of here. Let her speak to no one until I have personally debriefed her."

"Yes, sir. Immediately." One of the masked riflemen moved off to do Shirata's bidding. The other handed him the radio. "Team Two needs to speak to you."

Shirata took the radio. "What is your status?"

He could hear a roaring, rushing sound in the background as Team Two's leader reported from the roof. "Three of the uniformed security guards were overcome but not killed. One of my men has received moderate burns. All are now receiving medical attention. Two Nishiki-Tetsuo helicopters have been destroyed and a third stolen. An unidentified helicopter that I believe was used to land the enemy assault team was destroyed on the pad, as well. There is also a news helicopter orbiting the roof of the building. They are filming. I also hear sirens below, both police and fire."

"What actions are you taking?"

"We have hidden our rifles and two of my men are using the fire hose on the roof to contain the fires on the pads."

"Good. What happened to the Americans?"

"We reached the roof just as they were taking off. We exchanged fire with them, and I believe we damaged the helicopter they were flying. They then detonated the charges in the grounded helicopters, and my men and I were forced to take cover."

Shirata shook his head. For the moment there was nothing left to be done except damage control. "You have done well. Continue to contain the fire until you are relieved." Shirata handed the radio back to his man without waiting for a reply. He stormed into an undamaged office, picked up the phone and dialed the building's central security net.

An excited voice answered. "Yes?"

"This is a code-seven emergency. I want all security codes to the building and to all computer nets in the building changed immediately. I want you to delay entry of police and fire personnel into the building as long as possible.''

"We are already changing all codes."

"Good, now get me a secure line."

There was a moment's pause. "Line secure."

Shirata punched in a number and waited several seconds. The old man answered, and he didn't sound pleased. "What has happened?"

"The American has attacked us here, in Tokyo, at the corporate office. I saw him. He was in my office suite." Shirata's face split into a snarl, but his voice remained level. "I do not know how this was done. Somehow he had access to the building's security codes, and he knew exactly where my office was. He nearly made good on his promise to kill Taido."

There was a long moment's silence. "You said you spoke with Yukio earlier in the day?"

"Yes, I—" Shirata's snarl reached his voice. "Yes! Yukio!"

"Yes...Yukio." The old man's tone lowered. "You sent out men to get him?"

"I did. However, I suspect they will report in very soon, and tell me that he is in police custody."

"No," the old man said, "I believe he will be in PSIA custody. I have informants who tell me that elements of the PSIA have become very interested in our activities. Despite efforts that I and members of the board have made to draw attention in other directions, I am informed that there are members of the PSIA who know that Kojima Enterprises was attacked by foreigners, not Yakuza gangsters or religious terrorists. I am also told that there are those among them that believe that Kojima Enterprises and Nishiki-Tetsuo are connected in illegal activities."

"Perhaps something should happen to these PSIA agents."

The old man's voice rose. "No, not perhaps. Something *must* be done about them. Nishiki-Tetsuo has influence in the PSIA, but we do not own them like we own so many of the police. However, if these agents can be dealt with quietly, we can influence who they are replaced with, and we will ensure that they are replaced by agents who are more reasonable."

"I understand."

The old man's voice grew grim. "What kind of damage have the Americans done to us now?"

"They have destroyed two of our helicopters and stolen a third. I believe they broke into my office and attempted to steal my secure files."

"You of course had them guarded with destruct charges."

Shirata's eyes narrowed. "Yes, I did. However, the Americans were foiled at Kojima by the incendiary charges in the safes. I have to assume that when they attacked me here, they had some sort of plan to circumvent them."

"Is that possible?"

"I do not know. My office is currently on fire. They used white-phosphorus grenades. It will take chemical fire retardants to stop the fire, and by then it may be impossible to tell whether they got anything."

The old man's voice was as cold as stone. "We must assume they acquired everything you had. What would that give them?"

Shirata shook his head again at the implications. "Enough."

The old man's voice grew impatient. "Enough for what, exactly?"

"Enough to begin their war against the One Heaven in earnest."

THE DAUPHIN HELICOPTER was howling in its death throes. They had reached the outskirts of Tokyo on one engine, and it was howling into the redline while at the same time losing power. Slowly but surely they were losing altitude. Grimaldi fought the controls as he took directions from Tokaido.

"You should see a dark patch from the area, with some dimmer lights and a chain fence due west."

Bolan scanned the ground from the copilot's seat. They were out in the suburbs, and there were endless tracts of houses spreading in all directions. There was a patch of black, and Bolan could see fencing and some kind of platform.

"I see it, Akira. What is it?"

"It's a train station. They've closed it and a long section of track. Land as quickly as you can."

Burdick grunted from back in the cabin. "I think we have company."

Bolan craned his head around and looked behind them. There was a helicopter trailing them at about 250 yards. It was a small four-seat Hughes, and had no chin light. Bolan brought up his binoculars and his face tightened. It wasn't the police. It was a news helicopter for one of the Japanese networks. A man hung out on a chicken strap and stood on one skid like a door gunner, but instead of a belt-fed machine gun, the man was steadily training a zoom-equipped video camera on them.

Bolan moved back into the cabin. Burdick sat in one of the passenger benches and held his side. "Don't look now, boss, but I think we made the evening news."

The Executioner nodded. "It looks that way." He picked up his carbine and opened the breech of the underslung M-203 grenade launcher. "Let's give them some hot footage." Bolan jacked in a flare round and slid open the Dauphin's cabin door. "Grab my belt."

Burdick winced with effort but curled his hand around the back of Bolan's web belt. The Executioner leaned out and raised the M-4 carbine to his shoulder and fired. A moving helicopter at more than 250 yards would be an almost impossible shot, but Bolan didn't have to hit the news chopper. Most pilots he knew didn't enjoy being fired at. The M-4 rammed back against Bolan's shoulder, and pale yellow fire roared out of the M-203's 40 mm muzzle. Two seconds later the flare went off and the night lit up with incandescent white light. The news helicopter veered violently and dived away from the sudden brilliance of the flare. The Dauphin's airframe shuddered, and the remaining engine began to give out a continuous high-pitched yowl over Bolan's head.

Grimaldi shouted from the cockpit. "I have to land this bird! Now!"

"Do it!" Bolan nodded, and Burdick yanked him back into the cabin. The Executioner broke open the smoking breech of the M-203 and reloaded with a tear-gas grenade. The Dauphin was dropping like a stone toward a divided concrete platform. Two sets of railroad tracks ran between the platforms. Several tin shacks had been erected, and a small bulldozer was parked off to one side. Bolan braced himself, and Burdick grunted in pain as the Dauphin hit the ground hard.

"All right, we're down, but we're going to have company again real quick. What have you got for us?"

Tokaido sounded excited. His plan was working. "Go to the platform and look down the tracks toward the east. The tracks should head toward a hummock about five hundred yards away and then dip into a tunnel."

"Hold on."

Bolan glanced at Burdick. "Let's make tracks."

The sergeant winced as he rose and followed Bolan. Grimaldi was already out of the chopper and scanning the area with his silenced MAC-10 submachine gun in his hands. Bolan grabbed a nylon gear bag and moved to the platform. Directly below, three Honda dirt bikes sat parked on their kickstands. A helmet was hanging on the end of each one's handlebars. "All right, I see the bikes. Where did they come from?"

The young computer expert sounded insufferably pleased with himself. "Well, the CIA isn't allowed to give us any direct aid or shelter. But I made contact with their computer man when I first got into Tokyo and talked shop. Turns out 'he' was their computer girl. I convinced her that having some agents steal some motorcycles and then abandon them didn't count as direct aid if the agents were long gone by the time you arrived. Her superiors bought it. It seems the CIA Tokyo station chief has had it in for Nishiki-Tetsuo for some time. I think he's willing to bend the rules for us, if not actually break them."

Bolan shook his head. Akira's powers of networking were astounding. "What else have you been up to?"

"Like I said, I've been in communication with the local CIA, and I ran the name of the PSIA agent you spoke with, the woman."

"Honda Mitsuko. What about her?"

"The CIA has actually done some business with her. She's got a real thing for Nishiki-Tetsuo. She's investigated them on several occasions, and once about two years ago she even approached the Tokyo CIA office about sharing information about them. At the time the Agency didn't have anything on them or anything particularly against them. She really didn't have much to offer in return, either, so nothing really came of it. Also CIA observers confirmed that she was leading the team that picked up Yukio Tadashi back in Hongu. Apparently she's still on their case, and as gung ho as ever."

Bolan filed that away. It might prove useful. "All right. We've got to evacuate the area. Which way do we go?"

"Head for the tunnel. The track is being ripped up and replaced, but it should be negotiable by dirt bike. Follow it to the next station, two miles down. It's closed, too. I'll meet you there. I'll be in a dark green Honda 4×4."

"Got it." Bolan turned to Burdick. "You feel up to a short ride?"

Burdick clasped his side unhappily. "Do I have a choice?"

Bolan opened the gear bag. He pulled out a pair of night-vision goggles. "We're riding without lights. I'll lead." Grimaldi walked up and took a pair of goggles as Bolan pulled his own over his face and adjusted the straps. He hopped down, mounted one of the bikes and put on a helmet. The key was in the ignition. Bolan tightened his carbine's sling and kicked the engine over. The bike snarled into life. Bolan jerked his head toward the black hole of the tunnel ahead. "Let's get out of here."

11

Yukio Tadashi was unhappy. The Americans had held him captive for more than nine hours and then left him trussed like a pig at the inn. The Japanese police weren't known for their patience with criminals. But it wasn't the police who had come and gotten him. Most Japanese knew very little about the PSIA and its doings, but in the past three hours Tadashi had learned that its agents didn't have much patience with criminals, either. He was at the end of his rope and feeling very intimidated. Tadashi had been intimidated by the voice on the phone; he had been intimidated by large Americans with automatic weapons. It was quite possibly the worst twenty-four hours of his existence. Yukio Tadashi was a powerful man. He had killed with his bare hands without remorse. Now he was being intimidated by a woman.

Tadashi had never met a woman, much less a Japanese woman, who could look him in the eye. Only she wasn't. She was looming over him while he was handcuffed to a chair. She was snarling at him in the rapid, high-pitched dialect of the Japanese old-family upper class, which made Tadashi feel subservient against his will. She was telling him he was going to go to jail for a long time, and even if he didn't, he would have the PSIA watching him for the rest of his life. He didn't doubt that. Only one thing kept him from telling them anything they wanted to know, and that was the voice on the phone.

The PSIA might indeed see that he went to prison. Even if he squirmed out with a light sentence, agents would follow him relentlessly. He and they both knew that he was unlikely to find employment in any kind of legitimate business enterprise. Particularly at the level of compensation he was accustomed to. He would slide back into crime. He knew it. They knew it, and they would be waiting. There was one difference, however. The PSIA could indeed make the rest of his life a living hell.

The voice on the phone could erase him as if he had never existed at all.

Yukio Tadashi sat, sweated and kept his mouth shut.

Honda Mitsuko snarled in disgust and whirled on one heel. She stomped out of the interrogation room and kicked a wastepaper basket. She watched it tumble down the hallway without satisfaction. Agent Chaya Kenshin leaned against the wall and ground out a cigarette in the ashtray beside him. The stout, gray-haired agent smiled sympathetically. "So. Time for the 'good cop' routine?"

Mitsuko heaved a deep sigh. "Why not? Give Fatty a cigarette. Promise him immunity. Do what you can. If he doesn't go for it, I'll go at him again in an hour."

Kenshin nodded, loosened his tie and stuck his hands in his pockets. The small gestures instantly seemed to drape him in relaxed, fatherly understanding. He tapped on the interrogation-room door and walked in with a thoughtful expression on his face as one of the guards admitted him.

Mitsuko wished him luck. Kenshin was a master at interrogation. He could have the worst Yakuza killer convinced that he was talking to his long-lost beloved uncle in twenty minutes' time. But she didn't think he stood much chance with this fish. This one was scared to death. They had nothing to threaten him with compared to what Nishiki-Tetsuo would do to him, and both Tadashi and she herself knew that whatever the PSIA promised, there was no way it could protect him from Nishiki-Tetsuo's wrath for long.

Mitsuko shook her head. He was probably already a marked man. The phone call he had made, whether he had done it at gunpoint or not, would be enough to put him at the bottom of Tokyo Bay. She would use that argument with him when Kenshin failed, but she doubted that tactic would work, either. Fear and loyalty had been beaten into the very core of the overweight enforcer's being. He would keep his mouth shut and, when the opportunity presented itself, Nishiki-Tetsuo would have him killed.

Mitsuko's pager beeped. She glanced at the number and recognized it as the number of the Tokyo Chief Investigative Unit. She had, of course, heard of the strike on the Nishiki-Tetsuo building, but she had been on Tadashi and other agents had been sent to the site. That was one more thing that was burning her up. She walked to the phone on the wall. She had friends in the Chief Investigative Unit; perhaps one of them had decided to slip her some information. She dialed the number and waited. The line didn't ring. There were several seconds of silence, then the line clicked several times. A deep voice spoke.

"Agent Mitsuko."

The woman nearly dropped the phone. It was exactly the same scrambled voice that had tipped her off to Tadashi's location. With an effort she kept her voice professional. "This is Agent Mitsuko."

"I have usurped this line. If I detect any attempt to trace this call or transfer the line, I'll terminate communications immediately."

"What is it you wish to say to me?"

"You have Yukio Tadashi?"

Mitsuko's eyes flicked to the interrogation-room door. "Yes, we have Yukio Tadashi in custody."

"Is he cooperating?"

Mitsuko blinked as she was caught off guard. She considered her answer very carefully. Her instincts told her that her best gamble was the truth. "No. He is rightfully afraid that if he cooperates with us he will be killed. However, whether he cooperates with us or not, I suspect he will end up dead."

"Then perhaps you and I should cooperate."

Mitsuko's jaw dropped. The voice went on. "Nishiki-

Tetsuo has an illegal arm with global connections and the resources of the rest of the cartel to back it up. This arm is used in the trafficking of guns, drugs, espionage and assassination. As you know personally, the crimes they commit are unpunishable by domestic Japanese or international law. They're simply unequipped to deal with a criminal organization of such massive economic resources and influence. The scope of Nishiki-Tetsuo's crimes have become intolerable. I'm taking action against them. I attacked a warehouse of theirs in Naha, Okinawa. Kojima Enterprises was a cutout in their domestic distribution of drugs and weapons. I struck their corporate offices in Tokyo tonight. I suspect news of this has already reached you."

Mitsuko's stomach felt as if she had just crested the top of a roller coaster and was plunging downward. She worked saliva into her suddenly dry mouth and spoke as coolly as she could. "I am willing to accept what you have told me."

"I'll contact you again."

Mitsuko almost shouted for the voice to wait, but she strangled the impulse. She waited with her heart pounding for the line to cut, but it didn't. A moment later the voice spoke again. "Nishiki-Tetsuo will now be on a war footing. They'll use their influence to find out about any Japanese police officer or federal agent who is investigating them. You have Yukio Tadashi. It won't take them long to find that out, and to find out who you are. They'll suspect my having contacted you. They'll suspect our cooperation, whether you choose to do so or not. Your life is in danger."

The line clicked dead.

Mitsuko slowly hung up the phone and took several deep breaths. She walked down the hall to the elevator and pressed the button to go down. She passed the lobby of the building and descended to the underground floors. The door hissed open, and she walked down the hallway to a heavily insulated door. She took a card key from her purse and swiped it through the lock. The door opened and she walked across a tiny gray lobby. A sign on the wall said Hearing Protection

Must Be Worn On Other Side Of Door. She grabbed a pair of disposable earplugs from a small bin and plugged them into her ears. Mitsuko swiped the lock on the door, and her ears were immediately assailed by gunfire as it opened.

The PSIA indoor target range was small, but well designed. She walked past the firing line and smiled at a pair of agents who were firing 9 mm SIG-Sauer P-210 pistols at targets ten yards downrange. She kept walking and reached the range master's cage. Range master Toshiro Mori was a tall, thin man with wire-rimmed spectacles who usually didn't approve of female PSIA agents. He couldn't help approving of Mitsuko's marksmanship. The woman consistently had some of the best range scores among the investigating agents in the Tokyo branch. He nodded slightly at her.

"What can I do for you, Agent Mitsuko?"

She considered her response. Without wealth or political connections, the private ownership of firearms was almost completely forbidden in Japan. Even as a PSIA agent, she was required to check out a pistol when it was required, and then check it back in before she went off duty. The PSIA was a very professional outfit, and had some of the most modern firearms available in its small but well-equipped armory. Unfortunately Mitsuko wasn't a member of one of the fast-reaction teams. As an investigations agent, she was only certified to carry the standard-issue New Nambu Model 58 .38 Special revolver. Mori took his job as range master and armorer very seriously. Mitsuko knew there was no way she could beg, wheedle or cajole an Uzi or an M-16 rifle out of him. She had never even been qualified on them.

Agent Kenshin had told her of a trick, however. He had been a policeman before he had been a PSIA agent, and he had been to New York as an exchange officer and observer. For decades the New York City police had been forced to carry 6-shot .38 Special revolvers, even while many of the professional criminals in the city had begun carrying semi-automatic weapons and submachine guns. The police often found themselves having to stop and reload in a firefight while the criminals blazed away at them. Only recently had they begun to be issued semiautomatic handguns, and in the meantime they had countered the situation with the only way they could. Many of them had taken to carrying multiple duty revolvers. Drawing a spare revolver was many times faster than reloading one under fire, even with speedloaders, and it was a tactic that criminals never seemed to expect. Agent Kenshin was one of the few agents who had actually been in gunfights, and he swore the trick had saved his life.

Mitsuko gave Mori her most winsome smile. "I am going undercover. I need to check out a gun."

Mori nodded and began to type the paperwork into his computer. He talked to himself. "One Model 58 .38 Special revolver. Twelve rounds of ammunition."

"I need three of them."

Mori looked up. Mitsuko kept her smile at full wattage. "It has to do with the attack on Kojima Enterprises. The suspects appear to be heavily armed."

Mori's eyes narrowed. "That is highly irregular."

Mitsuko nodded. "The situation is highly irregular."

Mori grunted, and a smile almost creased his normally severe face. "You've been listening to old Chaya's war stories."

Mitsuko nodded. Chaya Kenshin was well loved by everyone in the Tokyo branch. Mori's fingers began to peck at his computer again. "Two Model 58 .38 Special revolvers, one Smith & Wesson Chiefs Special Airweight .38 Special revolver. One 50-round box of .38 Special ammunition."

Mitsuko blinked. Mori actually smiled. "Keep one here." He pushed his fingers into the front of his belt. "One here." He turned and stuck his fingers into the back of his waistband. "Keep the third on your ankle, and keep six spare rounds loose in your pocket."

Mori went into the back room and came out a moment later with a gun case full of revolvers. He pulled out two standard-duty revolvers and the American aluminum-framed snubnose. He went back, then came out again with a pair of clip-on belt holsters and a nylon holster with elastic webbing. "You're going to need to wear a stiff leather belt to hold these. Wear them with jeans. It will help keep everything tight against you." He took out a box of .38 Special ammunition, then passed everything through the slot in the wire cage between them. He took a clipboard and pen, and passed them through. "Sign here."

Mitsuko took the pen and had to restrain herself from trying to kiss Mori through the metal mesh. "I am in your debt, Toshiro."

"Indeed you are." Mori tapped his finger against his cheek in meditation as Mitsuko signed for the weapons. "Agent Mitsuko, have you considered requisitioning some soft body armor?"

12

The Executioner opened his eyes. Jack Grimaldi crouched at his feet and had just let go of the toe of Bolan's boot. He had shaken it, gently, once. Grimaldi had learned long ago that it wasn't wise to wake up a Special Forces operative in the field by grabbing him by the shoulder. If you woke him suddenly, he often came awake with a knife or pistol suddenly in his hand. Grimaldi grinned and waved the cup of coffee in his other hand. "Good morning, Mr. Striker, your coffee is ready."

Bolan rolled to his feet and accepted the steaming mug. "Thanks. How's—?" Bolan recoiled as he took a sip. He'd had instant coffee brewed in a canteen that had tasted better. "Jack, this is really bad."

Grimaldi pointed to the counter. There was a pair of slender cartons emblazoned with some sort of bizarre, bug-eyed infant superhero surrounded by Japanese writing. The single word Coffee was written in English and surrounded by exclamation points. Bolan glanced down at the dull brown liquid in his mug, then back at the kitchen. "Don't tell me you cooked this up in the microwave."

Grimaldi shrugged dismissingly. "It grows on you."

Bolan noticed the pilot wasn't drinking any of it himself. He checked his watch. He had been asleep for seven hours. "What's our status?"

"The CIA branch office here in Tokyo is arranging a full weapons resupply for us. We should be able to pick it up from a secure drop point within the hour. They're also maintaining twenty-four-hour surveillance on Agent Mitsuko for us. Akira's locked himself in the back room with those computer disks you liberated. I think he's in communication with the Farm at the moment.''

Bolan checked himself as he almost took another sip from his mug. "How's Burdick doing?"

"He's definitely got a pair of broken ribs on his left side, and that bike ride we took through the tunnel didn't do the soft tissues in his side any good. After you taped him up, I gave him some anti-inflammatories and a beer for the pain. He was asleep in the other room last time I looked in on him.'' Grimaldi's face turned thoughtful. "You know, he's actually done pretty well on this one, I think."

Bolan set the mug of prefabricated coffee substitute on the counter and stepped away from it. "He's still a criminal."

The pilot nodded. "Well, now, that's true. But, you know, I myself used to be a scumbag flying for the Mafia. That is, until I was reformed by the love of Mack Bolan."

"You're a sick man, Jack. You need help."

Bolan went to the back room of the safehouse Akira Tokaido had set up on his arrival in Tokyo. The safehouse itself was a converted loft in one of the industrial areas of Tokyo near the ocean. There was very little residential housing around, and at night the area was almost completely abandoned. No other building had a direct view of the back entrance, and Bolan and his team could enter and leave without being observed.

The Executioner knocked on the door to the back room and stepped in. Tokaido sat on a stool with a pair of computer terminals in front of him. There were several pieces of boxlike equipment Bolan couldn't immediately identify, as well as phone modems and high-speed laser printers. His setup had tripled in size since he had been working out of suitcases in the hotel room in Hongu. A Glock 21 pistol sat within reach next to a plastic bottle of water. His fingers flew over one of the keyboards in front of him, and Bolan could hear the music throbbing and howling in Tokaido's headphones from where he stood in the doorway. He walked around slowly so the young computer expert could see him without being startled. He looked up and pulled off his headphones. "Morning, boss."

"What have you got?"

He held up the heat-damaged disk. "The toasted one, well, it's toast." He pointed at a pair of hard drives in front of him. "Now, the other two you got, they seem to be intact."

"What do you make of them?"

Tokaido shook his head respectfully at the screen in front of him. It was a sea of numbers, letters and symbols. "Very interesting."

"How interesting?"

"Well, the code has been changed, but the architecture is very similar to the disk you pulled out of Libya. I would definitely say the same programmer who designed that code did this one."

Bolan nodded. It made sense. "Can you break it?"

"If I can't, the NSA probably can. And if they can't..." Tokaido grinned. "Well, I've already copied it and sent it off to the Bear." His grin faded, and he tapped the other hard drive. "Now, this one's different."

"Different how?"

"Just different. Totally different structure. Much more sophisticated. And the first one is as good as I've seen. The coding on this one..." The young man's eyes got a faraway look in them. "This one is next generation. It's got to be their latest stuff. Probably developed with being attacked in mind. The stuff on this disk has got to be sensitive, and I mean really sensitive. If we break this one, we can break into anything they have."

"You have a copy of the first disk?"

"Of course, several."

"And the second one?"

Tokaido raised a vaguely offended eyebrow in answer. Bolan nodded and smiled. "Sorry. Can I have the originals?"

He ejected both disks and handed them to the big man. "What are you going to do with them?"

"Score some brownie points with the locals." The Executioner looked at the screens full of data and listened to the vague hum of the linked computers, then tapped the disks in his palm as he regarded the younger man. "Tell me, how would you like to go outside tonight and get some fresh air and exercise?"

AGENT HONDA MITSUKO SAT on the train and watched Tokyo flash by. The train was crowded with people on their way home from work. It was ten o'clock at night, but that didn't keep the train from downtown from being packed. Tokyo was one of the busiest big cities in the world, and nearly everyone in the Tokyo area worked late hours. Mitsuko herself hadn't slept since she had received the phone call from Nishiki-Tetsuo's mysterious enemy the previous night. That enemy seemed to want to cooperate with her. She had almost wanted to keep this information to herself. She considered Nishiki-Tetsuo to be her case, and, being a woman, her fear of having it taken away from her once it became big was very real. However, she had one thing going for her. She had spoken with this faceless voice twice. Her superiors had wanted to put someone else on the case, but they were also afraid that if they tried to get another agent involved, whoever it was they were dealing with would drop out of contact. For the moment Mitsuko was still on the job, and the PSIA had turned her unique situation into its number-one priority.

The phones in her office and in her home had been wired, and the PSIA was ready to attempt a trace at the next contact. A great deal of the day had been devoted to anxiously staring at the phone and waiting for it to ring. The phone had stared back at her and the tracing team like a stone Buddha and refused to make a sound all day. The line in her home had been rerouted to a second phone in her office at PSIA headquarters, and other than an anticlimactic call from her mother, that phone had maintained a steadfast silence, as well. She had spent an afternoon and evening catching up on paperwork and vainly willing the phones to ring. Mitsuko was done in, and her superior had told her to go home and sleep.

Mitsuko rolled her head around on her neck and yearned for the train to ignore the next eight stops and deposit her directly into her bathtub at home. The train came to the next stop, and the press of the bodies shifted with the surge of people getting off and getting on. She was standing near the door and watched with vaguely weary interest as a smiling young man shoved his way through the doorway. Mitsuko didn't particularly care for ponytails on men, but the man was handsome by her standards, and he was so openly cheerful compared to all the professional men and women ignoring one another that she kept her eyes on him.

He looked her directly in the eyes, smiled and waggled his eyebrows as he spoke in English. "Hey, lady! Catch!"

The young man tossed a black object at her over the people between them, and Mitsuko was horrified at herself as her hands instinctively reached out to catch it. The young man shoved his way backward with authority as the train's doors hissed, and he hopped back onto the platform as they slid shut before him. Mitsuko caught the object as the train began to accelerate forward and she shouted at the top of her lungs. "Bomb! Get down!"

People on the train looked up in astonishment, and several people screamed. The passengers standing around her leaned as far away as the press of bodies would allow. Mitsuko crushed the black box against herself and twisted to face the wall of the train to shield the rest of the passengers with her body. Her heart hammered in her chest as she waited for it to explode. Long moments passed and nothing happened. The rest of the passengers gaped at her. Mitsuko took a quick peek at the object in her hands. It appeared to be a folding compact cellular phone. She stared at the phone, and it stared back without exploding. She took a deep breath and flicked the phone open. It still appeared to be a harmless cellular phone. She cleared her throat and pulled her badge from her jacket as she turned around. "I am PSIA Agent Honda Mitsuko. This has been a false alarm. Anyone who wishes to register a complaint may have my badge number."

The other passengers stared at her as if she were insane. Mitsuko felt herself redden and turned back to face the window. Her mind looped through the possibilities. It could still be a bomb, though it would be rather ridiculous to throw it at her if it required some kind of action on her part to activate it. She certainly wasn't going to punch any buttons until the bomb squad had looked at it. Of course, it was possible that somehow the bomb had some kind of radio detonation signal that had failed. Mitsuko scowled. What was most likely was that—

She nearly jumped out of her shoes as the phone rang. She took a deep breath and pressed the speak button. "This is Agent Honda Mitsuko. How may I be of assistance?"

Her whole body tensed as a voice spoke to her in slow, clear English. "You recognize my voice?"

"Yes, it is the same scrambled signature you used before."

"That's correct. Do you have another phone on your person?"

Mitsuko paused, but again, her instincts told her to stick with the truth. "Yes, I do. In my purse."

"Take it out and drop it on the floor. You're being observed. If you don't do so, if you attempt to contact your superiors or if this line skips or disconnects, there'll be no further contact between us. Do it now."

Mitsuko quickly turned and scanned the other passengers. There were well over sixty people packed into the train car. Many of them were still staring at her. Flashing her badge and telling everyone to follow her back to PSIA headquarters for interrogation would pose interesting problems. There was a very real possibility that whoever was observing her would have a story as airtight as any other passenger's, and there was the very real possibility that there was no one observing her on the train. But there was no way she could be sure. She knew that, and so did the voice on the phone. She was also very sure that if she screwed this up, she wouldn't be contacted again.

Mitsuko took her phone from her purse and dropped it on the floor from shoulder height. It fell with a clatter, and the batteries skidded across the floor of the train as the phone's black plastic battery cover popped off. A number of the passengers closest to her continued to stare at her latest act of insanity. Her face reddened again as she turned once more to face the window. "I have done as you asked."

"Good. Stay on the line. Get off at the next stop."

Mitsuko kept her tone cool and professional. "Why?"

"Because I took a number of sensitive, encrypted computer disks from the Nishiki-Tetsuo building when I attacked them. These disks came from an office that is directly linked with their illegal operations. I thought you might like to look at them."

Mitsuko's eyes narrowed. "Those disks were illegally obtained. Any information on them is very likely to be inadmissible in a Japanese court of law."

The voice didn't skip a beat. "You would know much more about that than I would. However, if you could break their codes, they would still make very interesting reading. Do you want them?"

Mitsuko let out a slow breath. "Yes. I believe my superiors would be interested in seeing them."

"All right. You should be approaching the next station. Get off and go to the street level."

The train whined to a halt, and Mitsuko kept the phone by her ear as she shouldered her way out of the train. The few other debarking passengers attempted to give her a wide berth as she exited. It was a stop she had never gotten off at before, and more passengers got on than off because it was in one of Tokyo's warehouse districts. She took the stairs to the street and glanced about. "I'm on the street."

"Start heading west. You are going to walk about three-quarters of a mile."

Mitsuko converted that to metric as she began walking down the street. "Where am I going?"

"To a drop-off point. There you will pick up the originals of the two computer disks I took from Nishiki-Tetsuo."

Mitsuko frowned again as she walked down the dimly lit street past massive warehouse buildings. "I must be honest with you. You have openly admitted to the crimes of theft, hijacking, illegal-weapons possession, illegal use of explosives, arson, kidnapping and assault with deadly weapons on Japanese soil. It is my duty to arrest you on sight."

The voice continued in an unperturbed fashion. "I am fully aware of both your duty and your reputation as a member of the PSIA, Agent Honda, and I respect them both. I'll make every attempt to prevent you from being put into a situation where either one would be compromised. However, I'll be honest with you. My own duty comes first with me, as well. I won't allow you to compromise my mission. I trust we understand each other."

"Yes, we understand each other." There was a great deal that Mitsuko didn't understand about the situation, but for a foreigner on a rampage, this man seemed remarkably reasonable. "I must ask you, do you—?"

The voice interrupted her. "Please continue walking. I have to put you on hold for a moment." Mitsuko stared at the phone as she was put on hold. The line clicked back on again after several seconds. "Agent Mitsuko, are you armed?"

The woman found her hand stealing unbidden under her jacket to rest on the wooden grips of the Type 58 revolver she wore in the cross-draw holster on her belt. Carrying three revolvers and wearing body armor had lost its romance after the first fifteen minutes, but their weight suddenly became a comfort as she heard the question. "Yes, I am armed. Why do you ask?"

"Things have just gotten complicated."

"What do you mean?"

"To your knowledge, is the PSIA having you tailed?"

To her knowledge, her superiors were tapping her phones,

but she didn't believe they would follow her without telling her. They knew she was armed, and it would be terribly embarrassing if she shot a fellow agent out of ignorance. "To my knowledge, no. Why do you ask?"

"My contacts inform me that they believe you are being followed by parties other than myself."

13

Mack Bolan grimaced. Things had just gotten very complicated. He spoke into his scrambled cellular phone. "You have a choice. You may disconnect with me now and call your agency or the local police. I don't know how quickly they can send you assistance."

There was a moment's pause, and the PSIA agent's voice came back. "Or I can continue to the drop point?"

"Yes."

The agent paused again. "You are nearby."

"Yes."

The woman's voice steeled slightly. "I am going to inform my superiors of the situation, and I am going to continue to your drop point."

Bolan considered this. "All right. Call your superiors. I'll call you back in sixty seconds." Bolan clicked the line off and spoke into his throat mike to the CIA agent on the rooftop that overlooked the PSIA agent's route. "What do we have?"

The CIA man from the Tokyo branch office spoke coolly. "You have approximately six individuals. No weapons in sight. Four are following with a loose tail. Two others are moving rapidly in parallel with Agent Mitsuko to the west behind a screen of buildings. I believe they are attempting to head her off."

"Affirmative. Maintain observation." Bolan calculated. Nishiki-Tetsuo had a six-man team in place at the train stop even though they'd had no way of knowing that the PSIA agent would have gotten off at that particular one. That meant they had to have a team in place at all fourteen train stations between the PSIA office and Mitsuko's apartment, and it meant that they probably had men shadowing her on the train, as well. Nishiki-Tetsuo was taking no chances, and it was clear that its agents intended to take out the woman. Other teams were likely converging on this spot now that she was on foot. Bolan ran a rueful eye over his surroundings. The warehouse district was an ideal place to make a clandestine drop. It was also an ideal place for an ambush. He frowned. The Tokyo CIA branch was proving to be an invaluable intelligence asset, but that was as far as they could go. No CIA agent could get directly involved without breaking presidential orders. This was supposed to have been nothing more than a friendly information drop, and Grimaldi and Burdick were back at the safehouse on the other side of town. Murphy and his law had struck again.

Bolan spoke into his mike again. "Akira, where are you?"

"I just got out of the train station."

"I need you here, ASAP. We have six possible unfriendlies behind Agent Mitsuko, and you and I are her only backup."

Tokaido's voice lost a great deal of its usually cheerful confidence. "Er, Striker, this was just supposed to be an info drop. I'm not carrying a gun."

Bolan realized that Murphy was having a field day. The obvious solution was to cut and run, but Bolan couldn't do that. He had put Agent Mitsuko in the warehouse district where Japanese police backup couldn't reach her. Abandoning her to Nishiki-Tetsuo's trained assassins just wasn't in the cards. He had to try to save her. If he failed, and they were both killed, then so be it. The other men from Stony Man Farm would have to step up and burn Nishiki-Tetsuo down in vengeance. "Hold on, Akira."

Bolan spoke to the CIA agent. "You have a gun up there?"

The agent's voice was cautious in response. "Yes, I'm armed."

"Good. A young man of Japanese descent with a ponytail

is going to come jogging by in about ten seconds. Drop it to him.''

There was a disbelieving pause. Mission protocol was being bent if not violated yet again. "What?"

"Just do it." Bolan glanced at his watch. Things were getting tight. "Akira, head past the CIA observation post on the east side. Our friend up there is going to drop you his weapon."

Tokaido didn't sound happy with the current turn of events. "Okay."

"Then run, as fast as you can. You're going to take the shortcut and parallel Agent Mitsuko on the east side. Our opponents are walking, but you're going to have to hustle. Run six blocks up. There'll be a cross street. We're going to hit the bad guys at the seventh block. I want you to sneak in behind them and help me put them in a cross fire."

Tokaido's voice steadied. "Hang tight. I'm running."

Bolan punched the automatic redial on his portable phone. "Agent Mitsuko?"

"Yes. I have contacted my superiors. They are sending police backup. Their estimated time of arrival is five to ten minutes."

"We don't have that much time."

"I suspected that."

Bolan glanced at the map in front of him. "All right. Proceed down the street you're on. You'll pass four more warehouses. At the fourth there's a narrow alleyway that cuts through on both sides of the street. When you reach that, run."

The agent's tone remained as cool as it had been at the start of the conversation. "Yes. I understand."

Bolan clicked off the phone. "Where are you, Akira?"

Tokaido's voice panted with exertion over the line. "I've got the gun. I'm in-bound."

The voice of the CIA man broke in. "Striker, the enemy is closing in on Honda."

Bolan slipped his map into a pouch of his web gear and

moved out of his hide. He had been positioned behind an empty stack of pallets a block away from the drop site, and now he moved at a dead run. Near the entrance to the alleyway, Bolan saw a large metal trash container and he sprinted for it. Agent Mitsuko would run right past it as she made her move. So would her pursuers. Bolan sprinted toward his chosen ambush position. As he did, he drew his Beretta 93-R pistol, then clicked its folding wire stock into place on the grips. He pulled down the folding forward grip from under the barrel and the pistol was transformed into a 9 mm shoulder-fired carbine. He flicked the selector lever to 3-round-burst mode, then dropped into the shadows behind the trash bin. The Executioner pulled his raid mask down over his face, then shouldered his weapon. He heard hard-soled shoes clicking on pavement around the corner. The footsteps suddenly broke into a run, and Bolan heard shouting out in the street.

A tall woman in jeans, boots and a brown leather jacket charged into the alley with her arms pumping for speed. The dull gleam of gun metal glinted in her right hand as she ran. Boots pounded on the street around the corner, and other voices, farther off, shouted in Japanese.

Bolan snarled low in his throat as the woman nearly passed him. "Down!"

The woman's head whipped around, then she threw herself to the ground without hesitating. Figures appeared in the mouth of the alley with weapons in their hands, and they shouted something unpleasant as they saw Mitsuko sprawl on the ground. They had target fixation, and it was going to be their undoing. The Executioner rose from the shadows behind the trash bin with his weapon shouldered and put the Beretta's front sight on the nearest man.

The Beretta rattled in his hand as he put a 3-round burst into the killer at point-blank range and dropped him. The other men shouted in surprise at the stuttering cough of the suppressed machine pistol. Bolan turned from the hips like a turret and walked a high burst from the Beretta up a second man's chest and neck. The gunner fell forward, and a revolver barked twice off to Bolan's right as Agent Mitsuko joined the fray. She fired as rapidly as she could pull the trigger and dumped four rounds into one of her would-be assassins.

The fourth man raised a silenced automatic and fired several bullets into Bolan's cover. Sparks shrieked as the rounds ricocheted away. A silenced .22 was an excellent assassination weapon, but it lacked penetration. The heavy subsonic 9 mm bullets in Bolan's Beretta didn't, and as he and Mitsuko fired at the same time, the last gunman twisted and fell backward in the cross fire.

Mitsuko's revolver clicked dry as the man toppled. She reached behind her back and whipped out a second revolver as a voice stage-whispered from around the corner. "Striker!"

"You're late, but you're clear. Come ahead!"

Akira Tokaido burst around the corner with a silenced .22 Walther PPK/S automatic in his hand. The gun was standard CIA spook armament.

Their CIA observer on the rooftop spoke urgently in Bolan's earpiece. "You have more company. I see a pair of vehicles moving in rapidly. They aren't flashing lights. I'm monitoring the police bands, and their cars aren't close yet. I don't think these boys are friendlies."

"What about the other two individuals who were flanking Mitsuko?"

"They're holding position. I think they're waiting for reinforcements. What's your situation?"

Bolan checked his watch with narrowed eyes. He couldn't afford a protracted firefight. He was about to be outnumbered and outgunned, and the police were on their way. "Agent Mitsuko is secure. I need alternative extraction, now."

"You've got it, Striker. Go back the way you came, then double south around toward my position."

"Affirmative. What do you have for me?"

"Two warehouses west of my position, you'll find an alleyway leading east. Two motorcycles will be there. Use them to extract, then dump them as soon as possible. They were reported stolen to the Tokyo police an hour ago.''

Bolan grinned. Someone in the Tokyo CIA branch deserved a merit badge in motorcycle theft. "We're moving. Keep me posted on developments." Bolan pulled the two computer disks from his web gear and handed them to Mitsuko. "We're extracting, now. You want to come along?"

Mitsuko looked up from pressing fresh shells into her revolver. "Yes, please."

"Let's move." Bolan took point as they moved back down the alley to the next street. They moved at a run toward the CIA lookout point.

The CIA agent spoke in Bolan's earpiece. "You have two cars coming from the west, Striker. They aren't flashing any lights, and I don't think the local cops are driving minivans."

"Understood." They continued running, and when they reached the lookout building they headed west down the alley. As they passed the second warehouse, Bolan could hear the squeal of tires as the vehicles took the corners of the narrow alleys. The enemy didn't know quite where they were yet, but that would change very rapidly. Bolan came to a door and tried the knob. It clicked open, and he could feel a vast empty space before him. Mitsuko and Tokaido came in behind him, and they closed the door. Bolan took out his miniflash and clicked it on. A pair of Honda Nighthawk motorcycles was parked in the middle of the floor.

The CIA man spoke in his ear. "A third van is circling in from the west, coming straight at you."

"Affirmative."

Bolan threw a leg over one of the bikes and flicked up the kickstand. Once he revved the engine, he would be announcing their location to everyone in the area. The Nighthawk was a street machine, not an off-road bike like the ones the CIA had gotten for them before. They would just have to be sufficient. Bolan ejected the clip in his Beretta and replaced it with a magazine full of conical, steel-jacketed, armor-piercing bullets. "Akira, you and Agent Mitsuko are going to take the other bike. I'm going out first to draw our friends' attention. When I do, you head out for the train station and drop off your passenger. Then get out of the area. Dump the bike. Dump the gun."

Tokaido straddled the other bike. "Right." He nodded at Mitsuko. "Mount up."

The woman glanced back and forth between both men while she pushed fresh rounds into her empty revolver. She nodded, then got on the back of Tokaido's bike with a revolver in each hand. Bolan rolled his bike toward the door with his feet, then spoke into his throat mike. "What've I got?"

"Three minivans combing the area. One of them is coming straight at you down the alley. I estimate the police will be here in a matter of minutes."

"Affirmative." Bolan glanced back over his shoulder. "Ready?"

Tokaido nodded. The Executioner hit on the starter, and the Nighthawk's engine snarled into life. He flung open the door and accelerated into the alley. Tires screeched, and Bolan yanked the bike around to face the oncoming threat. The van took up almost the entire alley, and its brights flicked on and threw their accusing glare on the big American. Bolan raised his Beretta in one hand and snapped off a burst into the van's front grille, then spun the bike. The rear tire screamed and laid down rubber as he turned, then it bit into the pavement and got traction. The Nighthawk lunged forward and yawed back and forth as it tore down the alley. Bolan leaned deep as he came to the side street and took the turn as hard as he dared. Behind him the van was tearing down the alley, and its brakes screamed to take the turn. Bolan pulled the bike up to a halt and twisted his torso around to face behind him with the Beretta machine pistol to his shoulder.

The van came around, and sparks flew from its side panel as it scraped the alley wall and lunged out into the narrow street. Bolan narrowed his eyes against the glaring high beams and began to fire steady bursts of 9 mm armor-piercing ammunition into the oncoming vehicle. He put a burst low into the driver's side of the windshield, then a second one into the passenger's side. The windshield riddled and cracked as the bullets punched through. When he put another burst into the driver's side higher up, the van suddenly slowed and began to veer off to the side of the street.

Bolan lowered his aim and put two more bursts into the front grille, then dropped the front sight of the Beretta to the two front tires and put a burst into each one. The left tire blew out, and the van crunched to a halt into the side of a warehouse as the Beretta clacked open on a smoking, empty chamber.

Bolan ejected the spent magazine and slammed in a fresh one. The van was disabled, but he doubted all of its occupants were. He gunned the bike and sped down the street as the van's side door slammed open. As he opened the throttle, he heard the roar of a shotgun blast in the street behind him. Bolan spoke into his throat mike as the wind tore at him. "One van down. What's the situation?"

The CIA man spoke with admiration. "You've still got two vans. Your partner and Agent Mitsuko are heading out of the warehouse district toward the train station. You've got a van heading your way from the east. If you don't hurry it's going to cut you off."

"Affirmative."

Headlights lit up the cross street ahead, and Bolan pushed the bike for all it was worth. Horns blared and the van's brights blazed as Bolan shot past. The van's tires squealed as it braked and turned to pursue him. As he turned hard down the next side street, he nearly laid the bike down as he braked to a screaming halt. The alley was a dead end. Bolan burned the bike around in a one-eighty and flew back the way he had come. Lights framed him again as he burst onto the street.

Bolan fired over his shoulder, and the crack of automatic fire sailing overhead answered him. He had fired off his one magazine of armor-piercing ammo. All he had left were subsonic hollowpoints, and they couldn't be depended on to penetrate the van or disable the engine. Bolan's lips skinned back from his teeth. This was supposed to have been a simple drop. His main concern had been breaking contact with the police if necessary. All he had other than the Beretta was a single tear-gas grenade and a flash-stun. They would just have to suffice.

The CIA man spoke rapidly. "The road you're on is going to T and then dead-end on both sides. You've got one more side street coming up on your left. Take it."

Bolan slowed as the side street approached and pulled the bike into the turn. "Affirmative—" Bolan hit the brakes as a parked semi filled his headlight and the side street from wall to wall. The Executioner yanked the bike around and pulled back into the street. The van bore down on him, and a man stood up in the sunroof and fired a burst from an automatic rifle. Bolan raised the Beretta to his shoulder and flicked the selector switch to semiautomatic fire. He took an extra second and aimed carefully as the gunman in the van fired off another wild burst. Bolan let out half a breath and squeezed the trigger. The Beretta's ravaged suppressor let out a coughing bark, and the gunner jerked backward and dropped his rifle. Bolan jammed the Beretta into his jacket and accelerated forward toward the van.

The van rushed forward to run Bolan down. The Executioner reached into his jacket and pulled out the flash-stun grenade. He looped the pin around the brake lever and hauled back to arm the grenade. Bolan watched the van bear down on him, and the cotter pin and lever pinged away from the grenade as he opened his fist. He counted one long second as he and the van closed, then he hurled the grenade.

The driver cut the wheel hard left as he saw Bolan throw, and the big American swerved in the opposite direction. The grenade bounced against the van's hood and detonated. Bolan squeezed his eyes shut and held the bike steady. Bright light pulsed orange through his closed eyelids, and he nearly lost the bike as the concussion hammered his eardrums. Bolan opened his eyes and yanked on the handlebars as the side of a warehouse flew toward him. The bike yawed but stayed up on its wheels. Behind him the van screamed and fishtailed as the blinded driver stood on his brakes. Bolan blinked against the wind and the flashes of light still pulsing across his retinas, and yawned to clear his ringing ears.

"What's my situation?"

The CIA man's voice was grim. "The other van is fleeing the scene."

"Tell me the bad news."

The voice was apologetic. "I couldn't observe both of you. I chose to direct you once I saw Akira and Honda were clear and heading for the train station. They ran right into the cops. Akira was boxed in. He stopped the bike, and both he and Honda got off. Honda is talking with the cops. They put Akira in handcuffs, and they're leading him to a car right now."

Bolan let out a long breath from between his teeth. "All right. Give me a bearing."

"Half the cops are clustered around Honda and the train station. Others are heading out into the warehouse district. Take your third left, then start heading south. It'll take you directly away from the police and into the suburbs. Give me a minute to pick an isolated location, and I'll send a CIA-friendly taxi to meet you there. Keep your line open."

"Affirmative." Bolan sped down the street and took the third left. The warehouses quickly disappeared, and the block towers of residential streets began. Out beyond them would be the Tokyo suburbs. Bolan took his speed below the legal limit and drove on into the night. He cleared his mind. It wasn't a total loss by any means. They had gotten the information to Agent Mitsuko, and saved her life. Akira arrested was better than Akira dead. Arrested they could work with, and they had also given Nishiki-Tetsuo another bloody nose. It was up to Aaron Kurtzman now. If he could break the codes on the disks, then it would be time to close with the enemy and take this fight to the finish.

14

"You work for the CIA! Admit it!"

Akira Tokaido sat handcuffed in a folding chair while a man who had identified himself as PSIA Agent Tadanobu yelled in his face. It was a small, dark blue room with a single folding table and a single shaded light bulb that hung from the ceiling and cast a harsh glare. Two uniformed men stood as silent as stones by the door and glared as they occasionally tapped the collapsible Japanese riot batons in their hands. It was an interrogation room right out of some bad spy movie, only it was an unpleasant reality, and Tokaido had very little notion of what his real legal rights were.

Other than eternal damnation and excommunication from the church, there was hardly anything that they hadn't threatened him with. He knew most of them were idle threats, except for the part about him having his stay in Japan extended by several years and spending them in a very small room with convict Yakuza scum who loved Americanized young men like him. Prison loomed ahead as a very real possibility. Tokaido grimaced inwardly at the thought. He had been held incommunicado for more than four hours, and he hadn't seen Agent Mitsuko since he had surrendered to the police at the train station. He steeled himself. The big guy was out there, and he took care of his own. Tokaido looked the interrogating agent in the eye and told the truth.

"I'm sorry, but I told you before. I don't work for the CIA."

Tadanobu looked close to bursting a blood vessel. "You do, too!"

"May I please contact the American Embassy?"

"No, you may not!"

"May I please talk to a lawyer?"

Veins pulsed in the PSIA agent's forehead. "No, you may not!"

Tokaido jumped slightly as he felt a buzz in his foot. The agent roared. "You will stay still!"

The young computer expert had been thoroughly searched, but so far they had left him in the clothes he had been wearing. When Tokaido had gone to Tokyo, they had factored in the possibility that he might be arrested. Gadgets Schwarz had modified the heel of his right boot with a simple communications device. It was really little more than a high-frequency pager. It would silently buzz when the proper signal was sent. Tokaido didn't move as he felt a second buzz against his heel. Two buzzes meant they knew he had been captured, they knew where he was and he was to hang tight until further notice. A third buzz would mean that they were coming to get him, and to be ready. He waited anxiously for the third buzz in his boot and hid his disappointment when it didn't come. He wished he knew Morse code. He could have received a lot more information that way, but he had never felt the need to learn Morse code until eight hours before he had decided to volunteer to go to Japan.

Tokaido considered the situation, and his options were very simple. He had been captured. This was the less glorious side of field work, but at least he had been captured by the police and not by Nishiki-Tetsuo, whose agents would probably be carving him like a Thanksgiving turkey right about now. He really only had one option. Bolan was out there. His instructions were to hang tight, and that was exactly what he was going to do.

"Stop daydreaming!" Tokaido jumped in his seat as Tadanobu's fist crashed down and nearly buckled the folding table. The agent rammed his face nose to nose with the young man and screamed. "I told you to stay still!"

"I'm sorry. You startled me."

Tadanobu purpled. "Scum!"

Tokaido kept his mouth shut and prayed that there was a "good cop, bad cop" game being run here, and that the good cop might show up soon. He was starting to need a bathroom, and he was sure that Tadanobu would take this as a sign of weakness on his part. "May I please contact the American Embassy now?"

"No!"

"May I contact a lawyer?"

"No! Now, admit it! You work for the CIA!"

Tokaido sighed. "No, I do not work for the CIA."

"Liar! You do too for the CIA! Your lying will not save you! This is not the United States. You are not a Japanese citizen! You have no rights here! No fancy lawyer can help you! You are a criminal! You are going to go to jail for a very long time! You will not be happy there! I will personally make sure of your discomfort! You will…"

Tokaido tried to ignore the spittle flying in his face as Tadanobu teetered dangerously close toward apoplexy. It was going to be a very long night.

IF SHIRATA HADN'T KNOWN BETTER, he would almost think that the old man was starting to sound desperate. His voice was as cold and calculating as ever, but there was an almost subliminal edge of fear to it. Shirata had no doubt that the old man was under tremendous pressure from the rest of the One Heaven board. The situation was out of control, and Shirata himself was starting to feel nervous. He was still in the main Tokyo branch building, but instead of being on the upper floors he had moved his operations room to the floors below ground. He was surrounded by the thick concrete walls and ceiling of a converted storage room. An entirely new suite of recoded computers had been installed, and makeshift personal facilities had been moved in for around-the-clock shifts. The entire floor had been sealed off and was guarded by nearly a platoon of men equipped with automatic weapons, body armor and gas masks. The old man and the rest of the One Heaven ring had moved out of Tokyo and gone north to their private stronghold. Shirata had been barricaded in the basement for two days without seeing the sun. Nishiki-Tetsuo had been driven to a bunker mentality. It was a flawed tactic. A static defense of waiting for the enemy to strike. It galled Shirata, but he could think of nothing better to do in the current situation.

The old man rattled on. He wasn't saying anything new or helpful. "These failures are intolerable."

Shirata had to agree. They had been beaten in Europe, and then again in North America. These had been tremendous, almost inconceivable setbacks, but in the end that was what they had been. Only setbacks. The downfall of the Western nations and the ascendancy of Japan as the number-one world power was, after all, a fairly large project. Their plans to destabilize Europe and biologically devastate the United States had been derailed. So be it. They could make other plans. Except the original plans had been nearly perfect. The European nations were backward and squabbled endlessly with one another. The irradiation of their capitals would have made their governments fall, and their economies ripe for takeover.

The Americans were fat, lazy and stupid. Americans were like wasps drunk on the honey of their material excess. They were only dangerous if you blatantly kicked their nest and stirred them up. Without a clear enemy, they became disorganized and foolish. The planned use of the flulike Ebola virus would have left them easy meat. Their population would have been devastated. Their armed forces would have been crippled. Their economy would have crashed. Nishiki-Tetsuo would have stepped forward with a cure at an opportune time for a devastated United States to gratefully accept Japanese aid in rebuilding its technological and industrial infrastructure. It would have become an economic satellite of Japan, and what's more, it would have been grateful. Japan would have become the most powerful nation on Earth in less than five years.

Shirata's knuckles went white. But one commando had stopped them at every turn. He undoubtedly had a massive resource base, but still, one man had stopped them cold. That man was here now, and rather than defending, he was relentlessly on the attack.

There seemed to be no way to stop him.

The old man broke Shirata's train of thought. "You are not telling me anything I want to hear."

Shirata knew that all too well. "Yes, the situation is critical. Now that Agent Mitsuko has been attacked, the PSIA will be on full alert. If they are not actively cooperating with the commando, they are at least receiving information from him."

"That is known to me."

Shirata searched for something positive. "The traitor, Yukio Tadashi, has been killed while in custody, as you ordered."

The old man grunted. "Yes. I understand the PSIA now has someone in custody involved with our attack on Agent Mitsuko."

"That is true." Shirata had been giving that matter a great deal of thought. "My contacts could not find out very much. He is an American of Japanese descent. His passport is in order. He is currently being held on charges of driving a stolen motorcycle. However, he was rescuing a PSIA agent from an assassination attempt at the time. I do not know what they intend to do with him."

The old man's voice grew cold and vindictive. "Use your connections. Have him killed, and in as ugly a manner as possible."

Shirata's eyes flared. "No! Wait. I have a better idea."

It was a measure of the old man's state of mind that he didn't immediately challenge Shirata's impertinence. "What is your idea?"

"You and the board have influence in the police and the government. I am sure the American's passport is false, but I am also sure that it will pass official scrutiny. I am sure they do not believe his alibi, but they cannot prove it wrong, either. His one real crime was riding a stolen vehicle, but he did so to save a PSIA agent in the course of her duties. Use your influence. Have the American released. I am sure you can do it. The PSIA will not like being told to do it, but they at least tacitly approve of what the Americans are doing. They will release him."

"And then we will kill him."

"Yes. We will decide the time of his release, and where and what conditions he will be released under. What's more, the commando must suspect we will kill his comrade on release. The American risked his operation to save Agent Mitsuko. I believe he will try to save his friend."

The old man mulled the idea over. "Yes, but we have no guarantee that he will do this. Now that one of their own has been captured and the mission endangered, his superiors may tie his hands."

Shirata smiled to himself as the plan came together in his mind. "That may indeed be so. But we have global resources at our disposal. It is time we used them effectively."

"What are you suggesting?"

"If we cannot lure the commando out, then I say we do not kill his friend. We have him escorted to a plane we control, with a pilot who works for us. That plane will experience technical difficulty and be forced to land someplace convenient to us. There we will have the American removed and he will disappear."

The old man sounded pleased. "And then we will interrogate this man about just who this commando is, how he is operating and who exactly he represents."

Shirata nodded with a cold glint in his eye. "Exactly. Even if we fail to draw out the commando with this man, I believe what he can tell us under the knife will be very interesting indeed."

MACK BOLAN PUNCHED the preset number on the portable phone. Agent Mitsuko answered on the first ring and spoke in Japanese. "This is Agent Honda Mitsuko, how may I assist you?"

Bolan had learned the phrase by heart and responded in English. "It's me."

The woman's voice had a slight edge to it as she spoke. "It is good that you have called me. There have been important developments."

Bolan was sure there had been. "It took me some time to maneuver back to a safe place. The detour took some time."

"I understand."

"What's happened?"

"Yukio Tadashi died in custody."

Bolan had expected that Nishiki-Tetsuo would have had it in for the traitor, but he hadn't expected their agents to act so fast or be able to intervene before he had been released or transferred to a regular prison. The fact that he had been killed while still directly in the hands of the authorities spoke of how high up the chain Nishiki-Tetsuo's corruption ran.

"How was he killed?"

"He was poisoned somehow. We are still not sure of the nature of the toxin or how it was introduced into his cell or into his body. We suspect some kind of nerve agent. When his body was found by the guard, it was in an extreme state of rictus that suggests violent convulsions. In its legitimate business enterprises, Nishiki-Tetsuo is known for the brutal way it treats executives who fail. One can only imagine the vindictiveness they reserve for operatives who fail in their illegal affairs, much less how they deal with traitors. Yukio Tadashi died a prolonged and agonizing death."

"What is the current status of the man you are holding now?"

Mitsuko sighed over the phone. "He is currently safe. He is being held at PSIA headquarters, and two armed agents I personally trust are with him at all times. At least for the moment he is safe."

Bolan didn't like the way she said "for the moment."

"What is his legal status?"

"He was arrested in possession of a motorcycle that had been reported stolen. His passport is in order, though I believe with enough cooperation from your government we would find that his current identity is a very elaborate fabrication."

Bolan reserved comment on that point. "What about weapons charges?"

Gun laws in Japan were extremely stringent. An American without diplomatic immunity found driving a stolen motorcycle and carrying a silenced handgun would automatically qualify for hard time in a Japanese prison. Mitsuko was silent for a moment. "Your man surrendered his weapon to me before he was taken into custody by the police. I..." She made a small perturbed noise in the back of her throat. "I have not reported it."

"So what exactly is his status?"

The woman made another unhappy noise. "He is under joint police-PSIA custody. This is very uncomfortable for both departments. The police know that we are not sharing all our information on the matter with them. They feel we are abusing our federal authority, and in a very real sense we are. They are protesting the matter, but now it is a moot point."

Bolan's tone went cold. "What exactly does that mean?"

"The man is being released."

Bolan could already sense the trap closing around him. "Released how?"

"The order came in an hour ago. He is to be escorted to the airport and put on a plane to the United States. His visa has been canceled. He is not to enter Japan or any of her territories again, or he will be arrested and prosecuted for the crimes of possession and transportation of stolen property."

The Executioner's eyes narrowed into slits. "Who is escorting him to the plane?"

"Tokyo vice."

Bolan felt the trap slam shut. In every big-city police force in the world, the vice departments were the most susceptible to corruption. It was the department that was directly involved with any metropolis's drugs, prostitution and gambling. It was where the big cash-money crime was, and more often than any department would admit, that money could buy officers. Tokyo was no different. Bolan shook his head. "Isn't transferring the matter to vice somewhat irregular?"

"Yes. It is highly irregular, but it is out of our hands. The order came from very high up the chain of command."

"Nishiki-Tetsuo is calling in their markers."

"Indeed it seems so." Mitsuko's voice grew slightly more hopeful. "We are doing everything we can to delay matters. It will take some time for the paperwork to be done, and we will stall and delay through every step of the transfer. However, his plane is scheduled to leave in three hours."

Bolan was silent for a moment. They were daring him to make a rescue attempt. That much was very clear. The Executioner looked at Burdick and Grimaldi, and they looked back at him expectantly. Bolan knew if he ordered the attempt, they would be willing to try, and he knew it would be suicidal. They were only three men. They would be attacking Japanese police officers in the performance of their duty. Nishiki-Tetsuo would have gunmen waiting almost every step of the way, and at the first hint of a successful rescue one of the officers surrounding Tokaido in the car would put a bullet in the young man's head. There was almost no chance of success whatsoever, and the price of failure would be astronomical. "What kind of plane, commercial or private?"

"A commercial jet. We insisted upon it, and there was no objection. He will be flying out of Tokyo International Airport, Japan Airlines flight L34, stopping in Singapore, and then continuing on to Honolulu International Airport, Hawaii."

Bolan could see the parameters of the trap very clearly in his mind. "How many officers will be escorting him on the plane trip itself?"

"Two plainclothes detectives."

"Vice, of course."

"Indeed, that is correct."

There were sure to be Nishiki-Tetsuo agents on the flight posing as regular passengers. Bolan considered the options. "The plane will be diverted somehow, due to technical difficulties or something, and forced to land in some isolated place in the Pacific. The passengers will be debarked, and my friend will be escorted off to some private place, and then he will disappear. Then Nishiki-Tetsuo agents will torture every last shred of information out of him and then they will kill him."

"Yes, that is what I would do if I was in their position. It is a nearly foolproof plan." Mitsuko's voice grew grim. "I want you to know that I requested that I be allowed to escort the prisoner onto the plane and into American custody. My request was denied, as were all other requests for PSIA involvement."

Bolan could have predicted that. Nishiki-Tetsuo was playing a full-court press. "I appreciate your efforts on his behalf, Agent Mitsuko."

"I wish I could do more." The agent's voice became stonily professional again. "However, I must inform you, your friend will be under official police escort on the way to the plane. Not all of those officers are in the pay of Nishiki-Tetsuo. Many of them will simply be doing their duty."

The threat didn't have to be spoken. If Bolan and his team attacked uniformed Japanese police officers in the performance of their duty, they would become public-enemy number one in Japan. "I understand."

There was a very long pause on the phone, and then Mitsuko spoke. "I do not expect you to answer, but what do you intend to do?"

"I'm not willing to kill innocent Japanese police officers."

"So you will sacrifice your friend?"

"No."

There was another pause. "What will you do?"

Bolan's counterplan was already forming in his mind. "Use the only weapons at my disposal."

"What weapons are those?"

"Speed and surprise. I'll contact you again. Thank you for your assistance in this matter, Agent Mitsuko. It won't be forgotten." Bolan clicked off the line.

Burdick looked at him with a furrowed brow. "And?"

Bolan turned to Grimaldi. "Rev up the satellite link. I need to talk to the Bear."

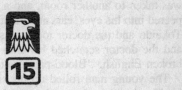

15

"Time to get up."

Akira Tokaido blinked up into the harsh light of his cell. He was most startled by the fact that Agent Tadanobu hadn't called him scum at the top of his lungs. Instead, the stout PSIA agent looked down at him in an almost kindly fashion. The young man's eyes narrowed warily. "What's happening?"

The agent sighed. "You are being sent back to the United States. You will be released from custody when your plane reaches Honolulu, where you will be remanded to United States federal authorities."

"When?"

"Now. You are going now."

Tokaido pulled on his jacket. There had been no further signal from the buzzer in his boot. His current orders were to hang tight, but if he was being released he couldn't very well demand to stay in jail. "All right."

He followed the agent through a corridor of holding cells and out into an office where he signed a number of extradition and release documents that Tadanobu explained to him in detail. The man behind the desk nodded and spoke in English as he took the forms back. "The contents of your suitcase and personal belongings found in your hotel room will be shipped back to your United States address within ten days." He produced another form. "Please sign here."

Tokaido signed and he was ushered past several more desks where he signed even more forms. Everyone seemed to be taking his time and was behaving in a friendly fashion. He was taken to another room, and a very short and thin doctor peered into his eyes, ears and mouth and checked his reflexes. Tokaido and the doctor took turns signing more documents, and the doctor scratched his chin thoughtfully. He spoke in broken English. "Blood-pressure test, please."

The young man rolled up his sleeve, and the doctor took his blood pressure several times. It suddenly occurred to him that everyone seemed to be doing his job as slowly as possible. It was suddenly very clear. They were stalling. Tokaido tried to decide whether that was a good thing or not as the doctor prodded him in the chest and asked him to cough several times. His first inclination was relief to be getting out of the holding cell that had been his home for the past day and a half, but doubts nagged at the back of his mind. If he was being released, someone from the American Embassy should have contacted him, or at least a lawyer sent by proxy. That hadn't happened. He was still being held incommunicado. A creepy feeling told him that something was wrong.

The doctor looked at the young man and then looked at his watch with a sigh. Apparently the little man was either out of time or out of ideas. He produced a final form, which Tokaido signed, then he gestured toward the door. Tadanobu was waiting for him outside.

He looked at Tokaido with grim interest. "Listen, right now, you are in PSIA custody. Once you step out into the main lobby, we must turn you over to Tokyo vice."

The young man straightened. He didn't like the sound of that at all. Tadanobu seemed to be able to read his thoughts. "Yes, I agree. It is highly irregular. You will be driven with police escort to Tokyo International Airport. Two officers will accompany you onto the plane, and deliver you to the American authorities in Honolulu. In my opinion, you will probably be safe as long as you are on Japanese soil. After that—" the agent's tone lowered "—you should be very careful."

Tokaido nodded. It seemed like very good advice. The agent nodded back. "Good. We can delay no longer. Let us go.'' The agent fell into step in front of him, and as they went out the door two burly agents fell into flanking positions. They walked out into the lobby, where two Japanese men in dark suits stood waiting with irritated expressions on their faces that their sunglasses did little to conceal. The taller one stepped forward without bowing and flashed his police badge. He spoke rapidly, and even in Japanese his voice sounded insulting to Tokaido.

Tadanobu nodded and stubbornly spoke English for his charge's benefit as he held up a clipboard. "Yes, please sign for the prisoner's release into your custody."

The detective snatched the clipboard and scrawled his signature on several lines and thrust the papers back at the PSIA agent. The shorter agent snapped a pair of handcuffs onto Tokaido's wrists and cinched them tight. The young man's only consolation was that they had cuffed his hands in front of his body rather than behind. He hadn't looked forward to sitting on his hands for the entire plane ride. The detective grabbed him by the collar and marched him outside. Tokaido blinked and squinted against the noonday glare as he was shoved into a car, the two agents squeezing in beside him. Two more men in suits sat up front. The car parked in front of them pulled into traffic ahead of them, and they followed suit. Behind them another car pulled out into a rear-guard position.

The taller detective reached inside his coat, and Tokaido tensed as he pulled out a revolver. The man sneered and suddenly drove his elbow into his prisoner's ribs with brutal force. If there had been room in the crowded back seat, Tokaido would have been doubled over by the sudden, dazzling pain. The detective's voice turned jovial. "Sit still and keep your mouth shut. If you move, I am going to shoot you through both legs. If we see any sign of your friends coming to help you, I am going to shoot you through the head. Do we understand each other?"

Tokaido grunted and with an effort kept his body upright

and his face rigid. The detective laughed. "Enjoy the ride, tough guy."

The ride itself was uneventful. Tokaido watched both sides of the road as they drove toward the airport, but he saw no sign of Bolan or any other members of the team. None of the preset signals buzzed against his heel. He was beginning to feel abandoned, and he was starting to feel genuinely nervous.

The detective laughed again. "Sweating already?"

Tokaido steeled himself as they drove into the airport passenger-loading area and pulled up to the JAL terminal. The men in the escort cars jumped out and formed a phalanx around him as he was shoved unceremoniously out of the car. They marched him into the terminal and went straight to the loading gate. The detectives flashed their badges and went through the metal detectors without stopping. The little platoon slammed to a halt as they came to the gate.

Agent Mitsuko stood directly in front of the gate and barred their way. Two of the largest Japanese men Tokaido had ever seen stood like brick walls in suits on either side of her. One of them held what appeared to be his suitcase. The head detective snarled at Mitsuko, and the PSIA agent took several steps forward and used her height to look down her nose at the detective as she snarled back at him. A heated debate began in incredibly rapid Japanese.

Mitsuko suddenly broke into English. "Very well, I will go back to my superiors! I will tell them that you did not comply with orders! You did not sign for the prisoner's personal effects, nor did you take their transfer into your custody! I will tell my superiors in the PSIA head office of your incompetence and reckless disregard for your duty!"

The detective said something nearly under his breath. Whatever it was had to have been personal. Mitsuko's face became a cold mask of rage. Tokaido fully expected to see guns drawn at any moment. The detective's face twisted, and he barked out a quick and condescending stream of Japanese. Mitsuko nodded once and replied in English. "Yes, of course you must be allowed to search his belongings, but I demand the right to examine the prisoner.''

The police detective and the PSIA agent glared at each other for a moment, then both of them nodded and looked back at their men. Tokaido was marched forward, and one of the massive PSIA men handed the head detective the suitcase. Two more detectives stepped forward and held the case while the head man yanked it open and began pulling out Tokaido's few changes of clothes and dropping them to the floor. Mitsuko faced the young man and spoke loudly in English. ''Hands over your head, now!''

Tokaido raised his manacled hands over his head, and the two burly PSIA men grabbed him out of the detective's hands.

The woman barked again. ''Turn around! Slowly!''

As he turned, the two agents patted him down as if they were looking for weapons. The head detective looked up and spoke angrily to Honda. She snarled back in English, ''I am not stalling! I am within my jurisdiction! This man is being deported! I—'' She suddenly whirled on Tokaido and shouted in his face. ''I told you not to move!''

He gaped. He hadn't moved. The two PSIA men clamped their hands on his shoulders like vises and formed a human wall that blocked him off on either side. Mitsuko began to wave her finger in his face and shout a stream of Japanese at him. Tokaido blinked in astonishment as she pulled a small pistol out from a holster just under her jacket. He recognized the PPK/S .22 automatic that the CIA lookout had dropped to him in the warehouse district. The sound suppressor had been removed. With magic-show deftness Mitsuko shoved the pistol down the front of his pants so that it disappeared into his underwear. He resisted flinching. It was an extremely unpleasant fit. The head detective dropped Tokaido's suitcase and strode forward shouting in Japanese. Mitsuko shouted back, and the two big PSIA agents spun the young man to face the vice cops.

Mitsuko went nose to nose with the detective as they hurled

more insults at each other. A number of the escorting vice cops seemed genuinely shocked by everything that was happening. Tokaido felt a gentle squeeze on his right shoulder, and one of the big PSIA men spoke softly without moving his lips. "You are in terrible danger."

That was becoming abundantly clear to Tokaido. Mitsuko suddenly looked down defeatedly and glanced at her men. They released their hold on the young man and gently shoved him toward the detectives. The head detective scribbled his signature on the form Mitsuko presented without even looking at it. He grunted at one of his men, and Tokaido's clothes were shoved back into the suitcase in a wad with the sleeve of one of his shirts trailing out of it. The woman gave the detective a final glare, and without a word or glance back marched away with her two men in formation behind her.

The head detective spoke to his men. They nodded and waited while he and his partner took Tokaido through the gate and loaded onto the plane. They marched down the aisle, and he was shoved into the center seat of the center row. His suitcase was crammed into the overhead luggage compartment, and the two detectives sat on either side of him. Without warning, the head detective rammed his elbow into Tokaido's side again. The young man folded forward, and the detective yanked him upright again and hissed in his ear. "All their goddamn stalling bought you nothing but pain, tough guy. We are going to be in international airspace for the next few hours, and you are in my hands. My orders are to deliver you alive, that is all. Do not get any stupid ideas. It is not just me and my partner on the plane with you. We have friends all over this flight, and I have no problem with taking you into the men's room and crippling you if you become a problem, understand?"

Tokaido nodded painfully as he tried to pull air into his lungs. The detective nodded and drove his elbow into the young man's ribs again. He fought the urge to throw up and kept his chest bent over his knees. The detectives rummaged through the inflight reading material in the seat backs in front of them. Tokaido sat in his own world of pain when he stiffened. There was a buzz against his heel, then a second, then a third. He took a deep breath and straightened in his seat. Bolan knew where he was, and his orders were to sit tight. Tokaido tried to ignore the pain in his side. He was fairly sure his ribs were cracked. He concentrated instead on the uncomfortable but reassuring mass of the pistol in the front of his pants. He decided he would wait until after take-off, then ask to go to the bathroom, where he would adjust the pistol for a more comfortable draw. Then he would sit tight and wait to see what Bolan had up his sleeve.

THE THREE TAV-8B McDonnell Douglas Harrier II jump jets cruised over the western Pacific Ocean. The TAV-8B was the two-seat trainer version of the Marine Corps Harrier II vertical-takeoff-and-landing fighter-bomber. The planes had taken off from the United States Navy amphibious-assault ship *Hornet,* which was currently in port at Subic Bay in the Philippines. Bolan hadn't wasted the three-hour advance notice Agent Mitsuko had given him before Tokaido's flight. The CIA had chartered a private Learjet from Narita International Airport in Tokyo and flown him straight to the Philippines.

The Japan Airlines flight that Akira Tokaido had been placed on had flown to Singapore as scheduled. CIA observers had been on station at the gate and reported that he hadn't debarked from the airplane. Bolan had been betting on that. Nishiki-Tetsuo knew that there would be observers, if not a rescue team waiting for them there. What they had done was pay enough money to make sure that no other passengers would be allowed to board the plane before it took off from Singapore again. The plane had taken off on schedule, and was currently on a heading straight for the Hawaiian Islands. The Harrier jets had taken off from the Philippines and intercepted the flight path of the JAL 747 from behind. They were currently tracking the plane with their radars and were hanging fifty miles back from the JAL jet, staying out of visual range.

Bolan knew at some point the JAL flight would divert to a Pacific island, and one that wasn't administered by the United States or a United States trust. He eyed the map on his knee. Given their current position in the Pacific, he was betting on either Kiribati or Nauru. Both islands were nearly midway between Singapore and Honolulu. Both were small, independent Pacific island nations. Neither one had any kind of United States military or administrative presence. With the massive wealth at Nishiki-Tetsuo's disposal, Bolan had little doubt that they could make almost anything they wanted happen on a tiny cash-poor island nation. What's more, whatever kind of reception they had in store for Tokaido would already be in place.

Once again the only real card Bolan held was surprise. The Executioner looked to his right and left from the instructor's position in the rear cockpit of the Harrier jet. Burdick flew behind a Marine Corps pilot off Bolan's left wing, and off to the right the third jet held two more Marine pilots. Grimaldi flew Bolan's jet himself. It had gotten to the point that the flyer from Stony Man was more familiar with the current United States warplanes in service than most Air Force test pilots.

On paper, the plan was fairly simple. They would shadow the JAL jet until it diverted. Electronic-warfare planes out of Subic Bay and Hawaii were already in the air and monitoring the air-traffic-control frequencies. When the JAL flight announced its destination, the Harriers would go to emergency power and swing around beyond visual range and clandestinely land Bolan and his two-man team on the beach. The spare Harrier would dump its extra Marine Corps pilot and take over Grimaldi's seat. The Harriers would then take off and head back to the Philippines. Bolan, Burdick and Grimaldi would be on their own after that. They would have to hump their way to the island's airport and intercept Tokaido before he could be tortured and killed. Assuming they could do that, the only problem would be getting off the island without getting caught.

On paper, it was a fairly simple plan. In reality, the plan was dangling by a string more than six thousand miles long. So far, it had gone as arranged. The three jets had experienced no mechanical problems. Harriers were short-range tactical attack aircraft, and their vertical-take-off-and-land ability made them fuel guzzlers. In-flight refueling had been arranged by dispatching tanker aircraft to meet them out of Guam. The in-flight refueling had been routine.

All that was left now was the wait, and the insertion and rescue itself. At this point nothing was going to be easy. Bolan sipped from a water bottle and waited. The seat in front of him was jammed with bags of gear he'd had delivered to meet him from the Philippines CIA branch office. It was going to be a daylight rescue, from an airport. They couldn't go in hard and armed to the teeth in armor and raid suits. Assuming they inserted and reached the airport without getting caught, they were going to have to sneak in posing as civilian tourists.

Bolan's thoughts were interrupted by the radio in his helmet. An Air Force electronic-warfare officer flying somewhere over the Pacific had found something. "Striker, we have intercepted a JAL flight L34 transmission. They have reported mechanical difficulties and requested emergency-landing clearance from Nauru International Airport, Nauru. Clearance has been granted."

"Affirmative." Bolan folded the map on his knee. "You heard the man, Jack."

"Affirmative, radar shows JAL L34 diverting south. New flight profile indicates they are on course for Nauru." The Harrier's wing dipped as Grimaldi swung them onto their new course. They were swinging wide around the 747 to avoid detection. The Harrier wasn't that much faster than a jumbo jet. The only advantage they had was that the 747 was flying at standard cruising speed. Only by taking the Harriers to full power would they be able to get to Nauru ahead of Tokaido and get in a position to save him.

The Harrier's engines roared as they went to full power, and Grimaldi's voice spoke in Bolan's ear. "ETA forty-five minutes, boss."

"What about Akira?"

"I'd say an hour and fifteen minutes, hour and a half at the outside."

Bolan calculated. A half hour lead, forty-five minutes tops. Nauru was barely four miles across at its widest point, but it was totally unknown territory. Bolan checked the gear in front of him a final time and then leaned back in his seat and closed his eyes. There was nothing he could do now but wait.

They were going to be cutting things very close.

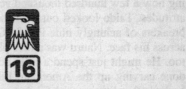

16

Nauru

Ryuchi Taido glanced at his watch, and on cue his portable phone rang. He clicked the line open. "Yes."

The Nishiki-Tetsuo secure-communications man spoke. "JAL flight L34 has been diverted. Emergency-landing request has been granted. ETA one hour and fifteen minutes."

"Excellent." Taido clicked off the phone and stretched his arms as he looked out from the veranda of his rental hut. Nauru was a fine little island. Small, isolated, no connections to old colonial empires. If the natives weren't so fiercely independent, and wealthy, Nishiki-Tetsuo could have easily bought the entire island nation with hardly a blip in the yearly financial report. Nauru had massive phosphate deposits, and exported over two million tons of it per year. It gave the tiny island nation one of the highest per-capita incomes in the world. Taido smiled. Of course, Nishiki-Tetsuo bought a great deal of those phosphates. Those phosphates weren't a renewable resource, and they were going to run out sometime shortly after the year two thousand. Nauru was looking to build up its tourist industry and facilities for offshore banking before that happened, and Nishiki-Tetsuo was very likely to be a heavy investor.

Nishiki-Tetsuo had a lot of clout here. As long as whatever the corporation did was quiet and didn't cause a local stink, none of the native authorities would really care what might have happened to one Japanese American who seemed to have turned up missing. Taido's smile widened. It was amazing how a few hundred thousand yen could change the locals' attitudes. Taido looked out over the white-sand beach to the breakers of achingly blue Pacific Ocean. A soft breeze blew across his face. Nauru was a nice place. The girls were pretty, too. He might just spend a little downtime here after he was done carving up the American. Like many native Japanese, he had very little regard for Japanese born and raised in the United States. Taido took a knife from the little table on the veranda and tested the edge.

The little four-and-one-half-inch Randall Chukkar blade was a shining arc of stainless steel. The blade was a deeply swept curve with a back edge as sharp as the front. The Chukkar was a classic American hunting knife, and ideal for cleaning, skinning and even caping small game. The stag handle made for a sure grip even when the handle was covered with blood. Taido grinned as he shaved a few hairs off of the back of his arm. Americans sure knew how to make knives. The knife he held was more like a surgical instrument than a camping tool.

Taido's smile turned cruel. He was going to operate on this American. He was going to carve every last shred of information the man had out of his body. The man was going spill just who he was, what his function was, who the commando was, what organization they belonged to, what location they operated out of, the names of everyone he knew who was even vaguely involved with the commando's operations. Then, when Taido was absolutely sure he had gotten every pertinent scrap of information out of him, he was going to go to work on the poor bastard for real. When he was finished, the mewling, sightless, tongueless, crippled thing that remained would be left someplace where its confederates could pick it up and see what happened to those who stood against Nishiki-Tetsuo's will.

Then they would take the information and destroy the commando and everyone associated with him.

Taido slid the knife back into its sheath and tucked it into the back of his khaki shorts. He pulled on a shoulder holster over his T-shirt, then securely snapped a silenced 9 mm Glock automatic into it. Taido pulled on an oversize Balinesian batik-print shirt and examined himself in the mirror. No weapons were visible. He picked up a small camera bag, inside of which were a stun gun and two syringes of sodium pentothal. Legally the American was still an undesirable alien being deported from Japan, but the stun gun and the drugs were just a precaution in case he tried to raise some kind of stink and had to be kept quiet. They also had four agents on the plane as backup to keep things running smoothly. Of course, they could use the sodium pentothal to make the American talk, but that would be too easy.

Taido wanted to do this job the hard way.

He stepped out onto the veranda. A few yards away six powerfully built Japanese men sat on beach chairs and drank fruit juice as they talked quietly and soaked up the sun. They were six of Nishiki-Tetsuo's best operatives. Taido had trained most of them, and they had been pulled from their field assignment and sent by Shirata's order to reinforce Taido and make sure nothing went wrong. He nodded to himself. These men were the best. They sat totally at ease with the start of their mission only minutes away.

Taido clapped his hands, and the men rose from their chairs as a unit. They were ready. "All right. The plane arrives in about an hour. I want to be in place well before then. Get your weapons, get dressed and be ready to go to the airport in five minutes."

THE NAURUAN MAN looked with forlorn hope down the barrel of a large and powerful-looking handgun. He was short with graying brush-cut hair, and his skin was the deep mahogany of a Polynesian who has spent his life working the South Pacific beneath the tropical sun. He looked to be in his late middle age, but except for a slight paunch his body looked accustomed to hard work. A lifetime spent on the ocean hadn't prepared him for invaders from Mars. Jet planes had flown up to the beach as he was working on his boat and landed almost right in front of him. Men in masks and coveralls had jumped out and pointed guns at him while others threw bags of gear onto the sand. The jets had flown away back into the sky. The whole experience had taken less than thirty seconds, and the man regretted the time he had spent gaping at the marvelous planes. Now he was gaping up at the muzzle of a 9 mm Beretta machine pistol.

Mack Bolan spoke quietly. "Would you like to survive this experience?"

English and Nauruan were the two languages spoken on Nauru, and the literacy rate of the islanders was an amazing ninety-nine percent. The man spoke his English with a slight British accent, and he spoke up without hesitation. "Yes."

"Good." Bolan jerked his head back to the beach where the sand had been blasted by the landing of the jets. "I don't have time to explain to you what is going on. We're here to rescue someone, and we can't afford to be interfered with."

The man's eyes didn't waver from the muzzle of the machine pistol. "I'll accept that."

"What's your name?"

"Saul. Saul Fuemana."

Bolan looked at the well-appointed hut under the trees. "You live here?"

The man spent a half second considering his answer, then seemed to resign himself to the truth. "No. I live in Yaren, the capital. I have a fish shop there. I own the hut. I rent it out to tourists sometimes. Sometimes I come out here to get away and do a little fishing for myself." He looked over at a little outrigger skiff that was up on sawhorses under the trees. There was an old army jeep next to it that seemed to be in good repair. "That's my boat."

Bolan nodded. "Is that your jeep?"

"Yes, that's my jeep."

"Is anyone renting the hut at the moment?"

The man shook his head. "No."

"Are you expecting anyone soon?"

"Just my daughter and my grandkids. But she doesn't get off work until tomorrow."

"Is anyone likely to drop by?"

"No, when I'm fishing, my friends know I like to be alone. There shouldn't be anyone, at least no one should drop by until evening."

Bolan nodded in satisfaction. "Listen, Mr. Fuemana, I apologize, but we're going to handcuff you and put you in your hut. Hand and foot, and gagged. With any luck, we should be back within an hour or two and free you. If not, we'll notify someone locally to do so. If that doesn't happen, it means we've been captured, killed or had to take an alternative route out of here. Worst case, if you're telling the truth about your daughter's visit, she'll be here tomorrow to free you. Understand?"

The man nodded warily. "I understand."

"Good. Please put your hands behind your back."

Grimaldi walked up and gently handcuffed the man's wrists and led him back into the hut. Burdick grunted with effort as he hauled at a deflated Zodiac pontoon boat from the transport pod one of the Harriers had carried on its centerline hard point. It was obvious his broken ribs were giving him trouble. Bolan walked over, and the two of them hauled out the Kevlar-armored mass of the inflatable boat. The Executioner threw the valve on the air tank and the limp mass began to bulge outward and inflate. Grimaldi came out of the hut and checked his watch. "Twenty minutes, Striker."

Bolan nodded. "Is he secure?"

Grimaldi nodded. "Hands and wrists. He's got a pretty solid wooden bed in there, so I roped him to that, as well. I used a loose gag, but I taped it in place. He can't shout out anything louder than a mumble."

Bolan looked over at the jeep. "What do you think?"

Grimaldi shrugged out of his coveralls to reveal a pair of shorts and a loud Hawaiian shirt. "It's a small island. Someone could recognize it as his jeep on the way in."

Bolan nodded. "We can say we rented it from him. I think we have to risk it."

Burdick pulled off his mask and wiped the sweat from his brow as the Zodiac boat inflated rigidly. Bolan shucked off his flight suit. He wore an oversize navy blue camp shirt and a pair of faded, sand-colored Gurkha shorts. He kicked off his boots and helped Burdick drag the Zodiac boat near the water. All three men kicked off their combat boots and strapped on all-terrain sport sandals from their gear bags. Bolan pulled on a battered Toronto Blue Jays baseball cap and slid a pair of tortoiseshell sunglasses onto his face. He wore a woven fabric pistol belt under the shirt, and he tucked the big .44 Magnum Desert Eagle underneath it. He attached the shoulder stock to the silenced Beretta machine pistol and clipped a two-power, eye-relief scope to a rail mounted on the slide. He put the converted weapon into a day pack that contained spare magazines and grenades.

Burdick concealed his red hair under a large straw hat and wore a threadbare dress shirt with the sleeves cut off and a pair of khaki pants that had been cut into clam diggers just below his knees. He looked like some sort of massive Huckleberry Finn. Bolan nodded. He certainly looked like a tourist attempting to go native. Grimaldi's tan shorts and white shirt looked as if they had just been cleaned and pressed. How he had managed this after a six-hour ride in a jet fighter's cockpit was beyond Bolan's understanding. Both Grimaldi and Burdick had .45 Colt automatics strapped under their shirts. Grimaldi had his silenced .45ACP MAC-10 in a duffel bag. Burdick had a stockless, pistol-grip shotgun and a folding-stock M-79 grenade launcher in a day pack like Bolan's. All three of them wore soft-armor vests under their baggy shirts.

The three-man team stowed their bags in the Zodiac and climbed into Fuemana's jeep. Bolan took the wheel. "All right, we're going to have to assume they're expecting us. We're pretty sure they have my description, and we know they know Burdick. Jack, they don't know you. You're our man inside the terminal. Burdick and I are going to drop you off and head toward the runway. When we spot the JAL plane, we're going to get in as close as we can. You give us the signal when you see some kind of movement from inside. The Nauru airport unloads planes with portable gangways, and the passengers have to walk a few dozen yards to the terminal. I want to try and get Akira before they can get him inside or to where airport security can help them. Legally Akira is still the vice cops' prisoner. Everyone got it?''

Grimaldi and Burdick nodded, and Bolan started the jeep. The airport was two miles away, and Akira Tokaido's life was hanging by a very thin thread.

TOKAIDO LOOKED at himself in the rest-room mirror and made sure the .22 pistol wasn't visible. He had pulled it out and readjusted it so that he could grasp the grips with his right hand. With his hands in cuffs, the draw would be slow, and awkward to say the least, but at least he now had a card he could play in deciding his fate. The warning lights came on with a chime in the rest room and signaled that the plane would be landing soon. He unlatched the door, and the Tokyo vice detective smiled and rammed stiffened fingers into Akira's midsection with practiced power.

Tokaido's vision blurred as he sagged to his knees. The detective grabbed him by his ponytail and yanked him to his feet again. "What, you could not manage to flush yourself down the toilet?" The corrupt cop laughed at his own humor. "Do not worry. You will end up in the sewer soon enough." He took a quick look around the tiny rest room to see if Tokaido had left any overt messages or clues about his situation, and grunted in satisfaction when he couldn't and closed the door. The young man stood hunched over gasping. His hands were resting on the .22 Walther automatic in his pants, and he fought the desire to draw and put a few rounds into Tokyo's finest. The sucker punches were really starting to get old.

The detective ground a thumb painfully into Tokaido's elbow joint in a come-along hold and led him stumbling down the aisle. A beautiful Filipina flight attendant looked at Tokaido's face and the handcuffs and then at the detective questioningly. The vice cop smiled sympathetically. "Our friend doesn't fly well. He's spent more time behind bars than in airplanes." The woman wrinkled her nose condemningly at Tokaido and moved aside as the detective shoved him back into his seat.

The detective grinned at Tokaido as the seat-belt sign came on overhead. "Not long now, tough guy."

17

Mack Bolan dropped off Grimaldi and pulled away from the front of the airport. Nauru International Airport was a small affair with one runway capable of handling jets and another for small planes and island hoppers. There was no fence around the field. Bolan took the jeep around the terminal toward the small-plane hangars, stepping beside a lanky man in coveralls who was wiping down the wings of a bright blue Cessna Skymaster.

The man looked to be about thirty and had sandy blond hair and a deep tropical tan. He spoke with a New Zealand accent. "'Lo there! Looking to rent out a plane?"

"Naw, just looking. I like planes," Bolan said as he got out of the vehicle.

The man smiled warmly. "You're a flyer, then?"

Bolan nodded. "Now and again, when I can get some hours in."

The man wiped his hands on a rag and gave Bolan a smile and a handshake that pilots reserved for fellow members of the fraternity. "Nick Corbolini."

"Mike Belasko." Bolan looked into the sky toward the west. At the limits of his vision he could see something in the sky. "Looks like you've got one coming in."

Corbolini nodded. "Yeah, heard about it over the radio. A JAL flight on the way to Honolulu has had some difficulties. It's making a short-fall here on our island."

Bolan frowned. "That's kind of unusual, isn't it? I mean

Kwajalein and Majuro can both handle jets, and they're a hell of a lot closer.''

The pilot frowned in return. "Too right, it's unusual. I've kind of been wondering about that myself.''

Bolan watched the plane as it slowly grew larger in the sky. Grimaldi's voice spoke in his earpiece. "I've got Ryuchi Taido in the waiting area.''

Bolan turned and stepped a few feet away to watch the incoming plane.

Burdick took the cue and stepped forward to accost Corbolini. "What kind of plane do you have there? I don't know planes like my buddy, but I like them. He's promised me he's going to teach me…''

Bolan took a few more steps away as the pilot began to extol the glories of the Cessna P337A and having an engine in the front and the back. Bolan spoke quietly into the microphone in his collar. "You're sure?''

They had both studied the pictures taken of the man in Mexico. Grimaldi's voice was positive. "Little guy, beard, shoulders like a fullback and arms like an orangutan. Definitely him. There are about six other Japanese gentlemen lounging around the terminal, and if they aren't special-forces trained, then bears have stopped crapping in the woods.''

Bolan trusted Grimaldi's eye. That meant seven highly trained hostiles. "Affirmative. Let me know when they start to move.''

"Roger.''

The Executioner watched the 747 descend and begin to make its approach. He could see the JAL markings on the plane as it came in.

"Well, her engines sound all right,'' Corbolini commented.

Bolan nodded, then turned. "How about your bird? Is she ready at the moment?''

The man nodded. "She's checked out, fueled up and ready to go. You want to take her up?''

"Just maybe.'' Corbolini's blue plane had just become Plan B.

The JAL flight made its final approach and hit the runway. The flaps went down, and the huge plane began to slow as it came down the tarmac without incident. The aircraft coasted nearly to a stop and began its turn to taxi toward the terminal.

Grimaldi spoke softly in Bolan's ear. "Taido is up, and so are the six others. They aren't even making a pretense at being casual about this. They're heading straight toward the gate."

"Affirmative." Bolan watched the plane come to a stop about twenty-five yards from the terminal. Two Polynesian men began to wheel a boarding ramp toward the plane. Bolan whirled on Corbolini with the .44 Magnum Desert Eagle in his hand. "Please put your hands behind your back."

The pilot's jaw dropped.

Bolan nodded at Burdick. "Cuff him."

Burdick pulled cuffs from his pack and snapped them on the stunned pilot's wrists. "Sorry about this. Nothing personal." The big Marine sat Corbolini in the hangar out of sight, then turned back to Bolan. "How do you want to play it?"

"There are two vice cops with Akira we know about. I'm betting at least two more Nishiki-Tetsuo agents are posing as passengers on the plane, possibly four to six. Then we've got seven in the terminal."

Burdick grimaced. "Long odds."

Bolan nodded. They were. "What do you have loaded in the M-79?"

The sergeant pulled the weapon out of his pack and snapped out the folding stock from over the barrel. "Flash-stun, like you said."

"Good. Here's how it goes down. Some of their plainclothes agents will probably disembark first to secure the area. The two vice cops will be right on top of Akira. One or two will probably be following behind. When we see Akira, I want you to put the grenade right on top of the loading ramp, right in the doorway if you can. Reload with a frag round, and hit Taido and his men as they come out. Watch out for civilians. You take the driver's seat in the jeep. When I say go, drive.''

''You got it.'' Burdick shoved the windshield down across the hood and climbed behind the wheel.

Bolan set the Desert Eagle on the jeep bed and pulled the Beretta out of his bag. The wire stock and folding foregrip turned the machine pistol into a miniature carbine. It wasn't an ideal weapon for sniping by any stretch of the imagination, but the plane was less than seventy-five yards away, and with the two-power scope attached, the Beretta ought to do the trick. The long eye-relief scope also allowed Bolan to keep both eyes open, and let him keep an eye on the surroundings, as well as on his target. The Executioner stepped into the back of the jeep and flicked the Beretta's selector switch from safe to semiautomatic fire. He raised the weapon to his shoulder, and the door of the 747 suddenly filled his cross hairs. "Be ready," he warned Grimaldi.

The pilot's voice was cool and steady. "I'm ready."

Bolan reached into his pocket and pulled out a small black box like a pager. He slowly pressed a button on it once, twice and then a third time. The signal should have gone straight to the heel of Akira's boot. They were coming for him. Be ready.

The door opened, and a flight attendant stepped onto the top of the loading ramp. She glanced about in the sunshine, and her face lit up in a smile as the first passengers began filing past her. Bolan kept his scope cross hairs steady and waited. More passengers disembarked. His eyes narrowed as two Japanese men came out together. They didn't smile, look up at the sky or gaze about wonderingly with the air of people whose flight to Hawaii had been diverted to a tiny tropical island. Their eyes scanned quickly from side to side. One man carried a newspaper, the other a briefcase. Both men held these articles close to their bodies with their left hands, while their right hands were held out of sight behind the objects they carried. Bolan smiled coldly. They were shooters.

A moment later two men in suits came onto the top of the

loading ramp with Akira Tokaido wedged firmly between them. Bolan spoke quietly to Burdick as he kept his own weapon on target. ''Ready...''

''Ready.''

The wedge broke up a bit as the top of the loading ramp narrowed into stairs. One detective was slightly in front of Tokaido, and the other slightly behind. Bolan spoke. ''Now.''

The M-79 thumped. Even as the 40 mm grenade flew, Burdick was breaking the weapon open to reload. The idling of the 747's engines helped mask the sound, and the hollow thump of a grenade launcher didn't sound like a gun to someone who had never heard one before. Through his scope Bolan saw one of the detectives look up at the sound he couldn't identify. Tokaido wasn't a field operative, but he had been to the Stony Man practice range many times, and he knew what the sound of a grenade launcher was like. Bolan saw the young cybernetics genius desperately squeeze his eyes shut and shove his manacled hands down the front of his pants. Bolan put his cross hairs on the detective behind Tokaido. He was the immediate threat to Akira's life. The Executioner squeezed the Beretta's trigger.

Several things happened almost at once. The rear detective jerked, and his eyes flew wide as he took the hit. Bolan squeezed his eyes shut so he wouldn't be blinded as the light pulse from flash-stun went off in his scope. The thunderclap of the grenade was definitely audible over the 747's engines, and Bolan immediately opened his eyes and swung his cross hairs onto the shooters. They had been down on the stairs, and partially shielded from the grenade's stunning sound and light. He squeezed the Beretta's trigger and put two rounds into one of the shooters as the man's newspaper fell away to reveal a silenced automatic pistol. The other shooter didn't see his partner go down, and he dropped his briefcase. He had a silenced automatic, as well, and he jockeyed for a shot at Tokaido past the other passengers on the ramp.

The young man put both his manacled hands onto the detective still in front of him and shoved with all his might.

The detective tumbled down the ramp and toppled the other passengers like dominoes. The shooter's gun fired into the air harmlessly as three businessmen and a Tokyo vice detective avalanched on top of him and he disappeared beneath them.

Bolan swung his sights back to the top of the ramp. Tokaido took a quick step and hurled himself over the rail of the loading ramp. He was already partway down, but 747s were tall planes. It was at least a twenty-foot drop, and Tokaido hit hard. He fell in a heap, and a small handgun went spinning out of his hands.

Grimaldi spoke rapidly in Bolan's ear. "Taido and his men are moving. They've all got guns."

The Executioner kept his sights at the top of the loading ramp. Two more men in suits had shoved past the shell-shocked flight attendant. Each had a silenced pistol in his hand and scanned the area for targets. "Affirmative! Wait for Burdick to engage, then hit them from behind."

"Roger!"

Bolan put his cross hairs on one of the shooters as he leaned over the loading-ramp handrail and spotted Tokaido. Bolan's first shot spun him, and his second one put him down. The second shooter looked about wildly, and as his eyes locked on Bolan, he swung up his pistol. The silenced Beretta chuffed three times and hammered the assassin to the deck.

Grimaldi's voice rose in Bolan's ear. "Here they come!"

Bolan kept his sights on the loading ramp. "Any civilians?"

Burdick kept his sights on the terminal door. "We're clear."

"All right! Hit them!"

The glass door of the terminal flew open, and the seven-man Nishiki-Tetsuo team immediately fanned out. The M-79 roared, and the men immediately threw themselves down. The grenade detonated with a crack, and the wide glass doors of the terminal gate spiderwebbed with fragment impacts.

Bolan shouted, "Drive!"

Burdick dropped the M-79, and the tires of the jeep

screeched on the tarmac. The sergeant reached down and put his stockless shotgun across his knees as he sped the jeep toward the plane. The hitters rose, some stumbling, most of them bloody. They were definitely wearing some kind of soft armor under their clothes. The terminal doors opened behind them as they charged forward, and Jack Grimaldi cut loose with his .45-caliber MAC-10. Two of the gunmen went down under the assault, and a third fell as they turned. Grimaldi faded back around the doors as they began to fire back into the terminal. "Akira's in trouble!" Burdick shouted.

Bolan whirled about in the back of the speeding jeep. Tokaido was crawling for his weapon, which had fallen a few feet away. The Tokyo vice cop and the Nishiki-Tetsuo shooter had extricated themselves from the pile at the bottom of the ramp and were moving around to take out the young computer expert. Both men had pistols in their hands.

Burdick raised his shotgun in one hand and fired. The sawed-off twelve-gauge nearly leaped out of his hand in recoil, and the shot went high and wide to strike sparks off of the 747's wing. But the shot had served its purpose. The two men spun and fired back at the jeep. Bolan tried to steady his aim, but firing a machine pistol from a moving jeep was an uncertain proposition at best. He swore as his shot went high. The two gunmen had no such problem. They steadied themselves and took careful aim at the jeep as it came at them straight on. A round tore into the hood of the jeep, and another slammed into Burdick's chest.

The jeep fishtailed and slowed as Burdick's foot automatically stepped on the brake. The tires shrieked as the jeep pulled up, and Bolan leaped from the vehicle as it rocked to a stop. A bullet spanged off the tarmac as the Executioner rolled with bone-jarring force across the concrete. Burdick had dropped behind the steering wheel and was awkwardly working the pump of his shotgun to chamber another round. Bolan brought up the Beretta to face his two opponents when the flat snapping of a small-caliber pistol began to fire rapidly off to his left.

Akira Tokaido lay on his side with the little .22 pistol held up in his cuffed hands. The range was less than five yards, and he pumped round after round into the Tokyo detective. The vice cop staggered back from the hits, and his revolver fired high and wide over the young man's head. Tokaido kept his sights dead on and continued to squeeze the trigger. The detective's revolver fell from nerveless fingers, and the man buckled and fell.

The Nishiki-Tetsuo shooter made the fatal mistake of snapping his head in the direction of the new threat. Bolan fired the Beretta, his first two rounds walking up the shooter's chest and the third snapping his head back and toppling him to the ground.

Bolan rose and bolted for the jeep. He opened his stride into a hurdle and slid over the hood. Hitting the ground, he squirmed behind the front tire as bullets struck the other side of the jeep. Part of Taido's squad had tracked their fire across the runway, while the others kept Grimaldi back.

Tokaido crouched and kept the loading ramp between him and the gunfire from the terminal. Grimaldi's voice was grim. "I don't think I can shoot my way past these boys, Striker, and I hear sirens."

Bolan shook his head. They were going to have to split up. "Get out of there, Jack. Break contact. Drop tear gas and retreat to the street side of the terminal. Hijack the first car you see. Don't go to the boat. Double back wide around the airfield and go to the small-plane hangar. There's a bright blue Skymaster fully fueled and ready to go in hangar number 2. Grab it and go."

"Roger, Striker. I'm out of here."

Bolan ejected the magazine from the Beretta and loaded a fresh one as he looked over at Burdick. The big man had dropped behind the jeep and was pale and sweating. "You all right?"

The Marine fumbled a fresh shell into his shotgun's action as more bullets struck the vehicle. He grinned painfully. "I think my armor held, but it didn't do my ribs any good."

The lopsided grin vanished into a grimace as Burdick coughed. Red bubbles flecked the big sergeant's lips. His body armor had held, but the bullet had still hit him like a sledgehammer. His already broken ribs had been driven inward. Burdick had blood in his lungs. The big man was hemorrhaging.

Bolan grabbed the M-79 and Burdick's bag from the back of the jeep. Bullets were striking the vehicle in sustained fire. He loaded a frag grenade and fired it in an arc over the jeep. It probably wouldn't hit very close to the gunman, but it wouldn't have to. Bolan leaped up and looked toward the terminal as he helped Burdick haul himself into the back of the jeep. The Nishiki-Tetsuo crew had definitely heard the M-79. They were charging back into the terminal and directly into an expanding cloud of tear gas.

"Akira!" Bolan shouted. "Let's move!"

Tokaido arose and limped so badly that he was almost hopping to the jeep. He fell into the back with Burdick and looked almost as bad as the Marine did. Bolan yanked the jeep into gear and pulled away under the 747 and headed straight down the runway toward the ocean. "You all right?" he shouted over his shoulder.

The young man grimaced in pain. "I think that bastard detective broke my ribs, and I think I broke my ankle jumping off the loading ramp."

"All right. Try to relax. We're getting out of here." Bolan took the jeep out past the runway onto the sand and turned south as he hit the beach. He had two casualties and was down to a fire team of one. So far the mission was less than a spectacular success.

Tokaido's voice was a little stronger as he spoke again. "Hey, Striker, you're leaking oil all over the place."

Bolan nodded. It was two miles back to Saul Fuemana's beach hut, and neither Burdick nor Akira could walk. It was going to be interesting.

RYUCHI TAIDO STAGGERED toward the front of the terminal with burning lungs and with tears streaming and blurring his vision. He swept his automatic from side to side and waited for the submachine gun of his enemy to cut him down. He nearly bumped into a small stone fountain, and he quickly shoved his head under the water and rolled his eyes. He came back up with water streaming from his beard, and his blood-shot eyes scanned the screaming people in the airport. Two of his men staggered past him to the left, and he shouted in Japanese. "Over here!"

The men stumbled over, and he rammed their heads under the water. They came up spluttering but with their weapons ready. Taido spoke rapidly. "They have their man back, but they had another man inside the terminal. If we can catch him, the mission is still a success even if the others escaped. He's an American with a submachine gun. Witnesses must have seen him flee! Find him!"

Taido whirled on a native man cringing behind a chair and spoke in English. "I am Interpol Agent Fujiwara! Which way did the terrorist go?"

The man blinked. "The man with the machine gun! He ran for the street!"

Taido nodded. "Let us move!" He and his two men charged out of the main lobby and out into the passenger loading area. People were shouting and shaking their heads. Taido roared. "I am Interpol Agent Fujiwara. There is an armed terrorist loose from the plane! Who has seen him?"

People began to wave their arms furiously and shout in mixed English and Nauruan. A native girl grabbed Taido's shirt sleeve. "Mr. Policeman! Mr. Policeman!"

Taido quickly knelt. "Yes! What did you see?"

The little girl pointed emphatically. "Over there! Them!"

A Caucasian man and woman in their late forties were al-most running toward him shouting. "The man! He took our car!"

"The terrorist, he took your vehicle? Which way did he go?"

The couple pointed their fingers at the same time. The

woman's voice was indignant. "He drove around the terminal and back out onto the airfield!"

Taido's stomach clenched. The shorter way was through the terminal, but he would have to go through the tear gas again, and he would be half-blind once he was out on the other side again. Taido broke into a sprint with his men following swiftly behind him. He rounded the terminal and skidded to a halt. A bright blue plane had taxied from one of the small-plane hangars and was accelerating down the runway. Taido's shoulders sagged as he watched the small plane pick up speed and gracefully pull into a tropical sky nearly the same color as the plane itself. He had seen the commando and Burdick.

This could only be their infamous aircraft-stealing pilot.

Taido's men came up behind him. They popped off a few shots with their pistols in frustration, but they knew as well as Taido did that the plane was well out of range. Taido holstered his weapon. "Get our wounded. Get to the boat. I want to be out in international waters before the locals have time to pull their heads out of the sand."

The men nodded and ran around the terminal to the scene of the firefight in front of the gate. They still had two men down, and it wasn't known whether they were living or dead. Taido pulled his radio off his belt to contact the boat when a thought struck him. The commando was almost certainly to be extracting by boat. Taido had no idea how the man had gotten to Nauru so fast, but there was only one airport, and the American was heading away from it. He had to be extracting by sea. Taido had a boat, and four of his operatives were still combat ready. Taido almost seemed to inflate with determination.

The mission wasn't over.

He clicked on his radio and called to Gun, one of his men helping the wounded.

There was a pause as Gun dropped what he was doing and got on his radio. "Yes, Taido-san."

"You are a pilot, are you not?"

"I am rated up to twin-engine aircraft."

Taido nodded. "Very good. Cease what you are doing. Go to the small-plane hangar and steal a plane." Taido considered. He was going assume that the commando's boat was close. "Take the plane and run an aerial search south of the airport and west of the island. The Americans cannot have gotten too far, and I suspect they will be in a small craft. We will go back to the boat immediately. You will direct us to them. Then we will destroy them."

Gun seemed to like the idea. "Yes, Taido-san! I will be in the air momentarily!"

18

The water of the South Pacific was so calm it was almost like blue glass as the Zodiac inflatable flew across it, throwing a perfect wedge of white water in its wake. Bolan checked his compass and adjusted his heading slightly. They were well beyond the three-mile national limit of Nauruan coastal waters, but he knew all too well that there was no white line drawn in the water. If the Nauruans figured out where their airport's attackers had gone, they just might send out an armed cutter and sink Bolan's little boat no matter what some little line on a map said. Naval vessels were known to get belligerent with people fleeing their coasts after committing crimes.

Bolan kept his heading. Somewhere to the west the United States Navy nuclear attack submarine *Los Angeles* was waiting to make the emergency pickup. He looked grimly at his gauges. The vessel was beginning to run low on fuel, and he hoped the submarine was somewhere close.

Burdick and Tokaido were in no condition to paddle. Burdick lay in the bow with his face shaded from the sun by his flight suit. He was pale and took rapid shallow breaths to try to ease the sawing pain in his lacerated lung. Tokaido crouched nearby holding his side. There had been no time for Bolan to tape his broken ribs, and his leg was stretched out in front of him with his fractured ankle still in its boot and elevated on a gear bag. The young man flinched with every bump of the boat.

Grimaldi's voice spoke over the radio. "We have company, Striker."

Bolan glanced at his gauges again. "What kind of company?"

"A plane, coming in fast from the east. I'm going to go take a look at him."

"All right, be careful." Bolan looked up into the sky. Grimaldi's blue plane was nearly invisible.

"Striker, I think we've got trouble."

Bolan pulled out his binoculars and swept the sky to the east. He stopped tracking as he caught a glimpse of a small white spot in the sky. "Is it Nauruan coastal patrol?"

"No, it's private. I recognize it. It's one of the planes that was in the hangars at Nauru International. I don't like it, Striker."

"Neither do I."

"I'm going to buzz him. Hold on."

Bolan watched as the plane grew bigger. It was a twin-engine King Air, a higher-performance aircraft than Grimaldi's Skymaster, with more speed and endurance. "Be careful, Jack. He's got more plane than you."

Grimaldi's voice was almost challenging. "Now, Striker, I've told you a million times. It's not the plane, it's the man flying it. And I'm betting this peckerwood has never been in a dogfight."

The King Air made no attempt to fly away from Grimaldi's aircraft as it continued on course toward Bolan's heading. The Executioner squinted through the binoculars as the two planes pulled side by side. Orange light suddenly flickered under the wing of Grimaldi's plane. Bolan realized the Stony Man pilot had stuck his MAC-10 out the window and dumped a magazine into the other plane.

The King Air nosed over into an evasive power dive. Grimaldi dipped his wing and gave chase, but the King Air was the faster plane and quickly leveled out and began to pull away to the west. Grimaldi's voice was jovial. "I don't think he'll be coming back."

"Did you make any kind of ID on him?"

"Well, I could swear I saw him fire a pistol at me earlier today at the airport."

"All right. He's seen us, and I don't think he was out here on a joyride. Keep an eye out for anyone headed my way."

"Roger."

Bolan turned on the inflatable's homing beacon and kept his heading for another uneventful fifteen minutes.

Grimaldi's voice spoke again. "You've got more company."

"What kind?"

"A boat. Looks like a motor yacht. A large one, with twin engines, and it looks like it's built for speed. It's moving fast."

Bolan looked at the needle as it went into the red. "I'm almost out of fuel."

"Well, I've got a couple of grenades left over. Want me to make a bomb run?"

"I don't know if that's such a good idea, Jack."

Grimaldi's voice was smug. "Got a better one."

Bolan sighed. "What the hell. Just be careful."

"Don't worry about it. I'm a pilot. They're swabbies. No problem."

The Executioner waited several minutes, then the radio crackled. "All right. I'm going in. I'm probably going to miss, but a willie pete will still burn on the water. It might put the fear of God back into them. Commencing run, I'm— Geez!"

"What's happening, Jack?"

"They've got automatic rifles, Striker! A bunch of them, and these boys know how to shoot. I'm going to—"

"You're going to pull out of there! Now! That's an order!"

"Roger."

Bolan took a deep breath. Short of having Grimaldi ramming the boat in a kamikaze attack, he was running out of options. He picked up the M-79 and unfolded its stock and broke open the action. He had two frag grenades left. They were antipersonnel weapons and not designed to take out vehicles or boats. He could clear their deck with them, but once they were gone, it would be rifles in a motor yacht versus handguns and a sawed-off shotgun in an inflatable boat, and that was assuming they didn't have heavy weapons of their own. The outcome was pretty predictable. Bolan and his team were about to get the short end of the stick.

He looked out across the water with his binoculars and began to make out the white shape of a boat coming out of the east. Bolan watched as it slowly drew closer. It was a decent-sized yacht. The frags would only scratch her paint and break windows.

"I tell you what, Jack. When they get close, I'm going to frag their decks. That should keep their heads down for a minute or two. You see if you can drop that willie pete and set her on fire."

Burdick coughed, then sighed heavily. "This is really getting thin."

Grimaldi seemed to be able to read the big Marine's mind, and Bolan's. "Striker, these guys are real bastards. How about I just ram them? I'm going to have to ditch anyway, so why don't I do it right down their goddamn throats?"

Bolan smiled wearily. He knew Grimaldi. The pilot wasn't bluffing. "Let's try it my way first for the hell of it. Get in position and wait for my signal."

"All right. I'm going to maneuver behind them. You give me the word."

Bolan throttled back the raft's engine and left it idling. The yacht was going to run them down anyway, and he wanted the raft to have a few seconds of fuel for evasive maneuvering if it came down to a firefight. He put down the binoculars when he could see the boat without them and flipped up the sight on the M-79 and waited. He decided to let them get in close, almost within rifle range. Bolan's lips skinned back from his teeth as he saw the yacht slowing. He looked through his binoculars again and found himself staring at a man who was watching *him* through binoculars.

It was Ryuchi Taido, and the little bearded killer was grinning. Men stood beside him with M-16 rifles. He could see Bolan's armament, and he lowered his binoculars and waved his men to the back of the boat, then pointed at the sky behind them. The men nodded, and two of them hoisted an M-60 general purpose machine gun out of a storage case and headed toward the bridge. Taido grinned again. He knew Bolan's plan. Taido turned and disappeared belowdeck. The yacht began to motor forward slowly.

"Forget it, Jack. They've got an M-60. You won't be able to drop anything on them."

"I bet I can drop a plane on them."

"Belay that. Get out of here. Find the sub, and then ditch. Go home. Get Able Team and get Phoenix Force. Then go to town in Tokyo."

"I don't like it."

"You don't have to like it. It's an order."

The radio was silent for a moment. "Roger, Striker. Aborting."

Bolan shouldered the M-79 as the yacht slowly pulled into range. He squeezed the trigger, and the grenade launcher's metal stock recoiled into his shoulder brutally. The grenade arced across the water, hit the yacht on her prow and detonated with a crack. The bow blackened, and bits of shrapnel shattered the windows of the bridge and scored the foredeck with furrows, but the yacht continued to surge forward. Taido knew he'd been fragged, and now he knew that Bolan didn't have any antiarmor or incendiary rounds. The yacht began to power forward at speed.

Bolan reloaded, and the M-79 thumped against him. He tried to loop the grenade through the bridge window, but the yacht was moving fast and began to swerve from side to side in an S maneuver to prevent him from doing just that. The grenade hit the roof of the bridge and tore up the rotating nautical radar dish.

Bolan dropped the spent grenade launcher and pulled out his Desert Eagle. The big pistol was loaded with armor-piercing .44 Magnum bullets, and at close range they would penetrate the yacht's cabin. But the yacht would be in rifle range long before that happened. Shooters had already come back out and were taking positions on the deck.

"All right, gentlemen," the Executioner said. "This is it. Get ready." Burdick took his .45 Colt in his hand, and Tokaido hefted the stocked and scoped Beretta. Bolan put his hand on the throttle and waited.

A voice spoke from the radio. "This is the *Los Angeles,* Striker. We see you. Please make a dash due west." Bolan rammed the throttles full forward, and the Zodiac raft lunged into a sprint. The yacht stopped its serpentine maneuvers and went to full speed. Bolan watched the needle on his fuel gauge as it sat solidly in the red and waited for the engine to die, and a grin split his face.

They surged past a metallic pole that was sticking up out of the water.

"Striker!" Tokaido yelled.

Bolan looked over his shoulder. The water was roiling behind them, and he could see a big dark shape manifesting under the deep blue water. Water foamed and boiled, and the long black hull of USS *Los Angeles* breached the water between the Zodiac raft and the yacht. Bolan kept up his sprint for another hundred yards and then cut the engine. The raft slid to a stop in the becalmed waters. The yacht behind them had been eclipsed by the long black shape in the water. The Executioner kept the big Desert Eagle in his hand and waited to see what developed.

RYUCHI TAIDO WAS ALMOST incoherent with rage as he stared at the black mass of the submarine standing between him and his prey. The commando had defeated him at every turn. Now, from the very jaws of death, the American had pulled another rabbit out of his hat and defeated him again. Taido was so filled with rage he felt like throwing up. He had known many of Nishiki-Tetsuo's field operatives who considered themselves latter-day samurai, and were almost eager to lay down their lives for the glory of the consortium. Taido thought all that modern-day Bushido was crap. He had never been willing to sacrifice himself for the company. He had never been willing to sacrifice himself for anything. He now found he was willing to die in the name of personal vengeance. There was nowhere to go. They were going to be blown out of the water. The other choice was to be boarded and captured, and Taido wasn't going to take out his knife and rip his belly to prevent it.

He was going to kill the American instead.

He turned to Yoshio, who stood gaping out the shattered bridge window with his rifle held in slack hands. "Yoshio, go get the rocket launcher and the spare rockets."

Taido had done a lot of business with the pirates and smugglers who operated in the Southeast Asian islands. They always kept light antiarmor weapons like RPG-7s and American LAW rockets close at hand. They were extremely useful weapons in short-range combat between small boats. Taido insisted on having such weapons on any boat he was using in a field operation. It had saved his life several times.

Yoshio looked at Taido as if he were insane. "Are you crazy? The rockets will not breach their hull. That is an attack submarine. Its hull is built to withstand thousands of pounds of pressure. You won't even penetrate the outer hull, much less the pressure hull beneath it!"

Taido decided to temporarily ignore Yoshio's impertinence. His voice was disturbingly calm. "Yes, you are correct. But they will blow a hole in their conning tower."

Yoshio blinked uncomprehendingly. Taido spoke quickly. "That is a modern U.S. Navy submarine. It has no deck guns. To attack us, they will have to send sailors up into the conning tower with rifles from their armory. I want to keep their riflemen down while we maneuver around the sub and kill the American. I do not hear his engine. I think he is out of fuel. I intend to go around the sub and blow him to hell."

"But they will torpedo us."

Taido nodded. "Possibly. But all torpedoes have a minimum range. They will have to fire the torpedo past us and then set it to return. I intend to hug their hull so that the proposition will be extremely dangerous for them. While you keep their riflemen off the tower with rocket fire, and they worry about firing vectors and hitting themselves with their own torpedo, I am going to kill the American.''

Yoshio's eyes grew bright. *"Hai, Taido-san!"* The man scampered for the weapons locker. Yoshio was one of those operatives who had that samurai spirit Taido usually so despised. It was going to prove very useful now.

Taido barked out commands. "Mas! Take the wheel. On my signal get as close as you can to the sub and then go around her. When you see the American boat, go for him full throttle. Ram him!''

Mas took the wheel and throttled the yacht forward. *"Hai, Taido-san!"*

Yoshio came forward again clutching a loaded RPG-7 launcher and three spare rockets under his arm. Taido picked up his M-16 rifle. He could see men's heads appearing over the lip of the submarine's conning tower and scanning the yacht with binoculars. He also saw men with rifles. "Yoshio, stay here. Wait on my signal. Then come out the other side.''

Taido strode onto the foredeck. The operative with a rifle looked at him expectantly. Taido made a wide cutting gesture with his hands, and disbelievingly his man put down his rifles. Taido waited a moment until he was sure that all eyes in the conning tower were on him, then unslung his rifle and let it clatter to the deck. Taido whispered, "Now, Yoshio!''

Yoshio swung out from the other side of the cabin and fired. The rocket hissed out of its launcher and streaked toward the sub's conning tower. Taido grinned and scooped up his rifle "Now, Mas!''

The yacht surged straight toward the sub, and Taido's men grabbed their rifles with savage grins on their faces. The RPG-7 rocket hit the conning tower and detonated with a boom. The men began to fire their rifles at the sub. Taido flicked the safety off his M-16 and shouted over the sudden gunfire. "Bring the M-60 forward! Now!"

CAPTAIN DARRYL Martinski's face was white with rage as he slid down the ladder of the conning tower. "Goddamn sons of bitches!"

The deck of the conning tower above was smoking, and one of his lookouts was unconscious and covered with blood. Two seamen tried to gently maneuver him down the nearly vertical ladder. The captain flinched as another rocket impacted into the top of the sail and orange fire and smoke bellowed into the hold. "Close that hatch!" the captain ordered. As he stalked back across into the attack center, he heard a metallic patter like hail hitting the hull. His lips skinned back off his teeth. The lunatic bastards were shooting rifles at his sub. The captain's body seemed to expand with moral outrage. "Weapons officer! Flood tubes one and two! Give me a firing vector on that goddamn yacht!"

The weapons officer's jaw tensed, and he didn't take his eyes off the control boards in front of him. "Captain, target is closing! Range is— Jesus! Range is three yards! They're right on top of us!"

The captain rolled his eyes disbelievingly. These people really were lunatics, and clever ones, as well. He looked at his weapons officer and knew that they were both thinking the same thing. They would have to fire the torpedo out to sea and have it double back to take out the yacht. If the yacht continued to hug their hull, the torpedo could very well hit the sub instead. Even if the torpedo was right on target, the Mark 48 was a very powerful naval weapon, designed to destroy enemy submarines and sink surface combatants. In comparison, the yacht wasn't a substantial target at all. The torpedo might well just sail right through the relatively flimsy pleasure boat and detonate against the sub's hull anyway. To date, Martinski knew of no U.S. Navy captain who had sunk his own boat with his own torpedo, much less while sitting still on the surface. Martinski couldn't imagine it looking very good on his permanent record.

The weapons officer shook his head. "Captain, the target is moving around toward our bow. He's skirting us, trying to get around to Striker."

"All ahead full! Block him as long as you can!" Martinski grabbed the radio. "Striker, head due south, as fast as you can! We're being flanked."

The bosun stood to one side with four seamen armed with M-16 rifles. The bosun was bloody, and some of it was his own. "Captain, you want us to go back up top and try to engage the target again?"

The captain shook his head. "No, we're—" the word stuck in his craw "—outgunned. But thank you."

He looked back at his weapons officer. "Where's Striker?"

"Six hundred yards south, Captain." The weapons officer frowned. "He's stopped. I think he's out of fuel." He looked up again warily at the captain. "You want the torpedo?"

The captain glared over the man's shoulder at the weapons display. His eyes flared. "No. The hell with this noise. I'm through playing games. Con, take on ballast!" He suddenly grinned at his weapons officer. "Ready a Harpoon!"

The lieutenant blinked. "Sir?"

"I said ready a Harpoon."

The Harpoon was an antiship cruise missile with a sixty-five-mile range and a 500-pound armor-piercing warhead. The lieutenant had never heard of firing one at a target that was within ten yards. The captain's eyes narrowed. "Just do it, Lieutenant."

"Aye-aye, Captain. Fire control acquiring target."

Martinski spread his legs and folded his arms across his chest. "Dive!"

YOSHIO HAD RELOADED his last RPG-7 round and shouted joyously, "Taido! The sub! It is diving!"

"Yes, it is." Taido's grin split his beard from ear to ear. "They must dive so they can get away from us and fire a torpedo. But by then it will be much too late for the commando.'' Taido watched the sea boil as the sub took on ballast and began to slide beneath the surface. The sub was still paralleling them, but it wouldn't delay them long enough to save the American in his little boat. ''Mas!'' Taido shouted, ''as soon as their hull is submerged, cut across her and make straight for the commando! We will not have much time! Ram them! They will jump, and then we will shoot them while they tread water!''

''Hai, Taido-san!'' Mas began to turn the yacht and throttle forward as all but the conning tower of the sub disappeared under the roiling sea.

Taido's eyes flared as he saw the little boat behind the sub. The commando was dead in the water. ''Yoshio! When we close within range, rocket them! If he still has some fuel, I do not want him taking evasive action while the sub fires its torpedo. I…''

Taido's voice trailed off as the ocean geysered upward in a tower of spume only yards from the yacht. A metal-and-plastic cylinder three times as long as a man flew into the sky trailing fire, then split apart. The two halves fell away, and a long, finned object shot into the sky. The spent booster rocket detached, and there was a high-pitched scream as its turbojet engine fired and the missile began maneuvering.

Taido's voice nearly rose to a scream of his own. ''Quickly! The American!''

The missile actually seemed to nose over and level out at Taido's words. It flew toward the Americans' little boat, then streaked past and began to execute a hard turn. Mas sent the yacht driving forward at full throttle as the missile streaked low across the ocean. From Taido's view it almost seemed to be moving in slow motion as it arced through its turn. The missile completed its high-G turn, and it didn't seem to be moving slowly anymore as it flew directly at them.

Taido lost his will to die. The mission was over. They had lost. The other operatives fired their rifles at the oncoming cruise missile desperately. Taido dropped his rifle and threw himself over the side of the speeding yacht.

He tumbled in the bow wake and swallowed salt water as he fought the turbulence. He popped up spluttering and bobbing as the yacht's wake calmed with distance. The yacht was still going forward at full speed, and Taido saw his men jump. The missile suddenly hopped at the last second, then shot downward straight into the speeding yacht's cabin. Taido dived under the water as the Harpoon's high-explosive warhead detonated and the yacht disappeared into a massive ball of orange flame.

Taido swam downward about ten yards and held himself under the water. Seconds later he could look up through the salt-water sting in his eyes to the bright vault above him and see dark objects hitting the water as flying debris fell from the sky. He stayed down until his temples were pounding, then smoothly stroked to the surface. He breached gently and only let his head stick up above the water.

The yacht was gone. There was little more than a slick of burning fuel on the surface where it had been, and lots of very tiny pieces of wreckage floated on the water. Taido looked off to his right and saw the submarine beginning to resurface several hundred yards away. He looked off toward the commando's last position.

He was still there, about a hundred yards away. The little boat sat calmly in the water, and a tall figure stood in the prow. The figure held some small, stocked weapon with a scope in the crook of his arm, and he held binoculars to his eyes with his other hand. He put the binoculars down and raised the weapon to his shoulders and sighted.

Taido felt like screaming, but the shot didn't come. The commando was simply covering him in case he had a weapon. Taido turned his head as the massive shape of the submarine slowly approached. For the first time in his life, Ryuchi Taido considered suicide for its own sake.

19

Bolan watched as Ryuchi Taido was led naked from the bridge down the conning tower ladder by two armed seamen. The sub had picked up Bolan and his team first and then gone back for Taido. At Bolan's suggestion they had forced him at gunpoint to strip while he treaded water. The Executioner had been on the wrong end of a number of the Nishiki-Tetsuo operatives' surprise attacks, and he was going to be sure that the little killer didn't bring any of his surprises onto the *Los Angeles*. His two surviving operatives had been ushered down in a similar fashion and been locked in separate compartments. Akira Tokaido and Burdick were already in the sick bay and receiving care. Burdick was in miserable but not life-threatening condition. Tokaido was having his ankle set and his ribs taped.

Bolan watched from the rather chewed-up conning tower as Grimaldi's plane slowly circled in a descending spiral. It was too bad that they were going to have to ditch Nick Corbolini's plane, but it couldn't be helped. There was no friendly airport close by. A pair of the sub's inflatable boats was in the water and waiting to pick up Grimaldi when he stalled the plane into the water. Bolan watched as the pilot took the Skymaster lower and slower over the water. He pulled up as the plane was about to stall and landed on the water almost as if it were a runway. He kept his landing gear up and slid across the water on the plane's belly. The propellers chuffed to a halt, and the plane slowed its forward progress. When the plane had stopped, Grimaldi threw open the door and dived cleanly into the water and stroked smoothly away from the slowly sinking aircraft.

Bolan shrugged. It was a shame to sink a perfectly good plane. At least Stony Man was a black organization. Officially it didn't exist. They had seized all kinds of cash from their enemies. It wouldn't be too hard to have an anonymous reimbursement sent to Carbolini.

Captain Martinski appeared at Bolan's elbow. The Executioner held out his hand, and the two men grinned at each other as they shook.

"Thank you, Captain. It was looking a little grim out there for a bit."

Martinski shrugged good-naturedly. "Not a problem. We were on a rather routine patrol when we got the call to assist you."

Bolan ran his hand over the twisted lip of the conning tower. There were two scored and blackened holes where the RPG-7 warheads had detonated, and the dark paint was scored with shrapnel scars. "Sorry about your boat."

The captain shook his head. "It's cosmetic. Besides—" the man leaned forward and lowered his voice "—I'm a mast-and-sail man myself in my days off." He shook his head in disgust. "I hate those goddamn motor yachts. Any idiot can pilot one. I've been wanting to blow one of them up for a long time."

Bolan smiled. Martinski had a positive attitude. The communications officer's head popped up from the hatch at their feet. "I have a priority communication for Striker."

The Executioner nodded and slid down the ladder behind the communications officer. The young man led him to a small room off the attack center. He pointed to the microphone in a bank of equipment, then closed the bulkhead behind Bolan.

The Executioner picked up the mike. "This is Striker."

Aaron Kurtzman's voice came across the satellite link crystal clear. He sounded extremely pleased with himself. "We've broken the disks."

"What did it give us?"

"What *didn't* it give us? I'm faxing hard copies now."

Bolan watched as the paper began to ream out of the console. He picked up the first page and scanned it. They had struck gold. "How much of this do you have?"

"A lot. I'm trying to edit the stuff so that what I send you is pertinent."

"Thanks. Keep it coming." Bolan looked up as if he could see past the bulkhead. "I'm going to read some of this, then wander down the corridor and cross-reference it."

SHIRATA WAS CALM as he spoke into the satellite link from his bunker at the bottom of the Nishiki-Tetsuo Tokyo office. "You are saying the commando was in Nauru, waiting in ambush?"

Shirata only knew Gun by his dossier, but his record and fitness report to this moment were extremely favorable. Nishiki-Tetsuo lawyers had been forced to bail Gun out of the jail in Nauru for stealing an airplane and then returning it, but the young operative was giving his report in a professional matter. "Yes, we have multiple confirmed sightings by team members, including Taido-san."

Nothing the commando did surprised Shirata anymore, but he didn't like the fact that the man seemed to be able to flout the laws of physics. "He was there ahead of the JAL flight?"

Gun paused. "Yes, that is what I told you."

Shirata shook his head. "That is not possible."

Gun was silent a moment before he contradicted his superior. "I believe I can explain it. We of course have been monitoring the activities of the Nauru police. An islander reported that he was kidnapped and his jeep was stolen by three men. He said three jet planes flew up outside his hut and 'landed on the beach like bugs,' and then flew away again. I believe the Americans were chasing the JAL flight with vertical-takeoff-and-landing jets. Most likely Harriers."

Shirata nodded. Yes, that was possible. Unthinkable. Unpredictable. But not impossible. They seemed to be the operating words of the commando. "So what happened?"

"They were there at the airport, waiting. They had the element of surprise, as well as grenade launchers and automatic weapons. They took their friend. One of them stole a plane. The others extracted from the island by boat. I stole a plane and followed to spot their boat for Taido in the yacht. We spotted them. We chased them. A submarine appeared and blew Taido out of the water with a missile. I was fairly far away, but I saw the explosion. The entire yacht just disappeared in fire. There was nothing left. I did not wait for them to drag a Stinger missile out of the hold and fire at me. I flew back to Nauru assuming you would want me to report to you as quickly as possible."

"I want a detailed report in writing, within an hour." Shirata clicked off the line as the full impact of what had happened hit him. The enemy had the disks. It was only a matter of time before they broke the code. Shirata looked at his phone and dreaded the call he had to make. He would have to call the old man and give him his report, and then give his recommendation. The old man wasn't going to like it, but it would have to be done.

They were going to have to flee. The vast majority of Nishiki-Tetsuo's holdings, members and activities were legal. Ninety-nine percent of Nishiki-Tetsuo employees had no idea that there even was an illegal arm; fewer still had any idea of what the illegal organization actually did. The Americans had disks and names. That in itself meant nothing, not if there was no illegal arm to find. They were going to have to disappear until a new infrastructure could be built. This war was over. They would have to bide their time and plan a new one for the future.

Shirata felt his insides turn to ice. They had failed. They had lost. He steeled himself. But the American had lost, as well. His goal was vengeance. He wanted to cut off the heads of those who had planned the attacks on Europe and released Ebola into the United States. The Americans would come storming in legally, illegally, clandestinely and in the world courts. The commando himself would come looking for blood.

The Americans would find nothing. Neither would the commando. All they would find would be genuinely confused Nishiki-Tetsuo executives who had no idea what anyone was talking about. The dust would settle. The stink would fade with the winds off Tokyo Bay, and sometime in the future, at a time of the One Heaven's choosing, the war would begin again.

TAIDO LOOKED UP at the sharp rapping on the bulkhead. He was being held in a tiny storage compartment that had been stripped of everything that wasn't bolted down. He sat on the floor wearing nothing but a towel, with his hands manacled behind him. Taido recognized the voice of the armed sailor guarding the door. "Prisoner! Step away from the door and sit against the far wall. If you move when we open the door, you will be shot!"

The Japanese already sat against the far wall. A distant part of his mind considered a flying side kick at the guard, but he didn't relish the idea of being cut in two with an M-16 by the other guards who were probably outside the door. "I am against the wall," he said in English. "I am sitting."

The door wheel spun and the bulkhead opened. The muzzles of two M-16s poked through the doorway, followed by the heads of two sailors. They faded back again, and Taido heard one of them say "He's all yours, sir."

"Thank you."

A tall man wearing khaki shorts and a Navy-issue undershirt stooped to clear the bulkhead and stepped into the compartment. The bulkhead shut, and the wheel spun to lock behind him. Taido looked up into the eyes of his mortal enemy. He had never seen the commando this close. The man was very big. Taido had been a field operative in the Pacific Rim for many years, and had personally killed many men, but facing the commando, this close, face-to-face, he couldn't help feeling intimidated. The force of the man's personality preceded him like a brick wall. The massive .44 Magnum pistol that didn't waver from the point between Taido's eyes wasn't helping matters, either.

The big man spoke in a casual but sincere tone. "If you move, I'm going to shoot you."

Taido didn't doubt that. His mouth was suddenly dry, but he managed to shrug indifferently. "You're here to talk. So talk."

The big man's casual tone didn't change. He didn't bluster or threaten; he simply spoke the truth. "Taido, you're dead. You know it and I know it. Your people think you're dead. That's the only thing keeping you alive, and the only thing that will continue to keep you alive."

Taido knew that was true, but he kept his poker face as the big man continued. "We can execute you. This is a black operation, and you're a confirmed terrorist. We can put you in Leavenworth in maximum security for the rest of your life, but once Nishiki-Tetsuo finds out you're there, even maximum security won't save you. Your friend Yukio Tadashi didn't last twenty-four hours, and he was in PSIA custody."

Taido knew this, as well. It was he who had seen to Tadashi's poisoning.

"For that matter we can just let you go. Hell, we can fly you straight to Tokyo if you like. But you and I both know that to Nishiki-Tetsuo, you're damaged goods. You've been captured. You've been compromised. Even if you don't tell me a single thing it won't matter. Even if they want to believe you didn't tell me anything, it won't matter. They can't afford to take the risk. As long as you as you're alive, Taido, you're a liability."

Taido met the big man's gaze and managed not to flinch. "So?"

"So you have a choice. You can stay alive, temporarily. Or you can stay dead. Refuse to cooperate, and I turn you over to someone else. You'll become a legal matter rather than a military asset. You'll end up dead, pretty damn quick."

"And if I cooperate?"

"Then you stay a military asset. You stay dead." The big man locked his eyes with Taido's and held them. "Listen, I'm not going to lie to you. I'm going to burn your employers to the ground. You give me information I need to do that, you get to stay officially dead and you get to live. I'm going to take what you give me and destroy Nishiki-Tetsuo's illegal arm. If I make it back alive, and if I found what you gave me useful information, then you get a new face, a new identity, some money and you get to drop off the planet. South America. We don't ever want to see you above the equator again, much less in the Pacific Rim. That's the deal. I want a yes or no. I want it now. I won't ask you again. You have five seconds."

The greatest instinct in Taido's life as an operative had been survival. That instinct spoke without hesitation. "Very well. I will cooperate with you." Taido's shoulders sagged slightly with the words. The die was now cast.

"Good. Now, if I were your employers, I think I'd be making tracks right about now until things cooled off. You know, I think you were pretty high up in the chain of security there, Taido. I want to know what kind of fallback plans they have." Bolan pulled a small tape recorder from his pocket, and he suddenly smiled in a disconcertingly friendly fashion. "Tell me everything you know."

20

Hokkaido, Japan

The One Heaven sat around a massive table of ebony. They were six men, each one of them well into his seventies. All of them were veterans of World War II. They hadn't been officers or men in command during that bitter conflict. They had been young men in their teens, soldiers and pilots, each fiercely determined to fight for the greater glory of the Rising Sun. They had been young fanatics who were willing to die to bring the four corners of the earth under one heaven. None of them had accepted the emperor's surrender after the nuclear weapons had fallen on Hiroshima and Nagasaki. Each one of them had risen from the ashes of the Japanese defeat to become men of tremendous wealth and power. For decades each man had nursed his own private dreams of vengeance even as he had built his wealth and power. As their wealth grew, and they began to move in the same circles of power, they began to share these dreams with one another. To them, World War II had ceased being a war. It had become a battle—a battle they had lost, but just one battle in a war that was to continue. These six men were now the generals in this war. It had been a war they had been slowly winning, a war their enemies didn't even realize they were losing.

Rinjiro Iasu sat at the table and was as grim faced as the rest of the men there. The Americans knew they were in a war now, and they knew who their enemy was. Not for the first time, Iasu was reminded of Admiral Yamamoto's words after the attack on Pearl Harbor and that first "victory" over the United States. Yamamoto's words were to prove grimly prophetic, and those words rang clear in Iasu's mind now: "I fear we have awoken a sleeping giant, and filled him with terrible resolve."

The United States was indeed a giant. Iasu had personally fought against the United States as a fighter pilot during the war, and he knew its might all too well. At present it was the only real superpower on the planet. Militarily and economically it was the most powerful nation in the world. Iasu shook his head in grim awe at his next thought. And in response to Nishiki-Tetsuo's worldwide series of attacks on the west, the most powerful nation on earth had sent one man.

It was inconceivable. Nishiki-Tetsuo was the most powerful business consortium in the world, and this one man had shut it down and forced its agents into hiding. Iasu sighed. In many ways he considered the present situation his responsibility. All of the men present were in effect generals in this war with the west, but Iasu was the man responsible for what they considered real "war fighting." He was ultimately in command of the field operations. They had been prepared to strike the final blows; they had been perched on the edge of total victory. According to their timetable, the capitals of Western Europe should have been radioactive ghost towns by now, and the United States on its knees in the grip of the worst plague the world had seen since the Black Death had swept Europe and the Middle East. Given these two failures, at the very least the commando should have been dead by now and whatever black operation he belonged to reeling and under attack.

Instead *they* were hiding.

Iasu glanced out the massive window at the evergreen forests outside the fortresslike mansion of stone that perched on a mountainside on Japan's northernmost island. The island of Hokkaido was Japan's frontier. Much of it was still heavily forested. It was mountainous and harsh, and inhospitable in winter. Compared to the other major islands, it was barely

populated at all. This secluded mansion was the only place
the One Heaven ever met together face-to-face. Few people
even knew of its existence. It was untraceable as a Nishiki-
Tetsuo asset. It was from here that the war against the West
had first germinated. It was here that the war would begin
anew.

Iasu swept his eyes across the vista of evergreens covering
the mountains as the men at the table considered plans and
tactics to save as much as they could from the rubble of the
operation. The walls were of thick stone. Shirata was personally in command of the heavily armed security detail. Even
with the disks, there was no way the enemy could know for
sure exactly who the members of One Heaven were, and there
was no way the enemy could know they were here. The only
people who knew of this fortress's existence were either here
or they were dead. Iasu's fingers trailed for the dozenth time
to the grips of the old 7 mm Baby Nambu automatic pistol
he had been issued as a pilot so long ago. He now carried
that pistol under his suit jacket. Iasu considered himself a
brave man. He had been an ace in the air war, shooting down
fourteen British fighters over Burma, and seven more American fighters over the Pacific in his Mitsubishi Zero before he
had been shot down himself. When the Americans had
dropped their nuclear weapons on Hiroshima and Nagasaki,
and invasion seemed imminent, Iasu had volunteered to be a
kamikaze.

Iasu looked out the window at the mountains. In his bones
he knew the commando was still out there, and the man would
never stop until he achieved victory. Rinjiro Iasu realized he
was afraid.

MACK BOLAN and Jack Grimaldi walked across the tarmac
toward the waiting airplane. The closest United States air facility was on the Kwajalein Atoll. The journey had been over
five hundred miles, and even running at full steam around the
clock, the voyage had still taken the *Los Angeles* twenty-four
hours. It was a day Bolan didn't like to give his enemy, but

it couldn't be helped. Nor could Bolan complain about the rest it had given him. He had slept for twelve hours, eaten a huge meal, told Barbara Price his plan and then slept again while he waited to hear whether the President was willing to approve it. Bolan had gotten the call even as the *Los Angeles* was pulling into Kwajalein. His plan had been approved.

The mission was a go.

Taido had told Bolan all about the mountain retreat on Hokkaido. Taido himself had helped put in the security system and had run infiltration exercises against it. A single road wound up the mountainside in a tortuous series of switchbacks. A few armed men could hold the road against a whole platoon. The mansion itself almost hung off the mountainside. Trees and rocks covered the mountainside, and climbing it to make an assault was a risky proposition at best. Insertion by air was the only real choice, and the defenders had planned for that eventuality. Except for the rooftop helipad, the roof had been designed as one sharp plane that slanted at an almost ninety-degree angle, and it was made of an almost featureless composite that was without purchase. A parachutist would hit the roof and slide right off down the mountain. The only flat spaces were the driveway and the helicopter pad. Both were monitored by infrared cameras, motion sensors and pressure sensors. There was no way to sneak in. Anyone dropping in by air would be discovered almost instantly.

Bolan didn't care. He had one advantage. According to Taido, there would be no civilians to worry about. There would be the One Heaven, and its security force. The Executioner wasn't going to attempt to sneak in. He was going in hard.

The three men he was going in with stood on the Kwajalein airport tarmac beneath the blazing South Pacific sun. Gary Manning, Calvin James and T. J. Hawkins stood at parade rest as Bolan approached.

Hawkins grinned. "Hey, boss, I hear we're going to Japan."

Bolan nodded. "That's about the size of it."

James folded his arms across his chest and grinned. Now that Bolan's attack was a go, they had all been briefed about exactly what Nishiki-Tetsuo had been doing. The ex–Navy SEAL was looking forward to dishing out some payback. "We read everything you sent to the Farm on the flight over here. Is there anything special we need to know?"

Bolan shook his head. "It's pretty straightforward. The second we hit the ground, they'll know we're there. Gary and I are going to land on the rooftop helicopter pad and blow a big hole in the roof and jump in. You and T.J. are going to be a little behind us. When you see the charge go off, you two are going to land on the driveway and blow open the front door. I'm not kidding you. This place is built like a fortress, and we're going to be using some really big charges."

James grinned. "That's okay. I like really big charges."

Bolan grinned back. James had been a crackerjack under-water demolitionist with the SEALs. Behind them a black MC-130 Combat Talon Hercules was warming up her engines on the runway. Bolan checked his watch. The enemy had had twenty-five hours to bug out and get to its retreat. It was time to strike now that their adversaries felt that they were safe. Everything was a go. The raid would either succeed or fail, but Bolan was going to have a little insurance in case he failed. When they were over Hokkaido, there was a phone call he had to make.

Bolan strode toward the plane. "Let's do it."

Three of the most dangerous men in the world fell into step behind him.

IT WAS WELL PAST midnight, and Honda Mitsuko was still at her desk at PSIA headquarters in Tokyo. At five o'clock in the afternoon an anonymous package had arrived addressed to her. Inside it had been a single computer disk, and on it had been the key to the Nishiki-Tetsuo codes. The information on those disks was shocking, to say the least. High-ranking politicians, well-known businessmen and members of

Japanese law enforcement were implicated in terrible crimes. The unknown entity called the One Heaven that was responsible for this web of crime was still out there, and they still didn't know just who the members of the cabal were. It was horrific beyond imagining. The One Heaven hadn't just committed heinous crimes in Japan, but it had also attempted to commit war crimes on a global scale. It had literally tried to commit crimes against humanity. The information was so shocking that only Mitsuko and her superior had read the information on their disk. They didn't know just whom they could trust with this. It was a bombshell that could well change Japan forever.

Mitsuko sat at her desk and tried to think of what should be done. Agent Minato was her direct superior, and she trusted him with her life. After much discussion, he had gone home to have dinner with his family. He had said, quite rightly, that after tomorrow morning it might well be weeks before he saw them again. Mitsuko had stayed at the office. It was the safest place she could think of while the One Heaven wanted her dead. She faced the real possibility of having a death warrant with her name on it following her for the rest of her life.

Mitsuko jumped as the phone chirped. It was the same phone the young man had thrown to her on the train. She had kept it by her side night and day since then, but it hadn't rung. Not even after two Tokyo vice detectives and a number of unidentified and armed Japanese individuals had been killed in Nauru International Airport, and a certain deportee who had tossed that phone to her had disappeared from their custody.

She caught the phone in midring and answered in English. "This is Agent Mitsuko."

A deep voice she immediately recognized spoke. "You received the code key I sent you?"

"I certainly did."

"Then you have some understanding of what I have been doing."

"I do. However, all I can go by is what I have observed myself so far of Nishiki-Tetsuo activities. They have covered their trail very well. I do not believe hardly anything I have at the moment would stand up in court, and while I believe the information on this disk is true, I have no proof of it. I do not know exactly how much of it we can even act upon legally. Of course, we will try, but I do not know how successful we will be. We will undoubtedly be able to cause Nishiki-Tetsuo a great deal of damage, and just knowing about much of their illegal operations—even if we cannot use the information in a court of law—will be enough to shut down many of them." Mitsuko sighed. "But as for the One Heaven, I do not know what is to be done. They are the serpent's head, and we do not know who they are. The disk does not tell us."

The voice on the phone spoke calmly. "There are six of them. I know the name of one, and I know where all six of them are at the moment."

Mitsuko nearly dropped the phone. The voice continued. "I'm going to take them out. When I begin my strike, I'll signal you. I suggest you have fast-reaction teams and helicopters standing by. Assemble them immediately. If I fail in my mission, I want you and the PSIA there to pick up the pieces and finish the job."

"I—"

"I'll signal you with the phone you're holding."

The phone went dead before Mitsuko could say anything. She took a long, deep breath, then dialed Agent Minato. He answered on the first ring. "Yes."

"I need permission to assemble fast-reaction teams, three of them."

Minato paused. "What is happening?"

"The American is attacking the One Heaven. I think he is doing it tonight."

The Lockheed MC-130 Combat Talon broke out of formation along the southern coast of Hokkaido. The island was close to the former Soviet Union, and the Japanese maintained a number of air-defense bases there. Fortunately American military aircraft flew into Japan all the time. A flight of C-130 transports was nothing Japanese air control would raise an eyebrow at. One of the transports was painted black, and as they moved along the coast it broke formation and headed inland, flying low under the Japanese early-warning radars. Jack Grimaldi's voice came over the intercom. "Half an hour, Striker."

They were jumping in LALO, low altitude, with a low opening of their parachutes. There would be almost no time before they hit the roof of the mansion. Everything would have to go right the first time, or not at all.

Bolan and his team ran a final equipment check. Each man was fully armed and armored for close combat with a Heckler & Koch submachine gun whose barrels and actions had been modified to fire the 10 mm Magnum pistol round. It would be impossible to silence such a weapon, but it wasn't important. The security on the mansion was such that once they set foot on the grounds, they would be detected. Bolan wanted stopping power, and the 10 mm Magnum round could be depended upon to tear through soft body armor and put a man down hard. Each man also had night-vision goggles, a personal knife and side arm and an assortment of grenades.

There were four small suitcases stacked on the floor of the

cargo bay, each one containing a shaped charge of high explosive. The mansion was made of heavy stone, and flexible charges wouldn't be enough to breach its defenses. The four corners of each case had a bolt gun that would fire a piton into the surface to lock the charge against the heavy stone of the mansion. The heavy charges were the key to the teams' entry. If they failed, the two entry teams would be stuck on the roof or out on the driveway. The brush and rock had been cleared from the mountainside beneath the mansion and along the road to create interlocking lanes of fire for the defenders. Retreat would be suicide. The only way to go would be forward. If they failed, they would be cut to pieces.

Bolan and Gary Manning each carried piton guns of their own. The plan was a variation on the attack on the Nishiki-Tetsuo building in Tokyo. They were going to blow their way in. Only this time they were going for the generator to throw the mansion into darkness.

The Executioner and his team finished their final equipment check as the black Combat Talon hugged the hills and climbed into Hokkaido's rugged mountains. Grimaldi's voice came across the intercom. ''Five minutes.''

Bolan looked to the back of the cargo hold. A large drop box dominated the back of the hold where it lay lashed down and locked on its rollers. Within the box were four Yamaha dirt bikes. Once the team was out the door, Grimaldi was going to circle back and drop the box. Its steerable parachutes and a microcomputer in the pallet allowed the package to be landed within a few yards of a designated target. The mansion's front driveway was a small but decent-sized target for the automated cargo-delivery system. But there would no room for error. Either the drop box would hit gravel, or it would continue dropping down the mountainside and leave Bolan and his team stranded. With the bikes and their night-vision goggles, they would descend the mountain road without lights and then head for the coast. Even now a team of Navy SEALs was secreting a Zodiac inflatable raft along a tiny stretch of beach for them.

"Approaching the drop zone, get ready!" The airframe of the Combat Talon seemed to vibrate in response to Grimaldi's voice. A moment later the lights dimmed to a dark red, and the rear cargo door began to lower. Air blasted into the hold as the plane opened itself to the sky. Bolan and Manning would be hitting the roof first, and Calvin James and T. J. Hawkins would hit the door immediately after the first charge went off. James would be the last man out of the plane, and that made him jump master. Bolan and Manning clipped their equipment to their jump harnesses and moved to the edge of the cargo door. It was an overcast night, with only a few visible stars, and all that lay below them was a sea of darkness.

James checked his watch. "Goggles on!"

Bolan and Manning pulled their night-vision goggles over their eyes, and the world became a flat greenish gray. The mountains and trees appeared below them. The amplified light in their goggles shifted slightly as a green light came on in the cargo hold. James shouted the jump command over the roar of the air rushing into the hold. "Go! Go! Go!"

The Executioner stepped into darkness and arched hard as he fell away from the MC-130. He stabilized himself with his arms and oriented himself to face south. The dim lights of the mansion were bright points of light in his goggles. Bolan pulled his arms and legs back and made an arrow of himself as he plunged toward the mansion. He plummeted for a few seconds, then hit his chute. The lines went tight, and his harness cinched hard against him as the parachute took his weight. Bolan grabbed his steering toggles and began to angle in toward the roof of the mansion.

Taido had been right. Other than the helicopter pad, the roof was built as steep as a church steeple. Anyone trying to land on it would slide right off into space. The only place to land was the helicopter landing pad, and once they hit it they would announce their presence.

The pad's landing lights weren't on, but Bolan could see

the pad well enough in his goggles. The pad rushed up at him, and Bolan spoke. "Gary?"

"Right behind you, Striker."

Bolan watched the pad come up at him. "Team Two."

James came through loud and clear. "Out the door and inbound. We're thirty seconds behind you."

The pad was at a difficult angle. It was surrounded by the sharp-edged roof. A helicopter could simply hover over it and lower itself straight down. The only way to come in by parachute was to angle steeply. Bolan began a slight slow spin to put himself in position, then hauled back on the toggles to stall the chute. He bent his knees as his boots hit and took several steps forward to stay on his feet. Even as he released his jump harness, Bolan knew that alarms were going off. Manning hit the roof right behind him and hit hard. The Canadian's knees buckled, and he rolled across the pad. Bolan took his charge, strode across the pad and set it right in the middle. He pushed down hard on a button on the top side of the case, and the piton guns fired and sank metal bolts into the pad to lock the heavy charge in place. Bolan heard Manning fire his own piton gun at the edge of the pad so they could secure ropes. He moved to Manning's side, and his hand moved to his remote detonator.

Calvin James spoke in his ear. "We're down, Striker!"

Bolan heard the bolts firing below as they secured their charge to the mansion's massive iron-bound oaken door, and he could hear shouting inside the mansion, as well. Manning raised his Heckler & Koch and fired a long burst at the conduit where the electrical power line ran from the roof down the mountainside below. Sparks flew and the line twisted like an angry snake and fell free. The lights of the mansion clicked off for a moment. They pulsed back on again almost immediately as the emergency generator came on-line.

Bolan nodded. They had been expecting that. "Firing charge one!"

The Executioner pressed the button on his detonator, and the roof shook beneath their feet. The roof was heavily constructed, and this section had to support the weight of visiting helicopters, as well. Twenty pounds of shaped high explosive exploded down and outward in a cone of destruction.

James's voice spoke in Bolan's ear. "Firing charge two!"

A second explosion split the night as James and Hawkins blew the door down below. Gunfire erupted immediately. Bolan clipped his rope to the piton and moved to the smoking hole in the roof. He pulled the pin on a fragmentation grenade and stepped back as he dropped the bomb into the mansion. The grenade detonated with a crack, and was met with the sound of screams. Bolan held his Heckler & Koch in one hand as he gripped the rope with the other and jumped down into the mansion. The grenade shrapnel had ruined all but one standing lamp in a large living area. Two men lay dead, and another twisted on the ground in pain. All three were armed with M-16 rifles.

Bolan pulled up his goggles as Manning slid down next to him, planted his own shaped charge on the floor and fired the built-in piton guns. The bolts sank through the carpeting and the wood and stone below it and locked the charge into the floor. According to Taido the emergency generator was on the third floor from the roof.

Manning spoke into his radio. "Firing charge three!"

The floor shook and buckled beneath the charge. Manning kept hold of his rope, then jumped on the blackened section of floor with both feet. Almost seven feet of floor broke apart around him and fell to the next floor below. Manning slid down the rope after it. "I'm on the generator."

Bolan moved into a hallway decorated with ancient Japanese murals of samurai fighting the Mongols and moved toward the sound of the firefight at the front door. He could hear the short hammerings of Hawkins's and James's 10 mm Heckler & Koch subguns and the longer, high-pitched snarls of M-16s firing in response. The door at the end of the hall was open and the sound of rifle fire was much louder. "Calvin, where are you?"

"In the foyer. We've got solid cover but so does the enemy. At least six hostiles."

"We're in. Gary's got the generator. I'm flanking your hostiles. Get their attention. Get down on my signal."

"Affirmative, Striker." The hammering of the H&K subguns at the front of the house went from short bursts to long strings of full-auto.

Bolan moved to the doorway and pulled another grenade from his belt. He could see four of the enemy behind corners of another open living area and behind carved stone pillars that dominated the center of the room. The men he could see were directing their rifle fire into the living area and into a large sunken foyer where people could remove their shoes. There was a splendidly groomed sand garden dominated by monolith-sized river rocks in the sand, and James and Hawkins were firing from behind them. Bolan pulled the pin and hurled the high-explosive concussion grenade as he spoke into his throat mike. "Down!"

James and Hawkins disappeared behind their rocks as the grenade exploded in the middle of the room. Bolan stepped back into the hall. The grenade had little shrapnel, depending, instead, on its explosive effect. In the closed confines of the room, the explosive effect was devastating. Thunder echoed through the house, and windows blew out in the living area. Bolan stepped back into the room. Two men were down and three more moved drunkenly from the effect of the blast. One brought his rifle around to point at Bolan, and the big man cut him down. These men were the One Heaven's most trusted soldiers, willing to go along with and to defend their atrocities. There was no room for mercy.

James and Hawkins resurfaced and took the other two men down with short bursts from their weapons. The sixth man rose and charged with a scream. His threw his empty rifle aside, and a knife flashed up high in his hand. Bolan put his front sight on the man's chest and fired a short burst. The knife fell from the fanatic's hand as the 10 mm rounds tore through him, and he collapsed at Bolan's feet.

Manning's voice spoke over the radio. "Goggles on."

A second later there was a muffled thump, and the lights in the mansion went out for the second time. This time they didn't pop right back on.

SHIRATA PULLED his soft body armor vest over his head and scooped up an M-16 rifle. Gunfire echoed through the mansion, and explosions shook the walls. He thrust a grenade in his pocket and whirled as a shadow fell across his open door. The front sight of his rifle was centered on the old man's midsection. Rinjiro Iasu stood in his pajama bottoms and a sleeveless T-shirt. He seemed much less old and bent than he ever had since Shirata had met him. His black eyes glittered, and he held a World War II–vintage Nambu pistol in his hand. He spoke with amazing calm. "The commando is here."

A grimace distorted Shirata's face as another explosion shook the walls. "Yes. But how? How could he have known we were here? The disk did not reveal who any of you are, and you all dispersed before making your way here. Everyone who knows of this place is here or dead—" Shirata's knuckles whitened where they gripped the M-16. "Taido!"

The old man nodded solemnly. "Yes. Taido must have been captured, and he must have capitulated."

Shirata's vision seemed to go red. "I will kill that little ape."

The old man sighed philosophically. "Ryuchi Taido is amazingly talented scum. It was what made him so useful to us. Survival is one of his highest talents. You have said so yourself." The old man's eyes slid to the ceiling as the sound of gunfire seemed to come from directly above. "We have larger matters to concern us than Ryuchi Taido's fate at the moment. Bring your rifle and come with me."

Shirata nodded and the lights promptly went out. A moment later the old man spoke. "You have night-vision equipment?"

Shirata had already moved to his dresser and pulled out both pairs of goggles he had stored there. He pulled a pair over his head and powered them up. He walked over to the old man. "Excuse me, Rinjiro-sama." He pulled the goggles down over the old man's eyes and turned them on.

"Ah." The old man glanced about the room with an almost childlike smile. "How remarkable." Shirata realized the old man was seeing things with the appreciation of a man who realized he was about to die. Like many modern Japanese, Shirata passed off the Bushido of the samurai and the spirit of the kamikaze as antiquated and fanatical. It was a thing of the past. He looked at the old man and saw a man who had lived these ideals his whole life. For the first time Shirata saw the old man as more than a brilliant, vicious spider sitting in the global web of Nishiki-Tetsuo. The old man was a soldier who was still at war.

The old man turned his goggled gaze on Shirata. "The One Heaven will be barricading themselves in the conference room. I believe I am going to go shoot an American instead, if I can. I would be honored if you would accompany me."

Shirata stared at the old man for a long moment. "Yes, Rinjiro-sama. I would be honored."

THE EXECUTIONER MOVED through the darkness. James and Hawkins split off with their last heavy charge and moved to take the upstairs while Bolan linked back up with Gary Manning. With Taido's information they knew that the mansion's conference room would be where the One Heaven directors would make their stand. They would expect the attack to come through the door or possibly by shooters rappelling from the roof above and crashing through the window. They wouldn't be expecting a charge to blow a hole in the ceiling above them. Bolan moved back to the original hole they had blasted and spoke into his throat mike. "Gary?"

"Right below you. Basement level is clear. There was no one down here. The generator is down. No one in the wine cellar or the two storage rooms. I'm coming up."

Bolan held the rope while Manning climbed up hand over hand. The Executioner swung his Heckler & Koch subgun and fired a burst down the opposite hallway. A burst of rifle fire erupted, and Bolan leaned to one side and fired back. The rope twisted in his hand like a snake, and he saw it rapidly begin to unravel where a bullet had struck it. "Gary! The rope's breaking!"

The rope snapped, and Bolan took Manning's weight for half a second, then quickly released it as a figure appeared down the hall. A pistol barked, and the big American returned fire. The burst of 10 mm rounds struck, but the gunman held his aim and the pistol snapped twice more. Bolan felt the punch of the bullet striking his frontal armor, and he put a second burst into his opponent. Even as the man fell, the second gunman opened up again with his rifle. The Executioner dropped prone and fired back, sparks spanging as the bullets struck the other man's weapon and he fell back around the corner.

Bolan pulled a grenade from his web gear as Manning's hands appeared on the lip of the hole in the floor and he began to pull himself up. The Executioner curled his finger around the pin as a hand appeared around the far corner of the hall and tossed an object.

"Down!" He dived into the hole in the floor and tackled Manning. The two men crashed in a tangled heap to the floor below, and a second later the hole above them lit up in a flash of yellow fire. Bolan stood and tossed his own grenade up through the hole to stop a follow-up on the attack, and a second flash of yellow fire lit up the hole as Bolan's frag detonated.

Manning stood with a groan. "Geez, I think you tore my arm out of the socket, Striker."

"Can you move it?"

The Canadian lifted his left arm a few inches, and his lips went tight. "A little, but it's messed up pretty good."

Bolan pulled a flash-stun grenade with a frown. It couldn't be helped. Manning would have been a lot worse off if he'd had his head sticking up through a hole in the floor as the frag came bouncing along the carpet. "Close your eyes."

He tossed the grenade up through the hole. Anyone wearing light-amplification devices would be blinded. When there was no returning gunfire, Bolan leaped and grabbed the lip of the hole in the floor. He pulled himself up and rolled to one side while bringing up his submachine gun. The body down the hall was gone. Bolan crouched and stuck his hand down the hole while he scanned the hallway. A second later Gary Manning's good hand clamped on to his wrist, and he heaved the man up. Manning had stuck his left arm into his webgear as a makeshift sling. He had slung his Heckler & Koch and pulled his .45 automatic from his belt as he stood up. His left shoulder seemed to tilt at a slightly unnatural angle. Bolan looked at him. "Are you all right?"

"It hurts like hell." Manning grinned. "Let's finish this and go home."

SHIRATA DRAGGED the old man into a bedroom and closed the door. Iasu was a bloody mess, and Shirata himself felt his own warm blood trickling down his arms and chest where shrapnel from the commando's grenade had hit him. He staggered and laid the old man on the floor. The bedroom's window blinds were open, and he could see the old man quite well through the night-vision goggles. Blood poured out of Iasu through the six ragged holes in his chest, but he still clutched the Baby Nambu pistol in his right hand. The old man coughed, and blood spilled over his lips and chin. His voice was very weak. "I hit him. I saw it. I hit him."

Shirata nodded. He had seen it himself, but the 7 mm Nambu was an anemic round by modern standards, and he doubted whether it could have penetrated the commando's armor. The commando certainly hadn't acted wounded. The old man's sigh almost sounded content. "I hit him. I've always been a terrible shot with a pistol, but I hit him."

The old man suddenly went rigid in his arms, and he spoke with great effort. "Shirata-san."

"Yes."

The old man sagged a bit. "Get the hell out of here."

Shirata was stunned. The old man nodded painfully. "Get out of here. You were born long after the war was over. It holds no shame or burden for you. We are old men, and we are doomed. You are young and clever. You have night-vision equipment. You can make it down the mountainside and escape."

Shirata opened his mouth to speak, but the old man cut him off. "Shirata-san, I order you to escape." The old man went limp, and his head slumped on his neck.

Shirata knelt for a moment and looked at the dead man as gunshots continued to ring throughout the mansion. He reached out and gently pried the dead man's hands from the still-warm pistol. Shirata felt a wave of nausea as he stood, and he reached out to the wall to steady himself. He couldn't tell how badly he was injured, but it really didn't matter. He would attend to that later or not at all. He moved to the window and gazed down at the jagged rocks and trees that stuck up from the nearly vertical mountainside. The window was one long sheet of heavy glass. Shirata tucked the Nambu pistol into the front of his waistband and picked up a chair. Jagged pain shot through the muscles of his arms and chest, but they obeyed him as he raised the heavy wooden chair over his head. Shirata took a step forward and hurled the chair through the window.

BOLAN AND MANNING moved toward the back of the mansion. The old stone building meandered as it clung to the mountainside. The conference room was at the far end, and its sweeping wall-sized window overlooked a sheer drop down the mountain. Taido had drawn Bolan a crude map from memory, and it had served well enough. The entry had gone as planned, and the generator was where he had said it was. Down at the end of the hall there would be an antechamber, and beyond that, the conference room. The security men had fought fearlessly, but they hadn't been prepared for the attack. They wore no armor and had no night-vision equipment. Bo-

Ian and his team had ruled the darkness with ruthless efficiency.

The gunfire on the floor above ceased, and Calvin James spoke in Bolan's ear. "Top floor clear, Striker. We're above the conference room. Do you want the charge placed?"

Bolan frowned. "Hold your position."

"Affirmative. Waiting on your signal." Bolan looked down the hallway at the door to the antechamber. Any remaining resistance would be there. Taido had said only the most loyal and fanatical of Nishiki-Tetsuo's clandestine soldiers served in the mountain stronghold in Hokkaido. At any one time it would be staffed by ten to twenty of them, serving as bodyguards, groundskeepers, cooks and personal retainers to the One Heaven. Bolan's team had accounted for sixteen of them, but he was betting that given the current state of affairs they would at least be at full strength, if not beefed up.

Bolan looked at the door. The guards would be in the antechamber, while the One Heaven would be in the conference room itself. He was curious why none of the guards was guarding the outside of the door. His gaze narrowed. They were waiting for Bolan's team to hit the door.

The Executioner let out a slow breath. "Calvin."

"Yes."

"There's something going on here."

"You know, I'm getting that feeling myself."

"What do you think?"

There was a moment's pause. "Well, it's obvious they're waiting on us."

"Kind of strange given that fanatical bent of theirs."

"I was kind of expecting to hear some kind of suicidal charge down there. I was thinking of sending T.J. down to back you up. You want him?"

"No, thanks." Bolan stared hard at the door for a long moment in the silence. Grimaldi would have dropped the extraction package by now, and it was either waiting for them in the driveway or it had missed and was lying broken open at the bottom of the mountain. Grimaldi would also have sent a signal to a satellite, which would have bounced the signal to a scrambling machine at the CIA Tokyo branch. That machine would have sent the signal back up to the satellite, and the satellite would have placed Bolan's prerecorded and untraceable call to Agent Honda Mitsuko. PSIA fast-reaction teams were probably already climbing into their helicopters.

"Calvin, the hall upstairs parallels the one Gary and I are in right now, doesn't it?"

"Affirmative."

Bolan nodded. "Fall back from your position." The Executioner's brow furrowed as he calculated. "Ten yards. Place your charge over the hallway."

"Affirmative. We're moving."

Several long seconds passed, then Bolan heard the thumps in the ceiling up ahead of him as the built-in piton guns fired the shaped charge into the floor above. "Charge secured. Ten yards back. Waiting on your signal."

Bolan turned to Manning. "You have any high-explosive grenades left?"

"I've got two."

"Give them to me." Bolan took the grenades and quickly taped them together. He pulled the pins and carefully held down the cotter pins with his thumb. "We're going to entice our friends out by making them think we're coming in." He handed the grenades to Manning, who gingerly put his thumb on the pins as he accepted them. "I want you to throw these with your good arm when I say to."

Manning nodded. "Give me the word."

"I'm taking your ten."

Bolan took the Heckler & Koch from around Manning's neck. The Executioner placed his own weapon on the floor and took careful aim as he flicked the selector switch to semiautomatic. The submachine gun began to bark as Bolan put several rounds into the hinges of the door. The hinges buckled and creaked as the heavy high-velocity slugs impacted. He slipped a fresh magazine into the smoking weapon.

"Get ready, Gary."

"I'm ready."

"Calvin, I'm going to shout now, but I want you to wait until I say 'do it' to you over the radio. Fall back out of the hallway completely."

"You got it."

Bolan flicked the Heckler & Koch's selector to full-auto and aimed at the center of the door. He took a deep breath and then roared at the top of his lungs. "Now! Go! Go! Go!"

The Executioner fired all thirty rounds from the Heckler & Koch in long bursts of full-auto into the door and nodded at Manning. The big Canadian wound up and threw a respectable fastball with the double grenade pack as Bolan scooped up his own weapon from the floor and faded back around the corner of the hallway. Manning stepped back and drew his Colt .45 and took the other corner. The grenades bounced against the door and detonated.

The door shuddered under the blast and fell inward. A great roar arose from within the chamber beyond, and men boiled out. There were six of them filling the hall. All of them toted M-16s, and all of them had bayonets fixed. They halted for a fraction of a second as they saw no one was outside the door, then the leader screamed in Japanese and charged down the hallway. His men echoed his scream so that it filled the hallway, and the men charged. Bolan pulled back around the hallway and counted to three.

"Do it!"

The ceiling erupted as twenty pounds of shaped charge exploded through the roof and blasted down into the charging men. A moment later a second, larger explosion rocked the mansion to its foundations. A fireball shot down the hallway and flame belched past Bolan and Manning. James's shouted "Goddamn!" rang in Bolan's ears above the thunder. The Executioner coughed and looked around the corner. The northern section of the house was gone. The hallway ended in burning rubble, and smoke drafted into the sky from where the roof had been. The stench of burning phosphorus was overpowering as flames clawed upward into the night. The One Heaven had heard the breaching charge, and they had set off their own in response.

"Calvin, are you all right?"

James's voice came back a little shaky. "That was a really big charge. Yeah, we're okay. We fell back as ordered."

"What can you see?"

There was a moment's pause. "I can't get too close. A lot of the floor is gone, and the flames are pretty intense. But from what I can see, the conference room and the room above it are gone. I mean nothing left. I see burning beams and mountainside."

Bolan peered through the smoke and fire. James had better ventilation up top, but what the Executioner could see confirmed it. The One Heaven had blown themselves sky high. If Bolan and his team had assaulted the antechamber, they would have gone up with them. "Good work, Calvin. We're extracting now."

"Affirmative."

Bolan turned to Manning. "Think you can ride a bike?"

Manning grinned. "Not really. You got a bicycle built for two?"

The Executioner slipped a fresh magazine into his weapon. "Let's go see if we have any bikes at all."

EPILOGUE

PSIA Agent Honda Mitsuko stood among the smoldering rubble as the sun rose above the mountains of Hokkaido. The fire and rescue teams were still pulling burned and twisted corpses off the mountainside. The mountain was very steep and the work slow and treacherous in the dark. Mitsuko had her doubts that any of these men would ever be identified. The ones on the mountainside were burned and blown apart beyond recognition. Whatever kind of charge had gone off had been both high explosive and incendiary. It had been intended to turn the room where it exploded into an inferno of blast and heat.

She jumped as the portable phone in her jacket chirped. She took it out and flicked it open. "Hello?"

There was a pause, then a familiar voice spoke in English. "Am I speaking with Agent Mitsuko?"

"Yes, this is she."

"You have found the One Heaven?"

"What little you left of them."

"That was self-inflicted."

Mitsuko looked back at the charred remains of the house. "They killed themselves?"

"Yes. I believe they did it because they had lost and knew that even if they held out behind their barricade, they would be captured by the police and the PSIA. We were only able to identify one of them, but I suspect the rest were some of Japan's ranking industrialists, and perhaps politicians. They had families. I believe they killed themselves the way they did because they didn't want their bodies to be identified. I believe you're going to have some high-ranking disappearances in the next few days, but they will have taken steps to assure that nothing can be proved."

Mitsuko let that sink in. "We did find one identifiable body."

"That would probably be Rinjiro Iasu."

"That is correct."

"He was the one we were able to identify as One Heaven through an informant."

Mitsuko grimaced. She had seen the old industrialist's body. "Yes, he was shot to death."

The voice on the phone was solemn. "Yes. Our intelligence told us that he was a World War II veteran, a decorated pilot and had volunteered for kamikaze duty right before the end of the war. He is a widower, and has no surviving children or family to be shamed or face repercussions. I believe he preferred to die fighting."

Mitsuko looked out at the rising sun. "Yes, I think you are right."

"It was a pleasure working with you. You're a hell of an agent."

Mitsuko found herself blushing. "Thank you." A line drew down between her eyebrows. "Someday I would like to know more of what exactly what happened here in my country."

The voice grew quiet. "Agent Mitsuko, you'll be fortunate indeed if you never hear my voice again. It'll never mean anything good."

Mitsuko smiled grimly. "Yes, I suppose that is correct. However, it is not very satisfying."

"The One Heaven is finished. Japan has avoided a scandal that would have rocked it to its foundations and brought about international censure. You no longer have a death sentence hanging over your head, and you have my profound respect."

Mitsuko opened her mouth to say thank-you again, but the

line clicked dead. She put the phone back in her pocket. She doubted it would ever ring again, but she suspected that she would keep the batteries charged and keep it on her desk for the rest of her career as a PSIA agent.

A powerful cult leader triggers a countdown to terror....

STONY MAN™ 36

STRANGLEHOLD

Trouble is brewing in the Land of the Rising Sun as a powerful cult leader has assembled a fanatically dedicated following, ready to do his bidding and deliver his gospel of death on the rest of the world.

It's up to the counterterrorist commandos of Stony Man Farm to act quickly to keep the world safe from this displaced doctrine.

Available in September 1998 at your favorite retail outlet.

James Axler

OUTLANDERS™

DOOMSTAR RELIC

Kane and his companions find themselves pitted
against an ambitious rebel named Barch, who finds a
way to activate a long-silent computer security
network and use it to assassinate the local baron.
Barch plans to use the security system to take over
the ville, but he doesn't realize he is starting a
Doomsday program that could destroy the world.

Kane and friends must stop Barch, the virtual assassin
and the Doomsday program to preserve the future....

One man's quest for power unleashes a cataclysm
in America's wastelands.

**After the ashes of the great Reckoning, the
warrior survivalists live by one primal instinct**

JAMES AXLER

DEATH LANDS®

Way of the Wolf

Unexpectedly dropped into a bleak Arctic landscape by a
mat-trans jump, Ryan Cawdor and his companions find
themselves the new bounty in a struggle for dominance
between a group of Neanderthals and descendants of
a military garrison stranded generations ago.